ALEX SHAW spent the second half of the 1990s in Kyiv, Ukraine, teaching Drama and running his own business consultancy before being headhunted for a division of Siemens. The next few years saw him doing business for the company across the former USSR, the Middle East, and Africa.

Cold Blood, Cold Black and *Cold East* are commercially published by HarperCollins (HQ Digital) in English and Luzifer Verlag in German.

Alex, his wife and their two sons divide their time between homes in Kyiv, Ukraine, Worthing, England and Doha, Qatar. Follow Alex on twitter: @alexshawhetman or find him on Facebook.

D1076917

Also by Alex Shaw

Cold Blood
Cold Black

Cold East

ALEX SHAW

ONE PLACE. MANY STORIES

HQ
An imprint of HarperCollins*Publishers* Ltd
1 London Bridge Street
London SE1 9GF

This paperback edition 2018

First published in Great Britain by
HQ, an imprint of HarperCollins*Publishers* Ltd 2018

ISBN: 9780008310196

MIX
Paper from
responsible sources
FSC C007454

This book is produced from independently certified FSC™ paper
to ensure responsible forest management.

For more information visit: www.harpercollins.co.uk/green

Typeset by Palimpsest Book Production Ltd, Falkirk, Stirlingshire
Printed and bound in Great Britain by
CPI Group (UK) Ltd, Croydon, CR0 4YY

*To my wife Galia, my sons Alexander and Jonathan,
and our family in England and Ukraine*

Prologue

'I can't see them yet.'

'They'll be here soon, he said so.' Vitaly Blazhevich peered into the distance towards the besieged city of Donetsk. Smoke rose from tower blocks on the outskirts, the result of early-morning shelling by Russian-supplied Grad rockets. The ceasefire agreement between the Ukrainian government and the Russian-backed insurgent organisations of the Donetsk People's Republic (DNR) and the Lugansk People's Republic (LNR) had been in operation for several months, yet attacks continued. The men around Blazhevich were a mixture of regular Ukrainian infantry and young, hastily trained members of a volunteer battalion. Despite the cold, the Ukrainians kept their spirits high as they rotated manning the vehicle checkpoint, cooking, and resting. Blazhevich had nothing but respect for the volunteers who, until recently, had been carrying on normal lives as university students, mechanics, bus drivers, doctors, and businessmen. Every now and then the group would spontaneously start singing Ukrainian folk songs or old Soviet tunes in Russian. They were Ukrainian and what mattered to them most was one country,

1

not one language. The checkpoint was to the north of the small town of Marinka and straddled the road towards Donetsk. The adjacent flat fields of fertile black earth had been left barren in the conflict zone. A click away, the road forked and the treeline started.

'Here.' Nedilko handed Blazhevich a mug.

'We should be doing more to help him,' Blazhevich replied to his SBU colleague before sipping the bitter-tasting army coffee.

'He likes pretending to be Russian.'

'That's true.'

Blazhevich saw movement ahead. He put his drink on the ground, raised his field glasses, and focused on the road. A white Toyota Land Cruiser appeared from the treeline. As it neared, the blue flag and markings of the Organisation for Security and Co-operation in Europe (OSCE) became visible on its paintwork. The Ukrainian soldiers manned their weapons, ever wary of a surprise attack. The checkpoint had changed hands several times so far; the men were taking no chances.

Nedilko's phone rang. 'Hello? OK.' He pointed at the SUV. 'It's him, or at least he's is in the vehicle.'

'It's four-up,' Blazhevich replied.

Nedilko removed his Glock from its holster. 'What's the saying? "Plan for the best, prepare for the worst"?'

'Something like that.'

As the Land Cruiser came to a halt, just short of the checkpoint, a series of rumbles rolled across the fields. The DNR were shelling again. A thin man, wearing a blue OSCE vest over a grey, three-quarter-length jacket, stepped slowly from the front passenger door. He held his arms aloft as a pair of Ukrainian soldiers advanced, weapons up. The rear door now opened and out climbed an Asian man followed by someone both SBU agents couldn't mistake: Aidan Snow.

'"Who Dares Wins",' Blazhevich said with a smile.

Snow led the trio towards the checkpoint. The man in the

OSCE vest held out his hand to Blazhevich. 'Gordon Ward, OSCE monitor. You must be from the Security Service of Ukraine?'

'That's correct, the SBU,' Blazhevich confirmed, shaking hands. 'Things getting busy back there?'

'Hairy is the word for it. The DNR are systematically violating the ceasefire!'

'We heard,' Nedilko stated.

'Well, here they are, safe and sound.' Ward turned to Snow. 'Don't make a habit of this, will you?'

'I'll try not to.'

Ward flashed a swift smile, turned on his heels, and got into the Land Cruiser. The Toyota crabbed across the road before quickly heading back towards Donetsk and the rest of the OSCE monitors.

'Vitaly Blazhevich, Ivan Nedilko, may I present Mohammed Iqbal,' Snow said.

'It's Mo, to my friends,' Iqbal added.

Snow was in Ukraine to facilitate the repatriation of Iqbal, a British citizen held captive for several months in Donetsk. Iqbal was one of many foreign students studying medicine at Donetsk University, but unlike the others he had been kidnapped by the DNR, who took exception to the colour of his skin. The news of Iqbal's plight had come from a bizarre post on the DNR's 'VKontakte' page. They used the Slavic copy of Facebook to inform the Russian-speaking world of their latest proclamations and 'successes' against the Ukrainian forces. Via VKontakte, Iqbal had been labelled 'a black mercenary' and 'a spy' by the self-appointed Prime Minster of the DNR. Iqbal was subjected to intimidation, beatings, and starvation by his captors. It was only after much negotiation that his release had been brokered and an agreement reached to hand him over to the OSCE. At least that was the official story, and the one that made the DNR look like humanitarians, but Snow knew otherwise. He still had the bruises and an empty magazine to prove it.

'Incoming!' A shout went up as a shell whistled overhead.

Snow grabbed Iqbal and threw him into the ditch at the side of the road as another shell flew past them to land with a thunderous cacophony further down the road.

'Bloody twats!' Iqbal's Brummie accent grew thicker with his annoyance, as he spat out a mouthful of cold mud.

'Stay down!' Snow ordered. He looked up and saw the source of the shells. What he took to be a Russian armoured vehicle, possibly a BMP-2, had appeared from the fork in the road. Too far away to return fire, the Ukrainians took cover as best they could. Still visible, Snow watched the OSCE Land Cruiser skid around the tracked vehicle and take the fork in the other direction. Then, just as quickly as it had started, the shooting stopped. The BMP-2 turned and followed the Toyota towards Donetsk.

'Nice of them to give you a sendoff,' Snow said as he pulled Iqbal to his feet.

'I'd have preferred a box of chocolates.'

Snow smirked. 'Come on. We need to catch a ride back to Kyiv.'

Chapter 1

Morristown, New Jersey, USA

As James East neared Morristown Green, a raw October wind battered his cheeks with icy rain like needles. For a dead man he felt very alive. In winter the snow that covered the park and storefronts lent a Dickensian feel to the otherwise drab, post-revolution architecture; today, however, rain was all anyone was getting. Saturday shoppers traipsed like herds of deer, umbrellas up, searching for bargains. East pulled up his coat collar. It wasn't the cold he disliked but the wind, which ravenously bit at his exposed flesh. He entered the green along a path that crossed the central square where a group of Latino youths dressed in baggy sweats were sheltering under the trees, smoking and taking snaps of each other. An elderly couple sharing a golfing umbrella joined East as he waited for the lights to change. They were holding hands and had probably been doing so since the Fifties. East felt a pang of jealousy. It had been three years since East had held his girl's hand; she'd loved him and he had left without a word. They hadn't spent much time together yet he remembered every second, every flicker of her eyelashes and how she curled her lower lip as she smiled. He closed his eyes briefly and could smell her perfume and feel her head upon his chest. East shivered – it was time to let her go. His eyes snapped open as a car horn sounded. The lights at the crossing had changed to 'walk'. Back to reality, his reality. The man she knew was dead, he had to be, but James East was very much alive. He crossed the road and entered the discount designer department store. Inside he nodded at the security guard; the man returned his nod solemnly. East undid his jacket, brushed his hand through his wet hair and looked around. To the left stood rows of handbags and on the right the cosmetics counter, where a middle-aged woman was receiving a makeover from an eager teenage assistant with make-up as thick as a circus clown. East moved past more women inspecting bags and reached the mens-wear section. Aisles of shirts stacked by designer, colour and size were neatly arranged. He selected a size bigger than he needed; he chose not to advertise the fact that he worked out. He took three shirts, no flashy colours, with ties to match, over to the 'tailoring' area, which was run by a white-haired man with an Eastern European accent. Much to the assistant's delight, he picked up a two-piece charcoal suit and entered the fitting room.

*

At the main entrance, Finch, the store security guard, fought to keep his eyes open. To say the former US Marine was bored by his job was an understatement. After ten years in the service of the good old 'US of A' he had been invalided out with a derisory disability pension. The irony was that the Navy had deemed him medically unfit to stand guard for long periods of time and therefore no longer suited to active service. Yet here he stood, a security guard in a department store, on his feet for eight hours a day. Where was the logic? Finch stepped outside for a blast of icy wind to wake him up. As he did so the detectors rang. Four men entered the store, while two women with heavy bags exited. Finch sighed and asked the women to step back inside; security tags left on again, he assumed. They moved to the jewellery counter where he started to remove their purchases to be checked one by one.

*

There was a scream and shouts followed by a series of loud staccato cracks. James East locked eyes with the menswear assistant. Both men dropped to the floor; they had heard the sound before – automatic gunfire.

'Stay down.' East's voice was controlled and firm. The elderly assistant bobbed his head in assent and crawled deeper into the dressing rooms. East worked his way, at a crouch, out of the alcove. What greeted him on the shop-floor was shocking. Two men holding Uzi submachine guns stood in the central aisle, firing off rounds indiscriminately at any shopper who dared move. The security guard, white shirt turned crimson, lay sprawled across a collapsed glass counter. Two women had been dropped next to him. As the store fell silent one gunman changed magazines while the second continued to swing his weapon in an exaggerated arc. East noted their actions: uncontrolled, jerky, and amateur. There was a sudden blur of movement as a portly woman ran from behind an overturned display. The gunmen tracked her with their weapons on fully automatic. Rounds spat from the barrels, showering her and the surrounding area. East hugged the floor as rounds impacted against the back wall, hitting fittings and spinning off at obtuse angles.

The woman, eyes wild, was thrown sideways, mid-stride, as white-hot lead tore into her flesh. She came crashing down with a sickening thud on the thinly carpeted shop-floor. Her eyes saw

East and her mouth moved; she reached out her hand. '*Pamageet minya.*' 'Help me,' she pleaded in Russian.

'*Nie dveegaisia!*' 'Stay still,' East hissed back in the same language. But it was too late. Her hand trembled, fell limp, and her eyes glazed over. East's jaw tightened – he was going to stop them.

*

There were footsteps on his left by the escalator. Two more gunmen were ascending to the upper floors, one a little ahead of the other. East craned his neck; the first pair now had their backs turned and their weapons pointing away. East moved with speed and stealth towards the disappearing gunman. Reaching the bottom of the escalator he launched himself up, two steps at a time, no longer caring about the noise he made, only the distance he covered. The nearest gunman turned, Uzi held upwards in one hand, the short barrel pointing at the concrete above. His eyes registered East but not before East's open palm crashed up into the underside of the gunman's nose, flattening cartilage and breaking bone. As if struck by a sledgehammer the man dropped the Uzi and fell sideways. East grabbed the weapon and squeezed the trigger. A three-round burst ripped through the gunman before burrowing into the side of the escalator.

There was more gunfire from above. East flattened himself against the metal steps and was carried upwards. As his head crested the shop-floor he saw that the fourth gunman, oblivious to his colleague's demise, had started to spray the room. East raised the Uzi and fired a controlled burst into the back of his target's head. The man fell instantly, body dead before it had stopped falling. Around him shoppers and staff cowered and wept. Two X-rays down, two more to go. East hit the stop button on the stairs and peered over the side at the ground floor. Save for sobbing, the area was quiet once more as both gunmen again changed magazines. One was silent and had a crazed expression on his face, while the other seemed to be quietly chanting. East had to act; he had to take them out now. He moved down the metal steps, took a deep breath, and then broke cover at the bottom.

The nearest X-ray looked up, eyes wide as East fired. The gunman stumbled backwards as rounds impacted his chest before he crashed into a counter. The second gunman returned fire and charged forward. East pivoted, fell to one knee to lessen his profile, and acquired the target.

'*Allahu Akbar!*' the gunman yelled.

East looked into the man's eyes and released second pressure on the trigger. The X-ray fell upon him and glass exploded around both men. The X-ray was history, but his momentum took East down with him. East's head hit the carpet-covered concrete shop-floor with a loud crack and his world went black.

*

British Embassy, Kyiv, Ukraine

Aidan Snow sipped his black coffee as he listened via the internet to the *Today* programme on Radio 4. The main news of the morning was an explosion at rush hour on the Moscow metro. It had happened at a station Snow knew well, one close to the international school he had attended as an 'Embassy Brat' twenty years before. So far the number of fatalities hadn't been released but Snow knew it would be high. The radio announced that the explosion had been confirmed as an IED and that a Chechen group, the Islamic International Brigade, had claimed responsibility. An expert on Russian security matters from the UCL School of Slavonic and East European Studies had been quickly found and, in heavily accented English, gave his opinion. He explained that the Russian authorities wouldn't accept that the real Islamic International Brigade had carried out the attack, due to the fact that the FSB had either captured or killed its leaders. Indeed, the leader of the group had been publicly put on trial and was at this very moment serving a full life term in Russia's most secure prison. The expert went on to say why he thought the bomb had been detonated and who else could be responsible. A splinter or copycat group using the same methods...

Snow clicked off the broadcast and continued to eat his breakfast in silence, even though he had now lost his appetite. Terrorism was senseless: innocent civilians were targeted based solely on the actions of their governments, whom they probably hadn't voted into power. Yet it was endemic the world over and it sickened him. Saturday had brought reports of a suspected Al-Qaeda attack on shoppers in a New Jersey department store and today it was the turn of commuters in Moscow. Snow shuddered as he imagined the horror created by the detonation and panic among the Muscovites. He pictured the metro station in his mind as he remembered it, with its scrupulously clean floors, advert-free walls, grand architecture, and fur-clad crowds. As a teenager he had frequently explored Moscow by jumping on the metro after school, much to the annoyance of the British Embassy driver. He had sat and listened to the Muscovites, often taking the train to the end of the line into areas that were strictly off the tourist path. In the late Eighties, just before the Soviet Union crumbled, Moscow had been an exciting place. There had been something in the air, a note of dissent those in power had chosen to ignore, to their ultimate cost.

Today, the people in power were jumpy; an attack in one European capital city put all the others on high alert. Moscow, having once again attempted to resurrect the Soviet Empire by illegally annexing Crimea and invading Eastern Ukraine, had made itself target number one. It had no one else to blame, but it was the Russian people who were suffering and not the warmon-gering cocks in the Kremlin.

The door to the room Snow was camped out in opened and Alistair Vickers entered. He sat heavily in an armchair. 'You've seen the news, I take it?'

'What next?'

Vickers shrugged. 'I have no earthly idea, but Jack's just called for a video conference.'

On cue, Snow's secure iPhone vibrated to show an incoming email from Jack Patchem, his boss at SIS. It contained just one word: *Moscow.* 'We'd better go to your office then.'

Vickers reluctantly dragged himself out of the comfy chair.

*

Several minutes later Patchem spoke without preamble as the video-link started. 'Terrible news from Russia. The last thing we need is the loony brigade annoying the Kremlin.'

'Do we know who's responsible?' Snow asked as Vickers pushed a plate of custard cream biscuits towards him.

'Only what the media is saying, but our man on the scene is confirming thirty dead now, some foreigners. The FCO doesn't know yet if this includes any Brits.'

'Was there any advance warning of the attack, any increased chatter seen by GCHQ?' Vickers asked.

'None, and that's what's so worrisome. The only chatter we have is after the event, the usual rhetoric praising the suicide bomber and thanking Allah. Allah the almighty, who invented Semtex!' There was a pause and Patchem apologised. 'I know, gentlemen, I know. Call me an Islamophobe, but you understand what I mean. These crazies want to blow us all up in the name of Islam.'

'Their view of Islam.'

'Yes, Aidan – you're right, of course.' In London, Patchem took a sip of water. 'Actually, one phrase has come up a few times: "The Hand of Allah". We don't have anything on it yet; it could be a new group aligned to Al-Qaeda or IS, or, who knows, perhaps the name of an operation or just a turn of speech.'

'If it's the name of a new group, that would back up what the Russians say.'

'That it's not the Islamic International Brigade? Aidan, you know as well as I do that the FSB and GRU would never admit some key members of the group might have evaded capture.'

'I'm surprised the Kremlin isn't trying to pin it on "Ukrainian Banderite fascists", Vickers said.

'I had a beer with Bandera's grandson once. He wasn't a fascist, he was Canadian,' Snow replied.

Patchem agreed. The Kremlin had labelled the new Ukrainian government fascists and called the protesters who had ousted the old Moscow-backed President 'Banderites' after Stepan Bandera, the Ukrainian wartime nationalist leader who had chosen the Nazis over the Soviet Union. 'We can't rule out anyone at this stage.' Onscreen, Patchem closed his eyes and pinched his nose. 'Look...'

'Everything OK, Jack?'

'What, Alistair? Yes, just not sleeping as much as I should.' Patchem drank some more water and then cleared his throat. 'So, Aidan, welcome back and congratulations on "collecting" Mr Iqbal. How is he?'

'He's still catching up on his sleep. They kept him chained up in a garage for most of the time, and if he wasn't chained up he was digging trenches.'

'Trenches?' Patchem frowned.

'Apparently the leader of the DNR is a World War One buff; he loves the idea of trench warfare,' Vickers added. 'Which is very odd, when you consider he's holed up in the middle of an industrial city!'

'The whole thing is very odd. Alistair, how long until we can get Iqbal back to the UK?'

'Midweek I'd say. He's going to be talking to the SBU today; they want a debrief on everything he saw during his time in captivity. They'll be chatting to Aidan too. It's all going to be taken down as evidence against the DNR. Of course, I'll be there to record the session.'

'Good. Aidan, finish writing up your report, and then, once the SBU are happy, bring Mr Iqbal home. In the meantime, keep a low profile, but have your "grab-bag" and passport handy.'

'I always do.'

*

New York, USA

The driving rain cut down visibility, which was good for concealment. He lay on the damp concrete under the truck, his left side leaning against the cold steel of the skip. His dark-blue waterproofs kept most of the rain out save for a continuous trickle working its way down into his cuff where it mixed with the sweat on his clammy skin. Lights came on in the timber warehouse as the first workers began to arrive. The business park, however, remained silent. Seven o'clock came and the sky lightened, but the rain did not, continuing to pound on the steel of the skip and the hood of the truck. His view was limited to what he could see directly ahead between the truck and the skip and to his right under the vehicle. If anyone approached on foot he would be blind until they were directly on top of him. His position was far from perfect. He put all thoughts of comfort to one side and continued to await his prey.

He felt rather than saw the first timber shipment arrive. Trucks could appear any time after the transporters had cleared customs at Newhaven port and been offloaded. For this reason the warehouse was always staffed. It was almost 8 a.m. now, and he stretched in an attempt to relieve cramped muscles. His mind started to repeat over and over the words he had been told... the target was the one who had carried out the orders; the target had burnt, torn, and tortured. Inside the overalls he sweated heavier as a white rage engulfed his body. The target would pay for his brother's murder. A vehicle approached, the distinctive growl of the AMG Mercedes engine competing against the rain. His mind was suddenly clear, focused, his breathing controlled. He craned his neck and saw the driver's door open. Positive ID. He moved with the speed and grace of a panther, springing up and away from its den. Uzi in his right hand, he narrowed the gap to his prey and hit him with a stiff arm. The target fell back against the hood of the Mercedes and, a split second later, he pulled the trigger. Intense flashes of light illuminated the stormy morning. The target convulsed, lightning bolts impacting his chest and upper body, forcing him into the car. The gunman stopped and looked into the eyes of the target with hatred. '*Za mayevo Brata,*' he heard himself yell in Russian. 'This is for my brother...' He repeated the proclamation as he emptied the remainder of the magazine into a lifeless corpse... the last time he had used an Uzi was... He felt a pain in his temples and a light flashed, the pain increasing as the light got nearer and brighter. He wanted it to stop; he wanted to move, to run away, but his legs wouldn't work. He tried to raise his hands to protect his eyes, but they wouldn't work either. All the while, the light got brighter and the pain intensified. His world changed from the blackest of black to a deep red. James East began to hear a voice speaking in a language he did not officially speak. The red gradually lightened and then the voice spoke to him.

'Can you hear me?' The Russian was flawless. 'You are safe; you are no longer in any danger.'

The doctor noted a flickering beneath the patient's closed eyelids. He spoke again. 'If you can hear me, can you try to open your eyes?' A note was thrust into the doctor's hand. He read it quickly. 'I need you to give me the name of your next of kin. We must contact your family to say that you are here and safe with us.'

Family? From somewhere inside East's mind, a light switched on. His mouth opened and several syllables of Russian rolled out.

'I am sorry, I did not hear that. Can you say it again?'

More Russian. '*Y menia bull brat...*' 'I had a brother...' East began to say in Russian, then stopped. The pain sharpened and the light became white. Suddenly conscious behind closed eyes, East realised his mistake. He started to groan and make unrecognisable sounds.

'I am sorry, but I do not understand. Can you say that again?' The doctor moved closer.

East opened his eyes and spoke in English; his throat was dry and his voice raspy, but his Boston accent, the same one he had used for the past three years, was unmistakable. 'Where am I?'

The two men standing over the bed momentarily seemed surprised before regaining their composure. The doctor spoke first, sticking to Russian. 'You are in hospital. You were involved in a shooting.'

East blinked, feigning incomprehension. 'I'm... s... sorry. What did y... you say?'

The doctor began to speak, but the second man touched him on the shoulder and shook his head. He asked in English, 'What's your name?'

'My... my name is James... James East.'

'Well, Mr East, my name is Mr Casey. As Dr Litvin was attempting to say, you were caught up in a terrorist attack.'

East tried to sit up, but a searing pain behind his eyes blurred his vision.

Dr Litvin placed his hand on his patient's arm and now also

15

switched to English. 'Try not to move too quickly; your body has suffered some trauma.'

East closed his eyes; when he opened them again his vision had returned. He assessed the room. It was a standard hospital white. He noted the badge on the doctor's coat but directed the question to Casey. 'Where am I?'

'You're in a hospital in Manhattan, Mr East. You were brought here after the shootings. Do you remember that?'

It was hazy, but he did. 'How long have I been here?'

'Just over forty-eight hours. You have a concussion.' The doctor touched his arm reassuringly. 'You are lucky, Mr East, that it was not more serious.'

'He must have a thick skull, eh, Doc?' Casey was jovial.

'Quite.'

'Mr East, there are a few questions I would like answered.'

The doctor frowned. 'If I could have a moment, Mr Casey?'

The doctor stepped outside and folded his arms. He waited for his visitor to join him. 'While I am more than happy to assist with your investigations, I do not think the patient is medically fit enough to be interrogated.'

Casey raised his eyebrows in mock surprise. 'Doc, no one's going to be interrogated. I just need to ask him a few questions.'

'Not today, Mr Casey. He is not going anywhere. You may question Mr East when I deem him to be fit.'

Casey's expression hardened. 'I need to question him in the interests of national security.'

'You came to me because you thought the patient might be a Russian and, indeed, I heard a few words. However, when he regained consciousness, he spoke English, just like you and me.' Litvin was an immigrant but didn't let that cloud the issue. 'I understand that Mr East is not a normal patient; however, he must be treated as one. Remember, it would be me in the firing line if he were to sue the hospital for any complications or malpractice.'

'Thank you for your candour, Doc.' Casey decided to push no further.

*

Scanning the room, East realised there was no TV in the corner, just an empty bracket. He tried to sit up again but felt as though a gigantic hand was squeezing his head.

The door opened and Litvin appeared. He smiled as he neared. 'Mr Casey is a government agent and wanted to interrogate you. I told him you were not well enough. You need to rest.' Litvin sat in the chair next to East's bed. 'Can you remember what happened?'

'I think so. How many did they kill?'

'Nine dead, and seventeen others with gunshot injuries. It was a miracle more innocent shoppers didn't die. Some people are calling you a hero. I, for one, agree with them.'

'Thanks, I guess.' Nine! Inwardly East cursed. Why hadn't he been faster? Why couldn't he have been by the entrance to stop them?

Litvin seemed to read his mind. 'I expect you are asking yourself why you couldn't have saved more people, or shot the terrorists sooner?' East nodded and Litvin continued. 'You are suffering from survivor's guilt, and everyone does. You wonder why you were chosen to live when others died, when others might have been more deserving of life. No one has answers to this, not down here at least. We are not party to the great plan. Tell me, are you a religious man?'

'No.'

'I see. I am from Moscow… and you, Mr East?'

'Boston.'

'Originally?' Litvin raised his eyebrows. East didn't reply, so the doctor continued. 'Where did you learn your Russian?'

'I did a course at college. It was either that or Spanish.'

'You spoke Russian several times while you were sedated.' In actual fact, it was when the sedation had begun to wear off, but Litvin wasn't going to admit the anaesthesiologist might have got the dose wrong.

East changed the subject. 'When can I leave, Doctor?'

'In about a week or so. There was some swelling to your cerebellum, which is at the base and back of your brain, and is responsible for coordination and balance. The good news is that the scans did not show any obvious damage. Until you regained consciousness, however, we could not be certain. Now you are conscious, you need to undergo further tests.'

East frowned. 'Why was Mr Casey here?'

'Mr East, there was a shooting; these things have to be investigated. I think it is best that you rest now. My colleague from the neurological team will be along to check up on you later.' Litvin rose and left the room. His patient needed rest and, regardless of who the men in suits were, they must let him be.

East closed his eyes. What Litvin had said was true; he wasn't worthy to live because of the innocent lives he had taken in the past. Any of the nine murdered shoppers had more to offer society than him. He closed his eyes for a moment. Were the painkillers altering his mood, making him morose, or did he really feel this way? He sat in silence. He had no idea. What he did know, however, was that he had messed up, and now he had to work on his escape.

Chapter 2

Kabul, Afghanistan

'Brothers, our Islamic Emirate is strong. The West cannot defeat us, for when we all shall die it will be with the grace of Allah, peace be upon Him! Those of us destined for martyrdom will die as Holy Warriors, leading the jihad against the infidel crusaders! On this sacred mission we shall be martyred on the infidel's own soil. For us there shall be no fear. It is the infidels who shall fear us and the anger of Allah!' The audience voiced their agreement. 'My brothers, you will continue to fight without fear, knowing that we have the blessing of our faith! Brothers, it is time for our journey to begin!' Mohammed Tariq stood and embraced in turn each of the men staying in Kabul, those who would continue to fight in their homeland while he and his five soldiers of Islam headed for the border.

The group of Holy Warriors left the dimly lit room and walked towards the bus. Although almost one in the morning, the coach station south-west of the Afghani capital was busy. Twenty-four hours a day, buses and trucks poured out of Kabul, taking migrants on the first leg of what they believed was their journey to new lives abroad. The bus Tariq's cell would take was known by locals as the 'border bus'. It ran nightly, travelling the four hundred miles west to Herat, a town near the Iranian border. At Herat, Tariq's men would be met by an Iranian contact, who would conceal them within his truck for the crossing into Iran at the Islam Qala border checkpoint. Once in Iran they would pass through Taybad and then on to Mashad, the resting place of the Imam Reza. It made no difference to Tariq that Mashad was one of the holiest cities in the Shia Muslim world, for in the name of Allah he had put aside all notions of Shia or Sunni. It was division that had held back Muslims and allowed the infidels to exploit them.

Tariq stepped onto the bus, followed closely by his trusted men. A sea of mostly young, expectant, Afghan faces stared back. They yearned to leave the country; they craved the embrace of the infidel, longed to be prostituted by the West. Unlike Tariq and his team, each migrant before him had on average paid $10,000 to a smuggler to get them into Europe, and some much more. Many would perish en route, prey to the elements, border guards, malnutrition, and bandits. Tariq fought the urge to spit, to lash out; these travellers were turning their backs on their duty to their country, their obligation to the jihad and, most sickening of all, their obedience to the Muslim faith. In his mind they were apostate, traitors to Islam and worthy of the death sentence. Tariq fought to keep his face a mask of calm. He and his men were hiding among the sheep, but they were wolves. They were wolves with the most mighty weapon of all; the Lion Sheik, peace be upon Him, had called it the Hand of Allah. Yet what was in the small case had been ordered by Moscow and created in Ukraine. The Hand of Allah had been requisitioned from the infidels who had attempted to destroy the Muslim Caliphate. Tariq enjoyed the irony as his group squeezed into the last remaining seats; the infidel's own weapon would be used to herald their ultimate destruction.

Tariq bent down to stow the case beneath his feet.

'Are you going to the West?'

Tariq looked up. A boy, too young to grow a beard, yet old enough to sleep with the infidel, was staring at him. 'My family has sent me to find work,' he said. 'I know it is hard but there is much opportunity in the West.'

'Indeed, there is much we can do in the West, my brother.'

'My father has paid for me to go to London. It is the best place. He has heard that France, Germany and Italy are racist countries, but England is good and the government is just. I will find work there.'

The Al-Qaeda operative's lips imitated a smile. 'London is a very popular destination. Perhaps one day I shall see you there, Insha'Allah.'

'Insha'Allah.'

With a scraping, caused by lack of maintenance and a build-up of dirt and sand, the outer doors shut. Moments later the engine coughed into life and the bus heaved out of the station and into the night. Once assured that they were away safely, Tariq closed his eyes. There was little to see and nothing to do. This night they would cross the blackness of the desert on highway one, stopping first at Kandahar before eventually reaching Herat in the heat of the following day. It was a tedious route, but one not many Afghan soldiers would think to monitor for an Al-Qaeda cell. Sheep were ignored by lazy shepherds, and he had been trained how to bleat.

*

British Embassy, Kyiv, Ukraine

Snow closed the laptop, his after-action report on the rescue of Mohammed Iqbal finished, and checked his watch. He needed some downtime away from anything to do with HM Government;

two weeks of intensive undercover work in and around Donetsk had left him drained. He lifted his iPhone from the desk and scrolled through the contacts until he saw a name which brought a smile to his face. He dialled the number.

An hour later Snow stepped out of a taxi in front of the salubriously named Standard Hotel on the corner of Horenska and Sviatoshinskaya Streets. On the outskirts of central Kyiv, the anonymous small hotel sat squat among the taller apartment blocks. It was a grey and cream two-storey structure and resembled a pair of gargantuan shoeboxes, placed one atop the other. The main hotel entrance was squarely in the centre of the ground floor, shaded by a burgundy awning, but Snow ignored this and entered via a door on the right-hand corner, itself under a burgundy sign which said 'Café Bar Standard'. He pushed through a heavy wood door and searched the dark, smoky interior for his old friend. He spotted a figure with craggy features, light-brown hair and wire-framed glasses sitting at a large corner bench, smoking and admiring a table of female customers.

Snow and Michael Jones had been ex-pat teachers together at a time when Snow had thought his gunfighting days were over. 'Look who it is, the drinking man's Gordon Ramsay!'

'Aidan, hokay?' The Welshman's accent invited strange looks from the nearest customers.

Snow stuck to the script and adopted a fake Welsh accent. 'Hello, Mister Jones, how are you?'

'Eh, not bad.' Jones beamed. 'Just look at the crumpet in here!'

Snow laughed out loud; Jones would never change. 'It's good to see you, Michael.'

'You too. How long are you back for?'

'Just a few days.' Jones knew Snow had been a member of the SAS, but not that he now worked for the Secret Intelligence Service. Snow stuck to his legend of being a senior teacher at an expensive Knightsbridge private school. 'The school's asked me to give a presentation to a few Ukrainian high-rollers.'

'Persuade them to send their kids to your place, is it?'

'Correct. I'm free this evening and then I've got meetings and business lunches until I fly out on Wednesday.'

Jones raised his eyebrows. 'Phew, I'm glad I just teach a few English lessons here and there. No stress and lots of time to drink, smoke, and observe the local wildlife.'

Snow shook his head at the fifty-something Welshman. 'How's Ina?'

'Not bad. She lost her job, though.' Jones's wife of sixteen years was a banker – and her husband's banker.

'Sorry to hear that.'

'Eh, but she got a new one with a Canadian investment group. She may have to fly out there next month. I don't mind, it gives me a chance to rest.' Jones's diction was lilting and slow, as always after he'd had a few pints. 'But great to see you, eh!'

'You too, Mr Jones.' Snow became serious. 'So, how have you been this last year?'

'Fine. We obviously skipped Crimea this summer and thought for a while of coming back to the UK. But then I saw the house prices. I can't bloody afford to get on the housing ladder at my age! So we didn't. Our area was pretty isolated from the violence and unrest, thank Christ. But eh, it's a shocking business, isn't it? Who are the Kremlin to say Ukraine can't join the European Union? Ukrainians are good people who were led by a corrupt president. Russians are good people but… people are people, let them live.' He waved his hand and then drained the remainder of his beer.

Snow agreed with Jones's statement, even if the wording was a little off, but he didn't want to get political or morose. For once all he wanted to do was sink a few drinks, reminisce, and relax. And from the look of it, Jones was several drinks ahead of him. Snow caught the attention of the barmaid, who trotted over with menus.

'Is this your friend, Michael?'

'This is Aidan. He used to teach with me.'

'Nice to meet you,' Snow said in Russian. 'Two beers, please.'

'Is Obolon OK?'

'Fine.'

She smiled pleasantly and returned to the bar with a wiggle that Snow tried but failed to ignore.

'Service with a smile,' Jones remarked happily.

'So, what brings you to this place then?' Snow asked.

'One of my students, Vlad, runs it. He's a good bloke and the beer is so cheap for Kyiv prices!' Jones was always counting his money. His love of bargains coupled with his love of alcohol had made him an expert on the cheaper watering holes of Ukraine's capital city.

'I'm not surprised it's cheap – it's in the middle of nowhere.'

'It's not far from the metro and if you're near the metro you're near everything.'

'That's true.' The beer arrived and Snow held up his glass. 'Cheers.'

'You too.'

'What time does Ina want you home?'

'Whenever. She doesn't mind me drinking with you. Thinks you're a calming influence.'

Snow smacked beer from his lips. 'I thought she knew me better than that.'

The door opened and a hulking figure ducked his head to enter.

'He's a big boy,' Jones noted, 'and I thought you were tall.'

'I am tall. He's a giant. Do you know him?'

'No.' Jones returned his attention to his beer.

The giant, dressed in a tracksuit under a leather box jacket, strode to the bar and, with a booming voice, ordered vodka. He knocked back his drink in one and then demanded a beer.

Snow's training kicked in as he scanned the bar. The other ten or so customers weren't making eye contact with the new arrival, especially the table of women Michael had been watching. Two of them discreetly turned their chairs away. The man was dangerous, and by the way people reacted to him, known as being such.

'Another?' Jones asked.

'Silly question.' Snow winked.

'*Pani!*' Michael called out the Ukrainian word for 'miss', also used to mean waitress. 'Two beers, please.'

The giant turned and leant against the bar, swivelling his large head to stare at them.

Snow involuntarily felt himself tense, ready for action. 'So, where is this Vlad then?'

'He's probably in reception; it's a family business. His dad owns the hotel; Vlad's just taken over here and his two sisters work in both. The one at the bar is called Svetlana.'

'I thought you said you didn't know him?'

Jones sniggered. 'Not the giant, the barmaid.'

'Here.' Svetlana brought the beers. She no longer seemed happy and hurried back to the bar.

Jones took a long swig and then stood. 'I'm sorry, I need a slash. Bladder can't keep up with me anymore.'

Snow continued to assess the threat and the giant continued to stare, until another man appeared in the bar. He wore black jeans and a black T-shirt with 'Café Bar Standard' printed on it in burgundy. On seeing the giant, he paused before walking to the bar. Snow watched as the new arrival started to polish glasses as the giant spoke to him.

'Hokay, Vlad!' Jones shouted as he emerged from the bathroom a minute later.

Vlad held up a tea towel but said nothing as the giant now glared at Jones.

Jones sat and noticed the expression on Snow's face. 'What's up?'

'I think the big fella is bad news, Michael.'

'What, him? He's just a bloke having a drink. You've been away too long.' Jones produced a new packet of Ukrainian cigarettes from his jacket pocket and fiddled with the polythene wrapper.

'Maybe.'

A glass smashed at the bar. The giant was pointing at Vlad with his index finger.

'Shit.' Snow sighed, getting to his feet. He'd seen enough shake-downs in his time to understand what was happening. 'Michael, stay in your seat.'

'What?' Jones looked up from his cigarettes. 'Oh, I see.'

Snow placed his empty glass on the counter. Svetlana was sweeping the floor with a dustpan and brush while Vlad stood, frozen like a rabbit in headlights. Snow spoke in Russian. 'Two more beers, please, and...' He studied the face of the giant. '... Whatever you're having.'

The big man's heavy forehead furrowed. 'Vodka.'

Vlad looked between the two men as he pulled the beer and then poured a shot of vodka.

'Two vodkas.' The giant grabbed Vlad's wrist and scowled at Snow. 'One for you, too, unless you do not want to drink with Victor?'

'I'd be honoured, Victor,' Snow said.

With a shaky hand, Vlad placed the glasses on the bar before retreating. Victor took his glass and Snow copied. There was a moment's hesitation and then both men threw the contents against the backs of their throats. Victor checked Snow's reaction to the harsh spirit. There was none.

'Who is your foreign friend?'

Snow shrugged. 'He's an English-language teacher.'

'I have always wanted to learn English.' Victor's face became whimsical. 'So I can tell foreigners to get the fuck out of my country.'

'That's a good reason,' Snow said.

26

'I am sick of seeing all these Westerners around Kyiv! They swagger like they own the place, throwing their money about while, in the East, our men without the correct clothing or equipment or weapons die fighting for Ukraine. And what do the foreigners do to help Ukraine? They call the Russian President and tell him he must stop!' Victor rubbed his face with his palms before placing them on the bar. 'Another!'

Snow knew Victor was right, but what could he say? He just nodded at Vlad who again quickly poured two shots.

Victor raised his glass. 'Ukraine.'

'Ukraine,' Snow repeated

Victor swivelled his head. 'I am from Kamyanka; it's a village to the south of Donetsk. The DNR have destroyed it. And why couldn't the Ukrainian army defend it? Because they did not have the equipment! Do you understand?'

Snow remained silent; Victor was dealing with some powerful emotions and likely to explode at any moment.

'I hate foreigners. They sit, drink, shit, and pay to screw our women. That is all.' Victor looked now at Snow and said mockingly, 'Thank you for the vodka.'

'You're very welcome,' Snow replied as he collected his beers and moved back to his table.

'You made friends then?'

'He's from the Donbas. He likes me, I'm a nice guy.'

'That's because your Russian is too good; ironic, eh?'

'What's ironic is that he doesn't like foreigners, and he thinks you're foreign.'

'Well, as an ethnic minority, I am offended! Does he not know about the significant historical links between Wales and Donetsk? Donetsk was founded by a Welshman who opened Ukraine's first mine and steel works. Ukraine's first state school was opened in Donetsk, and the first English-language school.'

'You looked it up?'

'Of course. Ukrainians like it.'

'Well, big Victor wants to learn English.'

'That's nice.'

'He wants to learn English so he can tell all us foreigners to eff off.'

'Make him the Minister for International Relations.' Jones puffed on a new cigarette.

Snow slurped his beer. 'Seriously, Michael, he's trouble, but he's not sober so his guard's down. I suspect he's part of a local protection racket.'

'Roof insurance.' Jones used a well-known euphemism. 'Aye, that's one thing I thought Maidan got rid of – the crime and corruption. I got stopped by a militia officer the other day who wanted to see my passport. I told him I didn't carry it around with me for security reasons. So he said I had to pay a fine of $50.'

'What did you do?' Snow was sure he'd heard the story before, but now it was updated for modern times.

'I did nothing. I was walking with Ina. She told him to piss off or she'd report him.'

Snow smiled. 'You don't argue with Ina.'

'Too right. When we got home she did report him.'

There was another crash at the bar and Victor wobbled. He staggered towards Snow and Jones. 'Teach me.' His two words of English were slow and slurred. He raised his voice. 'Teach me!'

Snow got to his feet and held up his palms. 'OK… OK, have a seat and we can discuss this. We're not the enemy.'

'Enemy?' A grin appeared on Victor's face. 'Tell the foreigner to give me his money, and you give me your money. You then can both fuck off.'

'I'm Welsh,' Jones said. 'A Welshman founded Donetsk!'

The giant frowned and, without warning, but with unexpected speed for a man of his size, dropped his shoulders several inches and shot his mammoth right fist out at Snow. Snow instinctively took a step back and, with both arms working at once, his left

28

palm swatted Victor's arm down while the back of his right fist slammed into the giant's nose. It was a simple but effective move; no one throwing a punch expected to receive another back before theirs had struck. Victor blinked and retreated a half-step. Snow reversed the momentum of his right fist and struck the man in the jaw. Victor's legs buckled and he landed on his knees. He had to go down; Snow didn't want him to be able to fight back, given his size and inherent strength.

'I am from Oleg. He says you don't come here anymore. Oleg is in charge here!'

'Oleg who?' Victor was dazed.

'Oleg.' Snow high-kneed Victor under the chin; his head snapped back, his eyes closed, and he fell. 'Michael, we're leaving.'

'Hokay.' Jones stood and shrugged at Vlad.

'Call the militia quickly. Tell them the SBU are on their way.'

Vlad looked at Snow in confusion. 'SBU?'

'Yes.' Snow reached into his pocket, withdrew a $100 bill, and handed it to Vlad. 'This is for your trouble; any friend of Michael Jones is a friend of mine.'

Michael stared down at Victor. 'Don't mess with the SAS.'

Snow grabbed Jones by the sleeve. 'Time to go.'

Outside, darkness had fallen and they took the path round to the front of the hotel. 'Who's Oleg?'

'There's always an Oleg.'

Michael pointed down the street. 'Sviatoshyn metro station is ten minutes that way.'

'OK, we'll go back to the centre and drink in a place full of foreigners.' Snow tapped Jones on the back. 'Don't worry – I'm on expenses.'

'Oh, that's great. But can you hang on a minute? I need another slash.'

'Fine.' Jones walked down the side of the hotel, opened his flies, and urinated into an evergreen shrub. Snow had ceased to be embarrassed by his friend's antics years before, so took the opportunity to call Blazhevich.

'Aidan? What's up?'

'I've had a bit of a problem with a guy in a bar – a giant to be exact. Can you send someone to collect him? I don't think the local militia would be up to the job.'

He heard the Ukrainian sigh. 'Where is the giant?'

'He's in a hotel on Horenska Street, not far from Sviatoshyn metro.'

'Was this giant called Victor?'

'Yes. Why?'

'Kyiv really is a small village. He's known to the SBU, and you were lucky.'

'Why?'

'Victor Krilov is a former professional boxer, a good one.'

'Nice.'

'Aidan, stay out of trouble. I'll see you and Mr Iqbal tomorrow, at the debrief.'

*

FBI Field Office, New York

Vince Casey looked up from the computer at FBI Deputy Director Gianni before placing his thick index finger on the laptop screen, the display changing colour under the pressure of his digit. 'This guy's a "pro", no doubt in my mind.'

Gianni stared at the frozen image of the member of the public who had taken down four gunmen.

'Look again at how he moves.' Casey clicked and rewound the surveillance tape.

Both men watched as the figure travelled with an economy of movement, without any hesitation or lack of purpose.

'So who is he?' Gianni asked.

'That's why your Bureau and my Agency are interested.'

Gianni sat back and folded his arms. The speed of the man was impressive, as was the way he had terminated the X-rays. 'Vince, what's your professional opinion?'

'I don't think it's any different to yours.'

'Humour me. Spell it out.'

'Definitely SF or SF-trained.'

Gianni valued the opinion of the CIA black-ops veteran. In the corridor outside the office they heard footsteps. Both men remained silent from force of habit until the footfall faded away. Gianni leaned forward, dragged his laptop nearer, and tapped the keyboard. He glanced across at his long-time friend from the Agency. 'The fingerprints come up as belonging to a banker from Boston.'

'Let me have a look at that?'

'Sure.' Gianni pushed the laptop back towards Casey. 'Just scroll down. All we have is there.'

'Thanks.' Casey read the report, although he already knew the basics. James East. Born in Boston, put up for adoption by his mother, no record of a father. Placed in a state orphanage, never adopted. There was a grainy photograph taken from a high-school yearbook, which showed East as a bespectacled, blond-haired teen. How was East's eyesight now, Casey wondered – he'd better check. He read on. After graduating from high school East travelled to the opposite side of the country to study at UCLA. Upon completion of his degree, he volunteered to teach English for charities in Romania and then Bulgaria before returning to the US several years later.

'Again, Vince, what's your professional opinion?' Gianni asked, deadpan.

'Again, the same as yours.'

'Too convenient?'

'Exactly,' Casey stated wryly. 'No family, no ties, out of the

US, and then no real job until three years ago when he comes back?'

'And, as you see, no record of any criminal activity, or military service.'

'So he's not one of ours,' Casey confirmed. His initial thoughts had been that East was a 'NOC', an agent with 'No Official Cover', a black operative. But his CIA database had thus far come up blank as regards any facial recognition match. In his experience even the blackest of NOCs left some record. He'd continue to search.

'So what do we have?' Gianni leant back in his chair and rolled his shoulders.

'Someone else's asset?'

'Perhaps, but we've got the local office in Boston digging deeper into his background; if there's anything fishy, we'll find it.'

The hard lessons learnt from the 9/11 terror attacks had now been fully implemented; the varying arms of the US intelligence and law enforcement services worked together, transparently and harmoniously. At least that was the official line, but Gianni and Casey did find the activity of their organisations more and more linked. The Bureau's remit was 'domestic security' and the Agency's the interests of the US abroad; however, each organisation was keen to keep tabs on suspects, wherever they might be.

Gianni continued. 'We got a court order to open his safety deposit box. There was nothing in it apart from a few thousand dollars in cash. I've asked the NSA to look for any recent calls made on the iPhone he was carrying.'

Casey got to his feet and helped himself to a cup of coffee from the pot in the corner of the room. 'Whoever Mr East is, he's got some explaining to do.'

'Oh, he'll talk. Hero or not, he's facing four counts of voluntary manslaughter at the very least.'

'And how many innocent shoppers did the bad guys get?'

Gianni held up his palms. 'I know… if it hadn't been for Mr

East we'd have had a full-scale massacre on our hands. The fact still remains, however, that he killed four men. Justice cannot be blind.'

Casey pretended to agree. 'How did we miss them?'

'Hey, if we knew that we'd have stopped them ourselves.'

'Why couldn't just one of them have lived? At least until we bled him a bit.'

It angered and annoyed Casey that the shooters had appeared from nowhere. The leads from the increased chatter following Bin Laden's kill/capture even now had them all chasing their tails. And, added to this, new threats from Islamic State to take their fight to the West had, in short, created so much chatter that it had become a shield. 'The bigger question is, how many more have we missed?'

'You know as well as I do how much traffic the NSA is looking at, the volume Echelon is sifting. My question is, why attack a store in Morristown, New Jersey? Why not hit the branch opposite Ground Zero?'

Casey had been wondering the same thing and had no answer. Was it random, opportunistic, a mistake, or personal? 'We may never know.'

'Yep,' Gianni agreed. The identities of the four men remained unknown. There had been no IDs found on the bodies and the fingerprints had thrown up fake legends, the origins of which were still being traced. 'How is Mr East?'

'Why?'

Gianni gave Casey his no-shit stare. 'I need to talk to him. Remember, we are in the USA; the rule of law has to be followed, otherwise we'll be no better than them.'

Casey raised his eyebrows. 'Hey, I'm not farm-fresh, remember? We have laws, and sometimes they bend.'

'OK.' Gianni sighed imperceptibly; he knew he was fighting a losing battle. Casey had an agreement with the Commander in Chief that Gianni wasn't meant to know about. 'Someday, Vince, you're not going to get what you want. This isn't a pissing contest; we've both known each other too long for that. East has to be under my watch. I'll pull my agents back a bit. After you've finished talking to him we'll resume our perimeter and he's mine. OK? Any intel you get, copy me in.'

'Thanks, Gino,' Casey said affably, 'but I wasn't asking you for permission.'

Gianni was about to reply when Casey's Blackberry pinged. Casey retrieved it from his pocket and read the alert. 'Shit. They've hit Moscow again.'

*

SBU Headquarters, Volodymyrska Vulitsa, Kyiv

The room chosen by the SBU for Iqbal's debriefing was much more elaborately furnished than any at Vauxhall Cross. The walls were clad in ornate, gilded, hand-painted panels, and the chairs were highly padded and covered in an array of exotic leather. The large table in the middle could hold twenty guests, but today it had seated only five: Mohammed Iqbal and the intelligence officers responsible for his rescue – Aidan Snow, Alistair Vickers, Vitaly Blazhevich, and Ivan Nedilko.

At the start of the meeting Vickers officially presented Blazhevich, who was deputising for Director Dudka, with copies of Iqbal's and Snow's statements. It had taken most of the day to meticulously go through these, the SBU being loath to miss anything that could potentially be of use in their ongoing anti-terrorist operation against the DNR and possible future international indictments. Photographs of known DNR members were shown in turn to both Iqbal and Snow, and videofits were created of as yet unidentified men. All in all, Iqbal's illegal incarceration had provided the SBU with valuable

Humint (human intelligence) they wouldn't otherwise have been able to gather.

Blazhevich signalled Nedilko to switch off the digital tape recorder as he closed the folder in front of him. 'Gentlemen, I think that's it. We have finished here.'

The official part of the debriefing complete, Snow let out a long sigh. 'I could murder a beer.'

'Me too,' Iqbal said.

Nedilko was confused. 'But aren't you a Muslim?'

'Yes, but some of us do drink, you know.'

'Unfortunately,' Vickers stated, 'we can't be seen in a bar together. People will wonder who you are, Mo, and then, well, you know how it is.'

'I see.' Iqbal had been made to sign the Official Secrets Act, the SIS's involvement in his rescue being classified and having to remain so.

'So, your flat it is then, Alistair?' Snow added quickly, filling the gap in the conversation. 'Right, votes for Alistair's place; let's see a show of hands.'

Vickers pursed his lips as all hands but his own were raised in the air. 'Very well, my flat it is.'

Blazhevich shrugged. 'Unfortunately, I am going to have to bow out on this occasion. My wife is expecting me home.'

Snow raised his eyebrows but made no further comment – it wasn't like Blazhevich to pass on a booze-up.

The five men left the conference room and took the steps down to the ground floor. Blazhevich hung back and pulled Snow to one side. 'By the way, my colleagues took "the giant", as you called him, into custody. It was the same guy Nedilko and I arrested a year ago.'

'Thanks for that.'

'He wanted to press charges against the guy from Kharkiv who'd attacked him.'

'Kharkiv?'

'He assured us that his attacker was a Russian-speaking Ukrainian.'

'Looks like my Moscow accent needs a bit of work then?'

'No, it's his cauliflower ears. So we've charged him with racketeering, for the second time. You do know you were extremely lucky? He was a dangerous individual before, but now that he's started to rage about the Donbas he's become completely unhinged.'

'Then I'm glad you've put him away.'

'So am I, but you did hit him quite hard.'

'Whoops.'

'So this used to be the old KGB building then?' Iqbal asked as he stared at the armed guard manning the reception desk.

'Yes, and I wouldn't like to think what happened in the underground levels,' Vickers replied.

'What, they've got catacombs?' Iqbal's eyes widened.

'No, a basement with cells.'

'Oh, I see.'

'Yeah, they threw me in one once,' Snow called out, catching up with the others.

'You were a person of interest, Aidan,' Blazhevich stated.

'What do you mean "were"; aren't I interesting anymore?'

'Did you meet the ghost?' Nedilko asked.

'Ghost?' Iqbal repeated.

Vickers enjoyed the banter which over the years had formed among the group as the SIS and SBU had been forced to work together. He'd miss it all when he was eventually forced to move on to a new post at a new embassy.

As they reached the door to the street, the guard's desk phone rang. He answered it and called over to Blazhevich.

'Hello?' the SBU officer asked. 'When? I see. Thank you, Gennady Stepanovich.'

Snow noticed the expression on his colleague's face was now grave. 'Bad news?'

'Yes. That was Dudka. He's just been informed that another terrorist attack has taken place on the Moscow metro system. They are still counting the dead.'

'Bastards,' Snow hissed; it was the height of rush hour in the Russian capital.

Vickers and Snow both felt their phones vibrate. Vickers checked his screen, a secure email. 'Aidan, we're needed at the embassy. Vitaly, Ivan – thank you. Mo, you have to come with us.'

Outside, a distinct chill hung in the air as winter tried to replace autumn. The British Embassy on Desyatynna Street was a brisk, five-minute walk away up Volodymyrska Vulitsa and across Sofiyivska Square, and at this time of day an embassy car would take much longer to negotiate the Kyiv traffic. Vickers led the trio through the commuters returning home, with Snow bringing up the rear as 'tail-end Charlie'. They weren't expecting any problems, but experience had taught both SIS men to be vigilant. Arriving at the embassy, Mo went to the room assigned to him while Snow joined Vickers in his office, where they called Patchem.

'Aidan, Alistair, it's the same modus operandi as before: a suicide bomber on a commuter-packed tube train.'

'Any warnings this time?'

'No, Alistair, none. None at all. Whoever is doing this is going to have the full force of the FSB brought down on them from a great height, and rightly so. These are innocent people, for Christ's sake.'

'Has anyone claimed responsibility?'

Patchem shook his head. 'Not yet.'

'What are the Russians saying, Jack?'

'Nothing new, Aidan. If it's not the same group then it's a very meticulous copycat, and when I say meticulous, I mean disturbed.'

'The SBU are now going to start to panic,' Vickers noted. 'After all, Kyiv does have a metro system built by the same people, but hopefully not the same enemies.'

'So,' Patchem reasoned, 'if there were to be any attack upon Kyiv it would be a copycat.'

'Or a false flag,' said Snow. 'The Russians getting in an attack and blaming the International Islamic Brigade.'

'Well, let's hope none of these scenarios comes true. Alistair, has the debriefing been completed?'

'Yes.'

'Good. Aidan, I'd like you to fly back here tomorrow with Mr Iqbal. The DNR have already started to talk about his "negotiated release" on their VKontakte page. I've had Neill Plato take it down and put the page offline, but even though he's a technical whiz, Neill doesn't know how long it will stay off for. That's the problem with this social media madness; anyone anywhere can retweet or repost. The last thing we want is a group of tabloid paps waiting for you at Gatwick.'

'Can't we fly into Brize Norton?'

'The simple answer is no. Our Director General has been told in no uncertain terms by the Foreign Secretary that we've spent far too much time and resources on Mr Iqbal's rescue.'

'I bet he wouldn't have complained if it was his arse I was saving!'

'Aidan, I wouldn't have ordered you to save his pompous arse.'

*

New York, USA

East opened his eyes. The room was dark save for a thin line of light spilling in from under the door. He tentatively sat up and removed the drip from his arm. The medical staff had 'settled' him for the night and, bar an emergency, wouldn't be troubling him for several hours. This was his window, his chance. Closing his eyes in anticipation of the pain that was about to hit him, East swung his legs out of the bed and let his bare feet make contact with the linoleum. He shook as a wave of cold shot around his head before turning into a hot pain at his temples. He opened his eyes and gasped, but managed to grab the metal bedframe and push himself to his feet as the pain moved to the back of his head. He swayed for several seconds and, had the room been illuminated, would have noticed the edges of his vision grey out as he fought to remain conscious.

Once steady, East took a step towards the exit, then another and another, until he was certain he wouldn't fall. He held his breath as he prized the door open a fraction of an inch. The light blinded him and made him nauseous. He stood stock-still until it passed and his vision adjusted. He opened the door further, looked left, and saw a corridor. Several other doors led off to what he imagined would be rooms like his; further along was a cleaning cart and then double doors at the end. The corridor led on to a junction – he didn't know what was around the corner. Unable to turn his head with his neck alone, he swivelled his shoulders to the right and saw two empty chairs. Whoever had been guarding his door was gone.

Taking a deep breath, East edged out of his room and towards the cleaning cart. It contained supplies and spare towels. He picked up a towel and held it over his arm, as though he were looking for a shower room, and continued forward. He heard a door open somewhere behind him. He didn't look back, but continued on, head throbbing as he tried to move faster. Just as he reached the double doors two large men in suits burst through them. Their eyes widened at the sight of the semi-naked man before them, the man they had been told to guard, the man who could not get out of bed. East saw the sidearms on both 'suits' and knew instantly they were there to guard him. Doing the only thing he could, he threw the towel. The first man automatically raised his arms to protect his face while the other took a half-step sideways. In the same instant, East moved forward and kicked the second man in the groin. Caught completely off-guard, suit two doubled up and dropped to the floor. Ignoring the lightning bolts of pain in his head, East reversed his momentum and stiff-elbowed the first man's throat. With both men down, East grabbed the nearest suit's sidearm and, struggling to remain conscious, pressed it into the man's forehead. 'Get up slowly and keep your hands above your head.'

Coughing, the suit pushed himself to his feet as his colleague continued to hold his throbbing genitals. East was about to speak again when a round impacted the door inches above his head, the repeat sounding like thunder in the enclosed space.

'Put the gun on the floor, Mr East.'

Dizzy, East did as he was told and within seconds the suits had secured him.

Casey approached and holstered his Glock. 'Very impressive, for a banker from Boston. Perhaps you were in ad-venture capital?'

'Thanks.' East's vision had started to blur.

'You OK, Beck?' A grin creased Casey's face.

'Yes, Mr Casey, just hurt my pride, that's all.' The former Navy SEAL continued to massage his groin.

'I'd get that seen to.'

'He's been asking the nurses to all day,' Needham, the other suit and a former Delta, croaked.

'Take Mr East back to his room. I'm gonna call the doc, Mr East, and have him give you a once-over. We'll talk tomorrow.'

East tried to reply but blacked out.

*

East's hospital bed had been raised, bringing him to a sitting position. Casey sat in a chair to one side, two manila folders resting on his lap. 'Who are you, Mr East?'

'Is that an existential question, Mr Casey?'

'If you like.'

'I'm an old soul in a young body.'

'Cute. Who are you, Mr East?'

'I'm an investment banker.'

Casey placed a folder on the bed. 'Your legend is good, almost too perfect. James East from Boston who runs his own start-up investment consultancy based out of Yonkers. You've got some great recommendations from current clients, by the way. Where did you receive your combat training?'

East felt his pulse quicken. He was hooked up to monitoring equipment so could do nothing to hide it. 'I'm a fan of the WWE.'

'Yeah, that Undertaker.' Casey didn't hide his sarcasm. 'James – I'll still use that name for the moment – let's not waste any more time. I know you're not a banker, and possibly not even an American citizen. Now, I'm no fluent Russian speaker, but I understand enough to realise you probably are. Dr Litvin certainly believes so.'

'I did a college course.' East reached for a glass of water on his tray table and sipped.

'I ran your prints through all our databases. I got one partial match. It was from an unsolved Interpol case. Would you like to take a look?'

'Sure.' He tried to stay calm.

'Here.' Casey handed him a folder.

East opened the dossier and saw a blurry surveillance photograph of himself at London's Gatwick Airport. He turned the page to a report on the assassination of a British businessman named Bav Malik. It had several graphic images attached. East sped-read the document without showing any outward signs of emotion. After this came an image taken by a camera in an Austrian restaurant; this one was clearer and showed him wearing glasses and enjoying a drink with a beautiful woman. East felt his pulse race at the sight of her. He turned to another report. It was written in Ukrainian, a language he didn't speak, and contained images of a second corpse – Jas Malik, Bav Malik's son. East raised his eyes and saw an odd smile on Casey's face.

'I know what you are, but not who you are, James.'

'What am I, Mr Casey?'

'I think you are a contract killer. Possibly former Spetsnaz, gone freelance.'

'Is that the official belief of the FBI?'

'Did I say I was with the FBI?'

'You didn't say who you were with.'

'*Touché!* I'm the only one who has this opinion, James. That's why we're having this conversation. You did a noble thing; you eliminated an Al-Qaeda sleeper cell – one we missed. You saved the lives of countless civilians.'

'Do I get a medal?'

'No medal, James. There are those who want to know more about you, the FBI included, and this file will come to light eventually. Unless I bury or lose it. I could potentially use someone like you, if you are what I think you are. I'm offering you a chance. I can protect you from all of this, the wolves here in the US, and Interpol, but in order to do that I need you to be honest with me. You are not James East. I need to know exactly who you are and what you were doing in New Jersey.'

East made a decision. 'My name is Sergey Gorodetski, and I was shopping.'

There was a moment of silence as Casey held eye contact with Gorodetski before he replied. 'The funny thing is, Sergey, I believe you. So, Russian or Russian speaker?'

'Russian.'

Casey tapped the file with his index finger. 'And so to this. Why did you assassinate these two British citizens?'

'What guarantee do I have that you are not taping this? That you will not turn me over to the Feds for rendition to the UK?'

'That's a fair point.' Casey took a Glock 19 from his jacket and placed it on the bedside table. He turned it so the grip was within the Russian's reach. 'Here, take it, it's loaded. You have my trust, Sergey, and I hope I have yours.'

Gorodetski slowly reached for the gun and was surprised to see that Casey didn't flinch. He aimed the sidearm at the American, felt the weight, and then carefully lowered it. 'It's loaded.'

'I told you it was.'

'I could have killed you.'

'You still can, if you want. I'm a good judge of character, Sergey, and I know you won't. Call me romantic – my ex-wife doesn't – but I know who you are… on the inside. I can tell. You're not a stone-cold killer. So enlighten me, ease my confusion, and tell me. Why did you assassinate that father and son, Jas and Bav Malik?'

'I was of the belief they murdered my brother.'

Casey was surprised. 'And did they?'

'No.' Gorodetski pushed the Glock back. 'They were innocent. I murdered them. I am a killer. I deserve a bullet to the brain.'

'I could shoot you, but I won't. I think I can use you, if you agree.'

'I agree.'

Casey smirked. 'Tell me more; treat this as a confession, not to a policeman but to a priest. Why did you believe these two men killed your brother?'

Gorodetski took a breath and recounted what he had been told was the truth. 'In 1989 my brother, Mikhail, was in the Red Army. His commanding officer said their unit was attacked by Mujahideen outside Kabul. Mikhail was wounded, captured, then tortured before being dismembered. Much later his CO told me he had found two of my brother's killers. They were living respectable lives with British passports.'

'Did you find the real murderer?'

'Yes.'

'Did you kill him?'

'Yes.'

'Who was he?'

'Mikhail's commanding officer.'

'How did that make you feel?'

'Empty.'

'I see.'

'I was fooled, but that is no excuse. I executed two innocent men. There is not a night that goes by without me seeing their faces.'

'We all make mistakes, Sergey – just ask my wife.' Gorodetski scanned his fingers for a ring. There was none. 'Exactly. Some mistakes are big, some small, and some monumental. I can give you a second chance, which no one else can; a chance to make a difference. Not many get that.'

'Why should I believe you? You have thousands of SEALs or Delta or Rangers or Activity guys to choose from.'

'Good question. I'm Agency. What I do, Sergey, is black – blacker than black. You could call it "Cold Black" – global counterterrorism. There are only four other men who know I have you, and one of those you kicked in the nuts. I get to choose my men, use Agency resources, and not get questioned. However, and this is where you come in, regardless of what you read in the press or see on WikiLeaks, we do not have unlimited resources – human or otherwise. In short, when the Cold War ended our threat radar was moved to point at the Middle East. Langley didn't see a need for Soviet speakers, let alone native Russian-speaking operatives. But then Russia invaded Georgia, and then they annexed Crimea, and then they shot down a passenger jet while invading Eastern Ukraine. Langley made a mistake and I had a problem. I was thinking about how I could fix it when you appeared.'

'Thanks.'

'Don't go getting any grandiose ideas; it was coincidence not serendipity. Are you a patriot?'

'To Russia?'

'Who else?'

'The people, yes. The country, perhaps. The Kremlin? No.'

'That's very good to hear, if you mean it. I need to assess you and, even if, after that, you were to pass, you'd be strictly on probation. Make a mistake or step out of line and this file gets updated and sent along with you on a one-way ticket to London. Or, failing that, perhaps I throw you in the nearest river; it all depends on whether I've had a bad day or not.'

Gorodetski allowed himself a half-smile. 'You should work at the Army recruiting office.'

'Who said I didn't? Here is your first test – an act of good faith you could call it.' Casey picked up the file containing the information on 'James East'. 'I need something for the FBI to, how can I put this, ease your transition into my custody and persuade me I'm not making a mistake with you.'

'I understand.'

Casey tapped the file. 'Who was responsible for your legend?'

Gorodetski frowned. 'Responsible?'

'Where did you get your false identity from?'

Gorodetski paused for a beat before he spoke. 'Tim Bull. He's a high-school science teacher in Miami and an old KGB asset.'

'And he's gone freelance?'

'For the right price. He doesn't like the current Russian President.'

'Who does?' Casey shrugged. 'I'm going to need everything you have on him.'

'Agreed.'

'It wasn't a request, Sergey.'

*

Penal colony No. 6 in the Urals town of Sol-Iletsk was known as 'Black Dolphin' and officially classified as a 'final destination' prison. It was one of five Russian facilities where criminals sentenced to death were held, but by far the most ominous. Inmates unlucky enough to be sent there had no chance of escape and, unofficially, no hope of parole. The Black Dolphin's seven hundred inmates represented Russia's most brutal criminals and included murderers, cannibals, rapists, paedophiles, and terrorists. One of the seven hundred was a Chechen, Aslan Kishiev. Sentenced to full life imprisonment for his part in terrorist attacks on Russian civilian targets, he was nicknamed 'mini-Laden'. Kishiev had been the de-facto leader of the Islamic International Brigade ever since its founder, Shamil Basayev, had been killed in 2006. Kishiev had continued the jihad against Russia until he was finally betrayed by a close friend. Outraged at the manner in which he had been captured, at his trial Kishiev had openly vowed revenge by offering a bounty for the informer's head. This, however, had only added to the charges levelled against him. To mock Kishiev further, the Prosecutor General ensured the weasel gave evidence no more than ten feet away from where he stood. Found guilty on all twenty-three breaches of the Russian penal code, which included murder, torture, hostage-taking, illegal arms trading, terrorism, and armed rebellion, he had then learnt of his fate. Kishiev would live out the rest of his days at the notorious Black Dolphin, where he would be monitored twenty-four hours a day, forced to sleep with bright overhead lights switched on, and, from 6 a.m. to 1 p.m. every day, forbidden to sit on his bed. He would be liable to be checked every fifteen minutes by a passing guard and would live in complete isolation from the outside world. The Prosecutor General closed proceedings by stating that Kishiev would not be a martyr, he would simply be 'forgotten'.

It had been a bitterly cold February afternoon in 2011 when Kishiev had arrived at his new home. Blindfolded with a black hood, he and the other new arrivals were made to walk from the prison truck to their cells, past a line of guard dogs barking viciously in their ears. Unable to see even his own feet, he had no idea if the dogs were on leads or if they would attack without warning. Once in his cell, a fifteen-day 'educational introduction' to his new life at Black Dolphin, a life that had been described as 'death in instalments', commenced. Each of the inmates of Black Dolphin had killed an average of five people; Kishiev, many more. The exact number of deaths his group were responsible for had never been truly calculated. He had been treated as a terrorist, but Kishiev saw himself as a soldier for Allah, a believer whose pacifist soul had been torn away, destroyed when his lands and faith had been mercilessly attacked by Russia. But as a terrorist, he had been thrown in with the worst filth Russia had to offer. He was forced to share a four-and-a-half-metre-square cell with a man from Murmansk convicted of cannibalism, a crime he hadn't known still existed. Locked away in a cell within a cell, behind three sets of steel doors, it was a bleak, isolated, and hopeless existence.

As the roll call started for cell #174, both convicts adopted the 'position'. Bending double they approached their inner cell door backwards, arms out to their sides with palms upturned, heads tilted up with their eyes closed and mouths open. The position made it impossible to move with any speed or launch an attack. It also made them look ridiculous. The prisoners in turn stated their full names, before two guards took a prisoner each and handcuffed them. Once done, each inmate was grabbed by the neck and pushed out into the corridor. They were then made to stand in a stress position holding their handcuffed arms above their heads, leaning forward with their foreheads against the wall. Kishiev heard two more guards enter his cell to commence the daily search and check protocol, while, no more than a metre away, he could feel the hot breath of an Alsatian pulling at its lead. Eyes shut until ordered to open them, Kishiev's day had started again.

The man in charge of Black Dolphin, Lieutenant Guard Grigori Zontov, stood with his men outside Kishiev's cell. It was exactly 6 a.m. It was his routine; he insisted on being present for morning inspection and roll call. Today, however, was not normal: they had a visitor. To be more specific, Kishiev had a visitor, something that was unheard of. A man from the FSB awaited them in Zontov's office. The visitor had orders, from the Russian President no less, that he be granted immediate access to the Chechen.

'Cell 174 at ease.' Zontov studied the human detritus before him with unhidden disgust.

'Yes, sir,' Kishiev and Rasatkin, the cannibal, replied in unison. It was an order to open their eyes, but not to relax the stress position.

'Do you have any forbidden items?'

'No, sir.' Without being ordered to, the men opened their jaws and stuck out their tongues while their mouths were searched for any concealed items.

Zontov had no sympathy for the pathetic pair of animals in front of him; to call them humans made his tongue curl. When the search of the cell was completed, he ordered 'Convict Rasatkin' back inside while his men placed a black hood over Kishiev's head. As he was taken under the arms and led away, Zontov felt no need to inform the Chechen of the reason why he was now being separated from the other inmates. After five minutes of twists and turns, in silence except for the heavy breathing of the guard dog at his heels, the hood was removed. Kishiev squinted and, to his surprise, found he was in an office. Zontov quickly closed the blinds and switched on the light; he didn't want his prisoner to have any idea where the office was located in the prison or to see the daylight outside.

The man at the table dismissed Zontov in a cursory manner. 'Thank you. That will be all.'

'I must stay here; it is what the regulations state.'

'You will leave the room now, Lieutenant Guard Zontov. This is what I state.'

Zontov bristled. It was his office, his prison, his command. But the man sitting in his chair, at his desk, had a letter which carried the presidential seal. 'Very well.'

Kishiev showed no outward sign of emotion but inside praised Allah as he started to realise his insurance policy might have been banked.

The man facing him wore an expensive suit and had a Moscow accent. 'I had hoped you were already dead, Kishiev.'

The Chechen's eyes burnt with hatred as he recognised the man seated behind the desk. It was the same FSB officer who had liquidated his brother Chechens and carried out a personal crusade against him. 'Strelkov.'

'There has been an explosion on the Moscow metro system. Many Russians have been killed and a further number wounded. Your group has claimed responsibility.'

Kishiev noticed a calendar on the wall with a red indicator showing the date. 'That is because they are responsible.'

'You knew this was going to happen, didn't you?'

'This is only the first. There will be a further attack tomorrow and then again in three days.'

'You will give me the details of the planned attacks in order for them to be halted.'

'No.'

'I do not think that you quite understand my position, Kishiev. I report directly to the Director of the FSB.'

'And I take my direction from Allah, peace be upon Him.'

49

Strelkov's rank and title meant nothing to him. What was important was what he could offer.

Strelkov's nostrils flared above his neat moustache. 'You will give me the information I want or face the consequences.'

'Shoot me.' Death would be a welcome release from the monotony of his current existence.

'I knew you would be unreasonable,' Strelkov stated smoothly. 'We are holding your wife and child. Unless I get the information I require their lives will become very uncomfortable.'

Rage flashed across Kishiev's eyes, then fear tugged at his chest. His family had been hidden, had been living well away from Chechnya in Abkhazia. 'I don't believe you.'

Strelkov held up a photograph of a woman and young girl standing with two masked FSB commandos. 'We found them in Sukhumi, enjoying the sea air.'

Kishiev's jaw hardened. 'I shall never leave this place or see them again, so I must accept that they are dead to me.'

'If you would like to see them dead that can be arranged. Shall I bring you another photograph showing just that?' He raised his voice. 'Do you want that? Do you want to be responsible for the death of your wife, of your own daughter?'

Kishiev noticed a vein in Strelkov's neck throb. 'What do I get if I speak?'

'A guarantee that your family will not be harmed.'

Kishiev shook his head slowly. 'No. What you will do is release me from here and reunite me with my family.'

'That is not possible. Now tell me about the next attack.'

'Those are my terms.'

'You are in no position to demand terms!'

'Then the attacks will take place, and the Great Sheik Al-Mujahid will hear of them and declare me a true warrior for Islam. He will proclaim that, even though I am in your most secure prison, I am still waging jihad, that I cannot be stopped! *Allahu Akbar!*'

Strelkov's sneer returned. 'By "Great Sheik" I take it you mean "Bin Laden"?'

'He who is all powerful, the Lion Sheik. The infidels tremble at his name.'

'Your Lion Sheik became a lamb to the slaughter. Bin Laden was captured by the Americans on the 2nd of May 2011. They executed him and tossed his body into the sea.'

Kishiev felt his jaw slacken and his mouth drop open. He had spent more than a decade training in Afghanistan, meeting and conversing with Bin Laden freely on several occasions. As a highly placed commander of an Al-Qaeda affiliated group, he was one of the few who had been privy to discussions on planning. 'You are lying. The Americans will never find the Sheik. He is a great warrior and moves as the wind.'

'He was living in Abbottabad, Pakistan. He was not living like a warrior, but like an old woman.'

There was a silence. Kishiev tried to read Strelkov's face. He could see that the intelligence officer was too conceited to hide the satisfaction he was getting from informing Kishiev of the news. He was too smug to be telling lies. Kishiev let himself smile and then laugh. He laughed hard until it turned into an uncontrollable cough. Strelkov did not understand. Kishiev recovered and spoke. 'If that is the case you have truly lost. The Hand of Allah shall be released and your capital cities shall burn to the ground!'

Strelkov shook his head dismissively. 'Enough of your religious rhetoric. Bin Laden is dead and so is your cause.'

'You speak of rhetoric; I speak of a real weapon.' Kishiev saw little point in keeping it a secret any longer. 'The Hand of Allah is a nuclear device. The Lion Sheik ordered it be deployed after his death.' His laugh returned, only this time harder than ever.

The man from the FSB was stunned. Had Al-Qaeda finally got its hands on nuclear material? Was the Chechen lying? 'What do you know of this device?'

'I know that it is a suitcase bomb, and I know its designation. I am extremely surprised that it has not already been detonated, but then perhaps the timing is the surprise?'

'Where is it?' Strelkov replied too quickly.

'What will you give me?'

Strelkov scrutinised the terrorist's face. This was a ploy, he was sure, a ploy to gain his freedom. It had to be a fabrication. But what if he were telling the truth? What if one of the world's deadliest weapons had fallen into the hands of Islamic terrorists? Strelkov had led raids against the terrorists in Afghanistan, in Chechnya, and in Dagestan. Rooting out and apprehending Muslim extremists had been the focus of his career, and he had won. But had they now achieved the impossible? Strelkov started to feel his heart beat faster and had to breathe deeper to control his rising fear. All the while the Chechen laughed at him like a circus clown, yet he had to take the statement seriously. 'What is the designation of the weapon?'

Kishiev became serious. He had a memory for numbers and specifications and had wanted to be an engineer before becoming a Mujahideen, before discovering a love for weaponry and the technology of weaponry. He knew how to dismantle, clean and repair any number of firearms and had created very effective IEDs. 'The designation of the device that I know of is RA-115A.'

Strelkov felt his blood chill and for a moment could not speak. What felt like a lifetime ago, when his employer had been known as the KGB, he had been assigned to a guard unit protecting the perimeter of a military base. Within the base had been a weapons-testing facility. He had never actually seen the device, or known where or if it had been developed, but talk among his unit, who met with other guard units at sporting events, was that a new type of atomic weapon called the RA had been created that was both deadly and portable.

'Where is it?' Strelkov demanded.

Kishiev remained silent.

Enraged, Strelkov leapt from the table and backhanded the Chechen across the face.

Kishiev slipped sideways and fell onto the floor. In his weakened state, after three plus years in prison, the once fearsome warrior could not fight back. He tasted blood in his mouth as he spoke. 'I know of the plans, the route it may take. I will tell you in return for my freedom.'

Strelkov rushed out of the door. He already had his phone to his ear as two of Zontov's men entered to secure the prisoner. Strelkov speed-dialled the FSB number, but it would not connect. He pulled the phone from his ear and stared at it before yelling at Zontov. 'Why is there no signal?'

'There is no signal for security reasons, Comrade.' It humoured Lieutenant Guard Zontov to see the self-important FSB agent lose control.

'What? Where can I get a signal?'

Zontov inclined his head. 'Two kilometres in that direction, I believe.'

Strelkov balled his fists, his knuckles turning white. 'Where is the nearest landline?'

'Back there, in my office.'

'Is it secure?'

'It is a telephone in my secure office.'

'That is not what I meant!' Strelkov snapped, turned on his heels, and went back inside. He picked up the desk phone and was about to make a call when he noticed that Kishiev was still in the room, standing between the two guards. 'Take that outside and wait.'

The room empty, Strelkov lifted the handset to make a call to Moscow but then hesitated. Moscow was almost sixteen hundred kilometres away and two hours behind Sol-Iletsk. He checked his wristwatch; it was almost a quarter to seven, which meant it would be a quarter to five in the morning in his Director's Moscow mansion. Strelkov sighed, shook his head, and called his chief,

Director Nevsky, on his mobile phone. It rang out to voicemail. Strelkov ended the call and immediately redialled. This time it was answered on the fourth ring by a slumber-thickened voice. Strelkov took a breath and explained what he had been told by the Chechen.

Several more time zones away at the headquarters of the NSA in Fort Meade, an analyst grabbed hold of his desk to stop himself falling from his chair. The Echelon system had picked up a phone call to a flagged and secure number, but, unusually, the caller was using an unsecured landline. This was surprising, but what was explosive were the keywords it had picked up on: Al-Qaeda... nuclear device... detonate... Western city... Hand of Allah...

Chapter 3

Mashhad, Iran

At the town of Herat, the group of six Holy Warriors were met without incident by their Iranian smuggler. A man well known to the guards on both sides of the border, he received his orders from an Egyptian, who since October 2001 had lived in Iran, immune to US attacks, and continued to serve as head of Al-Qaeda's security committee. The truck was used officially for cross-border trade, and unofficially to funnel foreign fighters through Iran. The relationship between Al-Qaeda and Iran was a complicated one, but one that for the moment favoured Mohammed Tariq and his team. At the Iranian border they were waved through after a perfunctory check while other potential Afghani migrants were hauled from trucks and beaten. Those who attempted to make a run for it were shot. Unlike the 'soft' borders of the EU, the Iranian guards were authorised to use lethal force to protect their beloved country from any undesirable visitors.

Tariq tried to settle his mind. In the semi-darkness of the truck he peered at his five men, all of whom had taken his advice and succumbed to sleep. He, however, could not. Although their route into, through, and out of Iran had been specifically selected by the late Sheik and the management council, Tariq couldn't get rid of the feeling that at any moment they might be ambushed by the Iranian Revolutionary Guard. However, he didn't let his fears show when his men were conscious; he was the leader of a holy mission and, as such, had to remain resolute about their chances of success. He stroked the case as though it were a pet, oblivious to the potential oblivion its contents could bring. Eventually, fatigue triumphed over fear and he fell into a fitful sleep only to be awoken what felt like minutes later by the truck's tyres crunching loudly on gravel.

In front of him, Reza Khan was the first to react; he sat up with a start and reached for his knife. By the time the back of the truck had been opened all six men were awake and alert. The driver informed them that they had arrived in the holy town of Mashhad. They hopped down to find themselves in the courtyard of a large villa. Above, the sky was a piercing blue and a slight breeze lightened the midday heat. This was the residence of Yassin al-Suri, the Al-Qaeda facilitator who, granted some leeway by Tehran, was permitted to operate discreetly within the country. This included collecting money from donors, to be transferred to Al-Qaeda's leadership in Pakistan, and facilitating the travel of recruits from the Gulf States to Pakistan and Afghanistan. Dressed in a grey, tailored suit, with neatly cropped hair that, if longer, would be curly, al-Suri resembled a banker not a terrorist. Yet he was both. He was one of only three men to know the true nature of the case Tariq carried. Any more would lead to security leaks and the mission being compromised. He was on hand to personally oversee their operation and grease palms. This was the highest-risk Al-Qaeda operation in history, surpassing even the New York attacks, for not only the infidels but the Iranians, too, would give anything to possess the device Tariq carried. 'Welcome, brothers!' Al-Suri held his arms wide to encompass the villa behind as he greeted them.

Tariq kissed al-Suri on both cheeks and introduced his team: Reza Khan, Sharib Quyeum, Ashgollah Ahmadi, Lall Mohammad, and Abdul Shinare. All of them were proven fighters, devotees to the cause, and resourceful. 'Is everything in place?'

The edges of al-Suri's mouth curled up. 'Everything. Now let us eat. Tomorrow you shall continue on your path to martyrdom.'

'Insha'Allah.'

'Yes, my brother, Insha'Allah.' Al-Suri's eyes wandered to the case. 'Is that it?'

'Yes.'

'Can I hold it?'

'No.'

'Good. Do not let it out of your sight and do not let anyone take it from you. Now let us all go inside. You must wash and then eat.'

Tariq beckoned to his men. 'Come.'

*

New York, USA

'This is most irregular.' Dr Litvin glared at Needham and Beck, arms folded defiantly.

Needham shrugged as though he had no choice in the matter. 'I understand, Doctor, but it's in the best interests of national security that Mr East be moved to a secure facility.'

'This is against my medical opinion. There are further tests that need to be carried out.'

'Rest assured they will be, Doctor. Our medical staff consists entirely of experienced specialists.'

'Really?' His nose had been put out of joint. 'What is the name of the medical institution he's being transferred to?'

'I can't reveal that, for reasons of national security, but he'll be well cared for.'

'Mr East, what is it that you want? Do you agree to be transferred?'

Gorodetski looked from one man to the other. 'I think it is best that I do go with them. Yes.'

Litvin shook his head slowly. 'Very well. Mr East, you have made a swift recovery thus far, but I warn you, head injuries are a very delicate area. Certain symptoms may be delayed in their onset for days after the time of injury. You may start to experience problems concentrating, have memory lapses, become irritable, unable to sleep, or be hypersensitive to light and noise. You mustn't overexert yourself, and if you start to suffer from any of these symptoms you must immediately report this. Do I make myself clear?'

Gorodetski nodded and was rewarded with a jolt of pain behind his eyes.

'Goodbye then, or as we say in Russian: *Dasvidaniya*.' Litvin held out his hand.

Gorodetski took it and replied in Russian. 'Thank you, Doctor, for your care and advice. I did appreciate it. Until we meet again, all the best.'

Litvin beamed at hearing native Russian. 'Moscow?'

'Tula.'

'Ah. Tula once had a hearing aid factory. Take care, my friend from Tula, and I mean that.'

*

Beck and Needham flanked Gorodetski as they entered the underground car park. Gorodetski felt unsteady on his feet but refused to let it show. Needham pointed his remote at a black Cadillac Escalade; the lights blinked to confirm the alarm had been disabled and that they could now open the doors.

Gorodetski glanced up at Beck as the taller man opened the sliding door. 'No hard feelings, I hope?'

'Not for a week, according to one of the nurses.' His face was unsmiling, but the eyes betrayed it wasn't an issue.

'Live by the pork sword, die by the pork sword,' Needham added as he climbed into the driver's seat.

On pulling out of the parking lot both operatives automatically scanned for possible threats. The NY traffic was heavy, but eventually gave way to the emptier roads of New Jersey.

'It's gonna be a while yet, James, I'd get some shut-eye if I were you.' Needham didn't know Gorodetski's real name, and nor did the rest of Casey's team. 'Sleep when you can, eat when you can, remember?'

'Yeah, I remember.' It was a Special Forces motto the world over. Gorodetski needed no encouragement; the cocktail Litvin had administered already had him nodding.

*

Camp Bastion, Helmand Province, Afghanistan

As one of the last units to leave Camp Bastion, Captain Mike Webster of the British Army Intelligence Corps had started to become bored with his posting. The frantic activity that had followed the target acquisition and execution of the Bin Laden kill/capture mission had long gone. There had been some infighting between rival groups, with splinter cells forming new alliances as their leaders vied to replace the late Saudi 'Sheik', but now, in Afghanistan at least, there was an eerie silence from Al-Qaeda. The West had turned its attention to the new threat: Islamic State, or IS, as British Intelligence officially called the new organisation. For their part, neither Al-Qaeda nor the Taliban had conducted any major attacks since the announcement that Camp Bastion was to close and ISAF were to pull out of Afghanistan. It was as though they were collectively holding their breath until Bastion's decommissioning had become a reality. Regardless of the lull in hostilities, Webster was sure that some very fanatical men somewhere were planning the next 9/11. It wasn't a matter of if – it was when. He supped his regulation milky tea and studied the US drone surveillance photographs. The most exciting things he had seen in months were the images in front of him. Known players in the Pakistani Taliban had been followed crossing into Afghanistan where they were recorded meeting local Afghani 'Talibs' and suspected members of Al-Qaeda. In Webster's opinion, the group posed a perfect target for a hellfire missile, but someone high up, undoubtedly American, had decided to let it play out, to see what the 'men in black turbans' were up to. Webster shifted the photographs to one side and sighed. His room was stuffy and he was tired. He closed his eyes and felt himself drift… He was suddenly on a beach with his wife, sipping rum as the sun set. He could taste the alcohol and feel the warmth of his wife's lips…

'Captain Webster.'

Eyes snapping open, embarrassed, he looked up. 'Just thinking with my eyes closed. What is it?'

Corporal Ian McAdam seemed a bit uneasy. 'We're holding a… er… local who wants to meet with a member of British Intelligence.' It wasn't an unusual request. Every Tom, Dick, or Halib thought they had vital intelligence, especially when rumours circulated about large cash rewards. What was unusual, however, was that Webster was being bothered. McAdam met his superior's eyes. 'This one is a bit different.'

'How so?'

'He says he's Russian.'

'Russian?'

'Soviet Red Army, sir.'

Webster raised his eyebrows. An unknown number of former Red Army soldiers had remained in Afghanistan after the Soviets had withdrawn. A few had been prisoners of war, others deserters who had gone native, and some bandits who attempted to make money in the 'Wild East' as the Soviet Union had crumbled. He, however, had yet to meet one.

McAdam held out his hand. 'He was carrying this.'

Webster narrowed his eyes. Puzzled, he studied the sheet of paper. It seemed to be some type of technical diagram. It was handwritten and contained words in Cyrillic. 'OK, lead on, Macduff.'

'McAdam, sir.'

Webster sighed. 'I know.'

McAdam led the way out of the dark seclusion of Webster's office into the dusty, blinding Afghan daylight and to an area designated for 'interviews'. Both buildings reminded Webster of a *Star Wars* set. Two armed squaddies had been placed, as a precaution, on sentry at the entrance. They saluted; Webster returned it and entered the room.

His guest was sitting with his arms folded and a hardness in his eyes. He was not to be intimidated. When the man spoke there was a recognisable Russian accent. 'You are Military Intelligence?'

'You can talk to me, Mr…'

'Then that is a "yes"? My name is Mikhail. I have valuable intelligence that you must pass on to your superiors in London.'

Webster kept his game face on. 'What would that be?'

Mikhail had no time for small talk. 'Al-Qaeda has an atomic weapon.'

'What?' Had Webster heard him correctly?

'Al-Qaeda has an atomic weapon. I brought it into this country in 1989. It is an RA-115A and is the size of a suitcase. The paper I have given you details the technical schematics of the device.'

Webster tried not to smile. It was best to humour the loonies, not make fun of them. He'd let 'Mikhail' talk and pretend to take notes. 'So you're saying that the Red Army brought nuclear material into Afghanistan in the Eighties?'

'That is correct. I was a lieutenant in the Spetsnaz. I was

assigned a classified order to bring certain weapons into theatre. I was to maintain them until they were needed.'

'How many?'

'How many nuclear devices?'

'Yes.'

'I personally had one such device. There may have been more in other bases that I was unaware of.'

Webster stared at the paper. He neither spoke nor read Russian, if that was indeed what he was looking at, but the more he studied the diagram, the more something started to niggle him; the more he started to feel that perhaps, just perhaps, Mikhail wasn't mental. What if this was real? 'How did you come across this document?'

'I created it myself.'

'From what?'

'From memory. I have perfect recall. What do you call it, "photograph memory"?'

'Photographic memory.'

'Yes. I was trained in how to use the device, how to maintain, and also, if necessary, adjust it. As such I saw the inner workings. If you have a basic technical knowledge it is really not complicated.'

Webster remained silent and studied the paper again. It meant nothing to him. He could see the shape of a case with a tube and several small boxes inside it, but that was as far as his technical understanding went. 'Mr Mikhail…'

'Just Mikhail.'

'Mikhail, this is of course a very serious accusation and one I will have to check the validity of before I take it further.'

'You do not believe me; you think I am a crazy man? Perhaps I am crazy to stay in Afghanistan, but I am not crazy enough to let terrorists detonate an atomic weapon.'

Webster noted Mikhail's unblinking eyes; there was still no reason to believe this was anything more than the imaginings of a heat-crazed Russian deserter. It wasn't his area of interest, but surely the notion that such suitcase nukes existed was one of fiction? 'Where exactly is the weapon?'

'Exactly, I do not know. Roughly? It is on its way to Europe, via Iran.'

'And what is the target?'

Mikhail shrugged. 'If I knew that I would have told you. I do not want a nuclear bomb to go off, anywhere.'

'Then why did you give the bomb to Al-Qaeda?'

'I did not give it to anyone. I had been hiding it away from the world. The terrorists took it and have decided to use it, and I have decided to tell you so you can stop them.'

Webster was confused. 'Why have you not informed ISAF before? Are you a member of the Taliban, Mr Mikhail, or perhaps Al-Qaeda?'

'I am a Muslim. These people of Afghanistan are now my people. I had no reason to believe that the device would be discovered.'

Webster pursed his lips. The idea that the bomb existed was wild enough, but the idea that, if it did, Mikhail could have at any time prevented its being taken or alerted ISAF but didn't was beyond him. But he couldn't waste any time on this now. What he had to do was report back to London just in case there was a shred of truth in what the Russian was telling him. 'Tell me everything about this weapon.'

'This of course I am happy to tell you, but in return I want safe passage out of Afghanistan.'

'Back to Russia?'

'No. I want to go to the UK.'

So that was his angle, the real reason why the Russian was sitting opposite him. He wanted to escape Afghanistan? 'I don't know if that's possible.'

'Of course it is,' Mikhail said slowly. 'There is a bomb heading for Europe and I know who has it. What information do you need from me to confirm that I am telling you the truth?'

Webster rattled off a stream of questions. 'I need your full name, the location of where you say the device was stored, the names of the men who took it, the names of the men who now have it, the name of your unit and where it was based, the name of your commanding officer, the name that was given to your operation, your...'

'OK.' Mikhail held up his hand and Webster stopped mid-sentence. 'Pick up your pen.' The Russian reeled off his answers and Webster noted them down. 'So now what happens?' Mikhail asked when Webster had finished.

'I need to check the information you have provided me with.'

'How long will this take?'

Webster had no idea. 'A few hours.'

'I shall stay here.'

Webster opened his mouth to disagree, then simply said, 'Very well.'

Webster left the room, giving the guards instructions not to let the Russian leave, and hurried back to his office. It seemed an improbable story and yet... and yet he now heard a voice inside his head telling him it was real.

*

Cabinet Office Briefing Room A (COBRA), Whitehall, London, UK

Abigail Knight, Director General of the Secret Intelligence Service, stirred her strong coffee as she mentally prepared for the emergency early-morning meeting. Her boss, the Foreign Secretary, Robert Holmcroft, sat next to her. Malcolm Wibly, the Home Secretary, was seated opposite with Ewan Burstow, Head of MI5, the Intelligence Service, by his side. The four did not attempt to make conversation. If the others knew the reason for the meeting they were remaining tight-lipped. In the early hours of the morning Knight had received an urgent message from GCHQ. The US's Echelon monitoring programme also fed GCHQ, and the same keywords – Al-Qaeda... nuclear device... detonate... Western city... Hand of Allah – that had the NSA worried had also alarmed the British.

Knight had immediately called Holmcroft and a matter of three hours later they were awaiting the arrival of the PM. It was almost 5 a.m. and the capital's streets were still dark and foreboding. Holmcroft turned his wrist to study his Rolex and tutted. Holmcroft was smug, happy to have been in the loop while his counterparts were not. He was, however, both impatient and pompous. He had been the candidate in the Conservative leadership contest against the PM; he was the man who should, in his own mind, now be king but was not. The door opened abruptly and Daniels entered. Even at this early hour he was in his customary shirt sleeves. As Knight looked on with red-rimmed eyes she had to admit that Daniels had an energy she'd rarely seen in a politician, but she put this down to his relative youth and exercise regime. He had become the most popular PM in decades. The opposition had been responsible for this when their attempt to lower the government's popularity by calling them 'the party of fat cats' had backfired. Daniels had caused outrage in the House of Commons by simply lifting his shirt and displaying his flat stomach to the chubby opposition leader. At the time Knight had found it amusing and the PM had been placed second in a UK women's magazine's 'fit list', beaten only by Daniel Craig. Today, however, there was no amusement to be had. The tone was one of urgent solemnity. A second man, wearing full RAF dress uniform, was at the PM's heels.

'Thank you for your prompt attendance.' Wibly half-smiled, while Holmcroft crossed his arms. Daniels continued. 'You all know Air Marshal Christopher Naylor, the Chief of Defence Intelligence?' There were nods and muted acknowledgements. 'This meeting will be classified as "No Eyes". Is that understood?'

Knight hid her surprise. 'No Eyes' was the highest security level in the UK and rarely invoked. So rare, in fact, that the general public were unaware of its existence. No notes would be taken, no record kept, and no documents distributed for the purpose of the meeting would leave the room. This was only the second such meeting Knight had attended.

The PM nervously pushed back a lock of his dark, dyed hair as he sat. 'We have had, over the last twenty-four hours, two pieces of intelligence which point to the existence of a rogue nuclear device.'

The shock was apparent on the faces of both Wibly and Burstow. It was the scenario security services the world over feared. It was the elephant in the room, a question of when, rather than if, it would happen.

'Two pieces of intelligence?' Holmcroft's tone expressed annoyance.

'That is correct. Ms Knight, please start by presenting your intelligence.'

'Very well, Prime Minister.' Knight looked at each of the men in turn before taking a deep breath and explaining the intercept from Echelon.

As soon as she had finished Daniels spoke. 'Home Secretary, Mr Burstow, I am sorry that you were not made aware of this sooner, but I decided it pertinent that we disseminate the information here. Since Ms Knight made me aware of this intercept I've received a further piece of intel that explains why I have asked the Air Marshal to attend. Air Marshal, over to you.'

Holmcroft folded his arms, his expression changing to one of indignation. He should have been informed.

Naylor cleared his throat. 'Thank you, Prime Minister. Yesterday an officer stationed at Camp Bastion received a piece of intel purporting that Al-Qaeda was in possession of a portable atomic weapon. A device often referred to as a "suitcase nuke".'

'Do such things actually exist?' Wibly asked.

'During the Cold War the US and the USSR were actively developing such devices. The smallest confirmed weapon was American and the size of a large rucksack. This device is believed to be Soviet.'

'Soviet? So you're saying Al-Qaeda has an old Russian bomb?' Holmcroft questioned.

'That is correct, Foreign Secretary; furthermore, we have been informed that this weapon was part of a Soviet programme and, as such, taken into Afghanistan in the late Eighties.'

'Programme? The Russians had more of them? What do the Americans think?' Holmcroft addressed the PM, who had become uncharacteristically quiet.

'Nothing yet. They don't know.'

'What?!'

'Robert, I haven't told the President about our piece of intel, and won't until we have positive verification that a real threat exists. We don't know if these two pieces of intel are related.'

Holmcroft all but threw up his arms. 'Prime Minister, with respect, if we're taking this matter seriously, we cannot for one moment longer pretend they are separate pieces of random intel that have just happened our way at the same time. We cannot and must not keep our allies in the dark.'

Daniels sighed. This wasn't the time for egos, but again the man was attempting to undermine his authority. 'Foreign Secretary, I thank you for your opinion. The purpose of this meeting is to decide how to move forward. This will undoubtedly involve our American allies. Air Marshal, do we have any idea where this suitcase nuke may be and, furthermore, who has it?'

'We believe the case to be in the possession of a man named as Mohammed Tariq. He is believed to be a member of the Tehrik-e-Taliban-Pakistan.'

Holmcroft did little to hide his anger. 'Believe? Believed, Air Marshal? We believe that he has a nuclear weapon?'

Wibly cut in before Holmcroft could continue. 'I'm confused. Are you saying the Taliban has the weapon, or Al-Qaeda?'

'The Tehrik-e-Taliban-Pakistan has aligned itself to Al-Qaeda, Home Secretary.'

'Forgive me for not being up to speed, but can you tell me a bit more about this group?' The PM furrowed his brow.

Holmcroft grinned, without sincerity. 'Prime Minister, they are the group that claimed responsibility for the 2009 attack on the CIA's Camp Chapman and the 2010 attempted bombing in Times Square.'

Daniels was embarrassed; he should have remembered. He cleared his throat. 'Thank you, I see. So we're saying that, for all intents and purposes, the Taliban and Al-Qaeda are the same? What do we know about this Mohammed Tariq?'

Naylor shook his head. 'Very little. JSOC has been targeting the known TTP commanders with drone attacks. It's possible Tariq is a foot soldier who was promoted in the field, or someone who's been keeping a low profile. Whatever the reason, his name doesn't appear on any watch list.'

'Do we have any idea where he is?'

'No, but our informer last saw him two days ago.'

'Who is our informer?'

'He claims to be the man who brought the device into Afghanistan in 1989.'

'Russian?' Holmcroft's eyes went wide. 'The intel from Echelon originates from Russia and our informer is Russian? Now to me this seems more than coincidental.'

Naylor was about to speak but the PM held up his hand. He pushed his chair away from the table and stood. It was his sign that he wanted a moment's pause. Burstow had been quiet throughout; Knight saw her own concern reflected in his face. He smiled thinly before looking down and knotting his fingers.

The PM held on to the back of his chair. 'Air Marshal, when can we expect to have our intelligence verified?'

'End of today. A team is already working on it.'

'Inform me immediately when you have any news, anything at all. Then, if needed, we shall locate and acquire the device.'

'With the support of JSOC,' Holmcroft insisted.

'I am well aware, Robert, of the role that the Americans' Joint Special Operations Command must play in this.'

'Again with respect, Prime Minister, we categorically cannot let this continue any further without involving the Americans.'

'I agree.' Daniels nodded. 'Ms Knight, Mr Burstow, I don't need to tell either of you how to run your organisations. All I ask is that we do not communicate this intelligence to our allies at this time.'

'Understood, Prime Minister.' Knight nodded slowly, while Burstow stayed motionless.

Chapter 4

Yuriy Kozalov bit into his black bread and gazed out into the frost-covered trees. His small house was directly opposite the edge of the forest that led to the Karachunivs'ke reservoir and his terrace offered a spectacular view. Depending upon the time of year he would see the odd eagle or hear the tapping of wood-peckers. The occasional wild boar had been reported by locals who, infused with vodka, imagined other exotic creatures too. Over twenty years after the USSR had finally stopped stripping Ukraine of its will to live, the country had started to regenerate, even here on the edge of a classified former weapons research facility. Kozalov was not a patriot; such things had been actively discouraged by both the Party and his former employer, which amounted to the same entity. What had been encouraged had been an unconditional love of and belief in the Soviet Union. He had not been a Ukrainian; he had been 'Soviet'. Kozalov finished his bread and washed it down with sweet black tea. He had seen on television that in the West many added milk to their tea, but to him this was a nonsense; it would be as unthinkable as adding fizzy Coca-Cola to Vodka.

Kozalov stood and stretched. His years of working as a physicist and weapons designer at the plant had left him drained and stiff. Others, although he hadn't liked to stay in touch with his old colleagues, had died of cancer – a hushed-up hazard of the job. He, however, was just tired. Tired and bitter, since his employer had cast him aside and his wife had left him. Although he still kept his apartment in the centre of town, he now spent more and more of his time at the *dacha*. Both properties had been given to him by the Party due to his status within the directorate. The old German clock in his living room announced, in its reliable and curt manner, that it was time for him to leave. He collected his breakfast things, washed them quickly in cold water, and headed for his boxy Lada Niva. In winter it was a ten-minute drive to the Gastronom he frequented. The fact that there was now a branch of the Austrian supermarket chain Billa four minutes further on made no difference to him; it was used by the New Ukrainians – those with more money than sense and cars as large as Soviet tanks. Not the type of people he wanted to mix with. At the Gastronom, with his battered Lada and fur hat, he was just another grey man, or he had been until he met Eliso.

He swung the 4x4 into the kerb, as near as he could get to the shop, and gingerly stepped out. Overnight, unseasonably early snow had fallen, melted, and then frozen as the temperature had dropped. Here the ice had been left to form large, glistening rivers to catch the unwary. So far it had been a very odd autumn. As he approached the pavement a trio of local Mafiosi looked on. Dressed in ill-fitting leather jackets over tracksuits and driving dated BMWs, they 'owned' the neighbourhood.

'What are you waiting for?' Kozalov muttered to himself. 'To see an old man fall over?'

'Nearly there, Comrade,' the nearest gangster wisecracked.

'Come on, Granddad, you can make it,' the second called.

Kozalov ignored them and reached for the door. Inside the grocery shop a couple of the 'real' elderly conversed with the fat woman on the meat counter, while another leather-clad bandit leant against the drinks counter and flirted with Eliso, the pretty, raven-haired Georgian girl. Eliso broke away from one admirer and addressed her next customer. 'What would you like?'

Kozalov was sixty-eight but looked older. Inside he wanted the same thing as 'Casanova'. 'I'll take two bottles of Kozatska Rada and one Desna.'

'You planning a party, old man? Maybe I should come,' Casanova jeered.

'You are not invited, but she is.'

'I doubt you could handle her,' the young man sniggered humourlessly.

'As I doubt that you could handle the drink.'

The girl blushed, placed the bottles on the counter, and told him the total. As Kozalov retrieved his money, Casanova's eyes narrowed at the sight of the KGB identity card which still remained on display in the ancient leather wallet. Kozalov put the exact money on the counter and placed his bottles into a crumpled plastic bag. 'Thank you. Goodbye.'

Feeling taller, he headed carefully back to his Lada. As the engine coughed into life he noted that the fourth gangster had now joined his friends outside and that they were glowering at him. He smiled to himself, satisfied that they were none the wiser. These posturing, third-class peacocks were unaware that he, a man of nearly seventy, was sleeping with the object of their desire. In fact, he had been sleeping with her for the past three months, almost since her arrival at the Gastronom. She was an immigrant from the Panski Gorge area of Georgia. He felt his heart flutter and his mouth become dry at the thought of her. He had been in love twice, once before and once after his marriage. At some point he might even have loved his wife; it had truly broken him when she left, but now his new love, Eliso, was repairing the damage. It had begun with a kind word here, a look there, and then he had met her unexpectedly near his *dacha*. She had been walking in the woods, collecting wild mushrooms, she said, for her mother, a woman who was gravely ill in bed. He had invited her into his home where she all but collapsed in tears and into his arms. She told him her life story. Her father had been killed when Russia invaded Georgia in 2008. Their village destroyed, she and her mother had left Georgia shortly afterwards and eventually found themselves in Ukraine, while her two sisters had been forced to stay. Her mother had now succumbed to a rare form of cancer, he knew not which, and she desperately needed to raise the funds for her to receive treatment. With this end she had taken the only legal job she could find and started working at the Gastronom in a vain attempt to start the process, but this in no way could pay for it.

'Is it money you are after?' he had asked her bluntly, thinking her willing to sell her body to him.

'Yes, but that is not why I am here. I am so lonely,' she had replied.

On the verge of turning prostitute for the locals, Kozalov had taken her under his wing and pledged he would do all he could. He had no children and paid nothing to his ex-wife. As a start he had given Eliso most of his savings, the money he had kept hidden in his rafters, squirrelled away over the years without his wife's knowledge. Eliso had then come to him one evening. He had not wanted to take her; he had not wanted to feel dirty, as though he had paid for her body... but she had reassured him that this was not the case. It was him she was interested in and not the ten thousand US dollars he had given her. In the morning, as he made them both breakfast, he realised he was in love with her. She was twenty-eight, forty years his junior, yet he was in love with her. He had found a new reason to live, a new reason to be. He would do all he could to help her, to help her mother.

In the next few months they had met up when she could get away from either the shop or her mother. Kozalov had agreed and understood that their relationship must remain secret. They had spent many evenings together at the *dacha* and talked about their lives. She had asked him much about his time at the plant and he had opened up. He had spoken of the secret work undertaken, words that if made public during Soviet times would have seen him sent to the gulags or shot as a traitor to the state. He spoke, too, of the equipment and parts he had taken from the facility. He realised he enjoyed talking about his past to someone who knew nothing of it, someone who had been just a child when the mighty Soviet Union had imploded. And Eliso listened. She listened like no one had before; his wife had had neither the intellect nor the interest to understand his work. It was conversation, he then understood, that he had been deprived of for all these years – conversation, compassion, understanding, and love.

Eliso spoke also, of her late father and his stories about Soviet times. He had been in a KGB guard unit and had worked at a facility; she said the name and Kozalov knew it. It was another closed area that had 'officially' developed rockets. Unofficially, it was a research centre just like his. Several such centres – even now he did not know the exact number – had existed during Soviet times. His interest was piqued. It was an unexplained coincidence, but he took it as a sign that they were meant to be together. Then one evening she had come to him with an idea. A man had approached her sister in Georgia, a man who had worked with her father. He had a proposal. It was unthinkable, outrageous, but a chance for them both. An opportunity for Eliso's mother to pay for the exorbitant treatment offered by an American private clinic in Kyiv and for Kozalov to live out the remainder of his days as a prince, with her at his side. Sitting on the terrace of his small house in the woods, he needed no time to think. His resentment of his former employer, of his former nation, had been bubbling under the surface for years, and now he was finally being given the means to strike back. 'Yes' had been his answer, and together they had decided upon a price. That night, elated, neither of them slept.

He slowed the Lada as he reached the start of the small village and bounced over the potholes as the tarmac stopped and the dirt track started. This would be the last winter he would spend in Ukraine for, if all went as planned, by the spring he would be a wealthy man with the ability to choose where in the world to sit and drink his tea.

*

Moscow

The Russian Interior Minister, Ruslan Pavlov, prepared himself to address the press. The media had been called to hear him make a statement on the spate of terrorist attacks in Moscow. The chubby Russian had a stern expression on his face as he stared into the audience. Numerous microphones adorned the lectern, each displaying the logo of a different news network. One of the most prominent was the green 'RT' of the Kremlin-sponsored Russia Today channel. Pavlov touched his tie, the flashes ceased, and he started to speak.

'Today a raid by Alpha Group, Spetsgruppa A, of the Russian Federal Security Service counterterrorism task force apprehended those responsible for the atrocities that have taken the lives of many innocent Russian citizens. The individuals guilty of these cowardly bomb attacks have been identified as Muslim extremists. We have been successful in destroying this terror cell without further loss of life. Let it be known that Russia is not a safe haven for any form of terrorism and we shall not let further outrages happen on our sovereign soil.'

Pavlov let his statement hang in the air and then again touched his tie, his idiosyncratic signal that he was now open for questions.

Safely back in London, Aidan Snow watched Sky News's live Kremlin feed with Jack Patchem. A simultaneous translation, given by a man with a monotone delivery, accompanied the audio feed. Snow, annoyed, tried to listen to the original Russian, as carefully vetted journalists asked Pavlov questions that he had rehearsed answers for. From these they learnt nothing new. As the conference drew to a close, a reporter who hadn't spoken before shouted a question. Unaided by a microphone her voice was lost. Pavlov pointed and snapped his fingers. The camera turned to show a young woman being handed a microphone.

'Please go ahead with your question.' Pavlov's voice could still be heard even though he was off camera.

'Ruslan Ivanovich, can you confirm that a convict transport carrying the Chechen terrorist Aslan Kishiev was ambushed yesterday?'

The camera quickly moved back to Pavlov; his face for the first time had lost its composure. His jowls wobbled as he shook his head, but his voice remained steady. 'That is not true. Where did you learn of this?'

The reporter was now off camera as the picture stayed with Pavlov. 'There were reports that Kishiev was being transported on medical grounds to a specialist facility. The same reports stated that, en route, his transport was attacked and he was freed.'

'I can confirm that you have been misinformed. Aslan Kishiev remains in a secure location; in fact, he is incarcerated in the most secure facility in our entire country.'

'But Ruslan Ivanovich…'

Pavlov held up his hand and the reporter's microphone was abruptly switched off. 'That is all.'

For several seconds the camera stayed with the minister as he exited the state room via a large set of ornate, gold-edged, double doors. The Sky News studio then reappeared on the screen. 'Some developing news there in Moscow and conflicting reports. I am joined now by Professor Oleg Gogol from the UCL School of Slavonic and East European Studies. Professor, tell me…'

Patchem switched off the screen. 'If the Kremlin says it's true, it must be so. The terrorist cell has been captured and now we've not lost a convicted felon.'

'It's a bit clumsy, Jack, if you ask me.'

'I agree. Pavlov is a professional; I've never seen him let the press get the better of him. He's a master at delivering propaganda. In Soviet times he used to be one of the bigwigs behind *Pravda.*'

'I never read it.'

'The crosswords weren't any good. Seven across, five letters, begins with L…'

'Lemon?'

Patchem smiled. 'Well, that's what Pavlov looks like. Whatever is happening is messy. First we have bombings the Islamic International Brigade claims responsibility for and then, apparently, the leader of said group is "sprung".'

'So what's really happening?'

'That, Aidan, is what we need to find out. Have you heard of the Black Dolphin penal colony?' Snow shook his head, so Patchem continued. 'It's where the worst cases are sent to rot. No one ever leaves. If there was a medical emergency it would probably be ignored; they would rather the inmate die. This story doesn't make sense. If Kishiev was moved, there was a very good reason for it.'

Snow thought for a moment. 'He gave up the bombers?'

Patchem contemplated Snow's words. 'That, I believe, is it. He gave them up, got a deal.'

'And then, what, escaped?' Snow smirked.

Patchem clasped his hands together. 'No one would know if he had or had not left Black Dolphin, security is that tight there.' Patchem's eyes narrowed as he tried to think through the permutations. 'Apart from an escape I see three scenarios: one, he's still at Black Dolphin; two, he really has been transferred because of a medical situation; or three, he's been moved because of a deal. Agreed?'

'Agreed.'

'So he's either on the loose or not, and he may or may not have escaped.'

'If he has escaped, the Russians wouldn't want to admit that their "most wanted" was on the run,' Snow said.

'So the FSB grants Kishiev a deal – "Give up the details of the cell and we'll transfer you out of Black Dolphin." They act on his intel, then he's fortuitously killed in an escape bid. But where is the body and why have a delay? Hmm, I wonder…'

Patchem pointed the remote control at the screen and then chose channel 512, Russia Today. Snow recognised the British anchorman who had previously worked on a satellite travel channel selling package holidays. He was talking to his own expert, a man dressed in fifty shades of beige and wearing glasses with Lucozade-orange-tinted lenses.

The expert spoke, his diction slow and his English pronunciation exaggerated by his Russian accent. 'It is impossible to escape from Black Dolphin. It cannot happen. But if we are to believe eyewitnesses, forces loyal to the Chechen terrorist Aslan Kishiev managed to overpower his guards and take control of a vehicle.'

Patchem and Snow listened in silence until the segment finished. Patchem spoke first. 'So, a state-sponsored channel is debating whether Kishiev has escaped or not. Why not give a definite answer? Why not just confirm either way? They either have him or they don't; they either plan on eliminating him or they don't.'

'Perhaps we're not looking at this the right way.' Snow frowned. 'Maybe we're meant to believe he's escaped and that the Russians are trying to cover it up?'

'But who is the "we"?' Patchem suddenly sat upright. 'Crafty sods! The Russians want the Chechens to think he's on the run! It's a message to them, but really Kishiev is working for the FSB and leading them to another cell. It's the only logical explanation.'

'That's a bit of a leap, Jack. Why would a Muslim fundamentalist negotiate with the FSB? If they were to kill him he would die a martyr.'

'They must have something he wants, something he values.

Family perhaps?' Patchem once again turned off the television. 'We don't have any answers here, but one thing is for certain: I don't need to send you to Moscow. If the Russians are cleaning house then we shall leave them to it.'

The desk phone rang. Patchem picked it up and listened. 'On my way.' He replaced the receiver in its cradle and glanced at Snow. 'Something's up.'

'To do with this?'

'No idea. Go to the canteen, have a second breakfast. I'll call you when I need you back.'

Patchem hustled the two of them out of the room. Snow took the stairs down as Patchem took a lift up.

*

As section chief for the Russian desk and one of her oldest friends, Knight trusted Jack Patchem completely. She smiled weakly as he entered the office and sat opposite her. It had been just over four hours since the meeting at COBRA had finished. In that time she'd had a separate discussion with Burstow and in Afghanistan a UKSF team had been sent to verify their informant's claim. It was as she had returned to her office, less than half an hour earlier, that she'd received a call from the Chief of Defence Intelligence. Naylor confirmed traces of radiation were present at the location the informer had provided. The radiation signature was consistent with that of U-235: enriched uranium. The threat, at least of a dirty bomb, was now verified. Knight's green tea seemed unable to quench her dry mouth as she sipped and composed herself. She felt uncharacteristically nervous; this was the most alarming piece of news she had ever had to announce. 'There is a Soviet nuclear device heading for Europe and Al-Qaeda has it.'

Patchem closed his eyes and let out a sigh. 'So it's happened. What do we know?'

Knight explained the two separate pieces of intel, including the Echelon intercept naming Aslan Kishiev.

'So Kishiev is allegedly on the run, but is actually helping Russian Intelligence?' Patchem asked.

'That would be a logical conclusion. We need to find this weapon. We believe it's an RA-115A.'

Patchem searched his memory. 'A suitcase nuke?'

'Yes. Do you know anything more?'

Patchem pointed to an open file on Knight's desk. 'Very little apart from that report I wrote for your predecessor. Arzamas-16 in Russia's Nizhny Novgorod region was where the majority of Soviet nuclear research and testing was undertaken, but there were rumours of other sites. There was an alleged experimental weapons research centre in Kryvyi Rih, Ukraine. The RA-115A was said to have been produced there.'

'It now seems that at least one of their weapons stopped being "experimental".' She took another sip of tea. 'Our informer states that, in 1989, he was tasked with taking a device into Afghanistan as part of a weapons cache.'

'Who is our informer?' Patchem asked.

Knight explained the details relayed to Captain Webster of the Army Intelligence Corps.

'So, project "Viru" did happen?'

'Viru?'

'It's Russian for "believe". The Soviets were trying to miniaturise their technology enough to fit a nuclear device into a suitcase. No matter how we tried, we could never get any intel on the project; we didn't have any assets in the area. Kryvyi Rih was a closed city, in a closed country. The CIA believed this thing did exist and that one or more of them would eventually turn up in the wrong hands.'

Knight frowned. 'So, is this report all we have on the RA-115A and the Kryvyi Rih facility?'

'Pretty much. The CIA went in disguised as weapons inspectors as soon as they could after Ukrainian independence, but the guy who "inherited" the plant from the state had already sacked the workers, stripped it bare, and sold off the land. There was no trace of any testing or design facility. As far as I'm aware the site was sold on quickly. Some of it was used for housing and the rest was later developed by an Austrian supermarket chain.'

'What became of the scientists and technicians?'

'The same old Soviet story: normal military records were mostly lost in the chaos of the Nineties. Classified documents, for personnel serving in black facilities, just vanished.'

Knight paused again to drink more tea and willed her fatigued brain to operate. 'How small could they have made this device?'

'At that time probably equal to a suitcase or perhaps even an attaché case, but your guess is as good as mine. The problem isn't the size of the housing, but rather what's inside – the fissile material. It degrades over time. If this bomb has been hanging around the Stan since the late Eighties, you can bet it hasn't been maintained. If it's out there, it's unstable.'

'Could it still detonate?'

'It's possible, but not probable. Remember, this is a twenty-odd-year-old experimental weapon. The best bet, as you mentioned, would be to use whatever radiological material that remains as a dirty bomb.'

'Or several dirty bombs,' Knight stated gravely. 'Jack, this is now a verified priority threat. Our intelligence has the device en route towards Iran.'

Patchem balked. 'Iran! It's going overland? Do we know what the target or targets are?'

'No. We have to assume that these are somewhere in mainland Western Europe. It could be any or several of our capital cities. GCHQ has been picking up some increased chatter mentioning an upcoming "spectacular". One phrase has been repeated: "the Hand of Allah". The PM is about to brief the American President and then EU leaders. The issue is that if the group holding the weapon gets the slightest notion we're onto them, they could detonate it, regardless of where they are.'

'If it were to detonate in Iran…' He let his sentence trail off. Both intelligence officers knew the implications. Iran would blame the US and Israel. Israel would claim the explosion as proof that the Iranians had atomic weapons. No one would accept it as an unrelated terrorist attack. The region would then destabilise as both Iran and Israel sought to annihilate each other.

'I think Al-Qaeda knows damn well that, even if we were alerted to their exact location, we wouldn't dare to either attack or apprehend them within the borders of Iran.'

'So they're taking the same route as the clandestines?' Patchem used a term coined by the UK Border Agency to refer to illegal immigrants. 'Afghanistan – Iran – Turkey – Greece, then up through Italy to France, and finally here?'

'That's the current assumption, but once in the EU they could go in any direction, strike anywhere.'

'Shit.' This was as coarse as Patchem's language ever became. 'So anywhere in the EU could be targeted at any time within the next, what, month?'

'Jack, this is what we've spoken about for all these years, our greatest fear realised. The PM wants me to activate all of our assets and get them out looking, chasing up the smallest scrap of intel. Someone must know something; someone must be helping them transport a radiological device across Europe.'

Patchem was silent for a moment. If the cell were being clever, once in Greece they would hide among the thousands of illegals who roamed the streets awaiting their asylum cases to be looked into. This could be in the Greek capital or one of the many shanty towns littering the ports. 'So we ask the Greeks to keep an eye out for anyone suspicious carrying a suitcase?'

'I know. It's not funny, is it?'

'No. Where do you want me to fit in?'

'You're head of the Russian desk, the device is Russian, and you are my most experienced section chief. I don't think you'd be treading on anyone's toes if you were to head this up.'

'Good.'

*

New Jersey, USA

Casey stood on the front porch swigging from a can of Coke as the sleek BMW M6 came to a halt at the end of the long driveway. The New Jersey mansion was one of many properties quietly acquired across the country by front companies for the Central Intelligence Agency after a spree of fortuitous bank foreclosures. Harris locked the vehicle. His nose was too large for his face and this, added to his unruly spikey hair, had once given him the nickname of 'Rod' – although, unlike Rod Stewart, he didn't wed or bed supermodels. He gave Casey a nod. 'Is he as good as you say he is?'

'You're here to find out.'

Harris removed his mirrored sunglasses. 'Damn right.'

Casey looked the operative up and down and shook his head. 'Is that the fashion now?'

'Hey, I've just flown in from goddamn Tbilisi,' Harris said to his boss and sometime drinking partner. 'This is haute couture over there.'

'Don't bother changing – you're flying back tonight.'

'Fantastic.'

Casey strode into the safe house, Harris following. What could not be seen from the outside was that the walls had been reinforced with ballistic fabric and the doors were titanium. They entered a drawing room; Harris sat on an overstuffed leather settee and helped himself to a file that lay on the coffee table. Casey let him read it as he finished his Coke and busied himself with his secure Blackberry. After five minutes or so Harris replaced the file.

'So?' Casey asked.

Harris shrugged. 'From his scores on the range I see he can shoot straight. But those things don't shoot back and sure as hell don't move. How's his fitness?'

'I didn't ask Doc Spence for details, just the bottom line. He's fully recovered from his concussion; no further complications or weaknesses have been apparent. He's given our boys a run for their money on the assault course – his times are impressive.'

Harris still had his doubts. 'His story checks out?'

'Yep. I had Scott Lewis pay a visit to his old CO from the GRU, now retired but still very tight-lipped.' The Moscow station chief's story was that Gorodetski had won a green card and the US authorities wanted to carry out further background checks. It was lame, and both sides knew it, but it was an opening.

'Let me guess, his lips were eventually loosened?'

'Scott met the Colonel at his *dacha*, shared a lot of Samogon, made a large "donation" to his pension fund, and got the intel.'

'So is he who he says he is?'

'He was one of the youngest ever Spetsnaz captains, an outstanding sniper, unbeaten in Sambo.'

'Ah, Sambo.' Harris grunted at the mention of the Russian martial art. 'So he's a real warrior.'

Casey ignored the sarcasm and continued. 'He's seen action in Chechnya, covert ops after the second war, mop-up operations in Dagestan, in addition to other CTU ops in the Caucasus and Moscow. He resigned his post just over three years ago.'

'Family?'

'Mother dead, father is a lecturer in English literature and teaches some ESL in Moscow. He had a brother, also Spetsnaz. The GRU confirmed he was KIA Afghanistan.'

'So the kid's reason for killing these Brits you told me about is real. It's revenge, not cash?'

'The kid's actual word was "justice".'

'But he was played.' Harris shook his head theatrically.

'His loss is our gain. We have a ready-made operative.'

'Really?' Harris became serious. 'You're certain he's not a ringer?'

'As much as I can be.' Casey had no problems with his second-in-command questioning him; he preferred that Harris be onboard and fully briefed. 'I think you should introduce yourself.'

'Just what I was thinking. You need a professional opinion.'

'Yep, I'm just an amateur.'

Casey stood and opened the door, and they exited and headed down the hall to 'the bubble'. Unlike the opulent, New Jersey housewife-style drawing room, this was a clinical white box, built with a 'shell' suspended inside the structure of an existing room to mask any sounds from escaping. The room was bare, save for a metal table and three chairs. They sat and, within a couple of minutes, Gorodetski appeared. He had been pulled from a PT session and was wearing sweats.

'James, come in.' Casey continued to call the Russian by his American moniker; it made the rest of the team feel more at ease. 'I have someone here who wants to meet you. This is Harris.'

As soon as Gorodetski entered the bubble the door hissed shut, sealing the men off from any potential form of electronic surveillance. Gorodetski regarded the newcomer and extended his hand. The man was about the same height as him, looked to be in his fifties, and was powerfully built, but had a stomach that strained at his belt. What he noticed most, however, was the hair and large nose. 'Hello.'

Harris shook the proffered hand. 'Have a seat, son.' Gorodetski sat. 'So you were thrown out of the Spetsnaz? What was wrong? Were you not good enough?'

Gorodetski blinked. He hadn't expected hostility. 'I didn't renew my commission.'

'Aw, c'mon, you can tell me. What was it, shit yourself on parade, or were you caught in bed with a junior officer?'

'Both. I have a bowel disorder, and I find young men appealing.'

Harris's nose twitched. 'I could tell, no offence, by the way you walk – like a fairy.'

'Thank you.'

'I'd like to get to know you better; tell me a little more about yourself.'

'Why? Do you find me attractive?'

'You,' Harris said, pointing his finger, 'are a goddamn funny man.'

'That would make you the straight guy, which I struggle to believe.'

Harris glared at the Russian for a moment before he spoke. 'So, tell me, where are you from?'

'Boston.'

'Boston, Russia?'

'If you like.'

'So, why were you thrown out of the Spetsnaz?'

'I told you; I left. I had to kill a man. It was personal.'

'Jas Malik?'

'No. I left to kill the man who murdered my brother.'

'Bav Malik?'

'I left to kill the man who murdered my brother.'

'You assassinated Jas Malik and his son, Bav Malik – you've admitted this.'

Gorodetski looked at Casey, who nodded. He fixed his eyes once again on the man Casey had called Harris. 'Yes. I believed they were responsible for the death of my brother.'

'So you killed them?'

'I was told they were responsible.'

'Do you believe everything you're told, son?'

'I do if it comes from a reliable source.'

'Well, this didn't. So you murdered two innocent men.'

'Yes.'

'How does that make you feel?'

'Empty.'

'And?' Harris could see the Russian was holding something back. 'And, what else did that make you feel?'

'Dead inside.'

'So you regret what you did?'

'No.'

'No?' Harris raised his eyebrows.

'I do not regret what I did. I regret who I did it to.'

'So for you was it just collateral damage?'

'No, you were correct when you called me a murderer. I am a murderer.'

Harris waved his hand dismissively. 'I didn't call you a murderer; I said you murdered two innocent men. So, back to basics. You left the Spetsnaz to find and kill the men who murdered your bother?'

'Yes.'

'But you were used, weren't you, son? They played you, made you do their dirty work. Pashinski had you kill two men for him.'

'Yes.' Gorodetski tried to hide his surprise at the use of Pashinski's name.

'Why did you come to the US?'

'To escape.'

'Who were you running away from?'

'Myself.'

'Why should we trust you... James, Sergey... or whatever?'

'I'm not asking you to.'

'Smug shit.'

'If you say so.'

Casey stood. 'OK, James, thank you.'

Gorodetski followed his lead and stood. Harris extended his hand. 'It was good to meet you, son.' Gorodetski shook hands. As he relaxed his grip to move towards the door, Harris twisted his wrist outwards and down while at the same time striking Gorodetski with a left hook to the jaw. Caught off-guard,

Gorodetski stumbled right and fell to one knee. He saw the arm draw back again, but swiftly rolled to the right and stood. Now out of striking distance, he didn't raise his guard.

'You a pussy, boy?'

Gorodetski remained silent. Annoyed. It was a test and he had failed.

Harris jutted his chin out. 'Aw, c'mon, give it a shot. You might get lucky.'

Gorodetski turned to Casey. 'Is that all?'

'Yes, James, you can go.' Casey pressed a button and the door hissed open.

'Have your boyfriend put some ice on that jaw,' Harris scoffed as the Russian made for the door. Once it closed he continued. 'He's Russian, he's wired differently.'

'Meaning?'

'He may mouth off, but has a greater respect for authority. We own him, we can beat him, and he won't bite back. As I said, he's a puss.'

Casey didn't agree; 'puss' wasn't the first word that came to mind. 'And?'

'He wants to make things right. He's crippled by remorse – and this NJ shooting thing has only made it worse. He'll give it his all, but if we ask him to do something he doesn't think is morally right… it'll come back and bite us in the ass. He's a soldier not an operative, Vince.'

Casey shrugged. Harris was no psychiatrist, but he had learnt to listen to his views, even if they were often roughly expressed. 'Thank you for your expert opinion.'

'So when does he go active?'

'As soon as we need him.' As Casey left the room his felt his Blackberry vibrate. 'Casey.' He frowned. 'Now? OK.'

Harris followed. 'Problem?'

'That was our contact at 1600 Pennsylvania Avenue; the President wants me to listen in on a conference call.'

'You'd better hurry; you wouldn't wanna keep the Commander in Chief waiting.'

'Thanks for that advice too.' Casey hurried along the corridor in the direction of the secure comms room.

Harris returned to the porch for a cigarette.

*

Vauxhall Cross, London

'Jack, this is serious.'

'I think that's an understatement, Vince.'

Casey snorted at the other end of the secure video-link. 'Yes, it is. So where do you think the nuke is now?'

'Our best bet is Iran or Turkey.'

'That's what your PM told my President. I've studied the intel and I concur with your assessment of their route: Afghanistan – Iran – Turkey – EU. And as for targets, take your pick of the usual suspects.'

'Have you heard anything at all?'

'Nope.' Casey shook his head. 'Just the same chatter as you, but I'm trying to get a bird repositioned over the Turkey-Iran border. If I can get it in place it should be able to pick up the nuke's signature, unless it's shielded.'

'And will it be?'

Casey paused before he spoke, making sure he had eye contact, albeit digitally, with his British colleague. 'I've been authorised to inform you that we, the Central Intelligence Agency, are in possession of an RA-115A.'

'How handy,' Patchem noted with undisguised sarcasm. 'And where did you come upon this one?'

'Now, that I'm not authorised to disclose, but I can tell you it wasn't Afghanistan. What the hell was a suitcase nuke doing in Afghanistan anyway? It's a city weapon, for God's sake.'

'They were testing it as part of project Viru.'

'Ah, of course,' the American conceded. 'Now, the casing of the RA-115A has been designed to prevent any radioactive signature from being detected. How effective that will be, after twenty-five years lying in a hole, is hard to say.'

'We found a trace reading at the location the device had been stored.'

'So that kind of answers that question, but the bird still has to be in the right place at the right time in order to read it. I'm emailing you now all we have on the nuke, its size and specs, etc.'

'Thanks. Adding your intel to my old report should make it quite comprehensive.' He and Casey had a symbiotic relationship in many ways, but both sides still had secrets. The CIA's being in possession of an RA-115A was one of them.

Casey grinned to acknowledge Patchem's sarcasm as he tapped his laptop. 'And send.'

A bleep informed Patchem the email had arrived. He clicked 'open' and there was a pause as the attached document was scanned, decrypted, and displayed. Patchem speed-scrolled through the file. 'So it actually looks just like a photographer's aluminium case?'

'Yep, but it's slightly smaller, more like an attaché case.'

'Does your one work?'

'No, there's a problem with the firing unit decoder. You'll find the details in the file, but that begs the question – is the Al-Qaeda bomb also faulty?'

'They were experimental. Did they ever operate correctly?'

'None has gone off – yet,' Casey said dryly.

Patchem looked again at the photograph of the aluminium case. 'The size is a moot point anyway; they'll have removed the fissile material and packed it into a new container. Unless the Afghan one is in working order?'

'Jack, I doubt it. You'd have to run a diagnostic on it and this thing is old and experimental. Why would Al-Qaeda risk it blowing up in their faces? I'd turn it into a small dirty bomb, let it off in a major population centre, and boom...'

'This makes me glad you're wearing a white hat, Vince,' Patchem said flatly.

Casey smirked. 'Some would say it was grey.'

'What assets have you got in the area?'

'Nothing doing in Iran. In Turkey we've got the usual teams at the embassy in Ankara and the consulate in Istanbul. There are a few "military advisers" down south on the borders with Syria and Iraq.'

'No other teams?'

Casey adopted his poker face. 'Jack, I'm going to be absolutely transparent with you on this. The President has put my group on standby to extract the nuke if it's found anywhere in Europe. I'm having a team move to an FOB in Romania. I'll order them in if the threat is confirmed.'

'Thank you for your candour.' Patchem smiled thinly. So the US had decided it was going to take care of the device once located? This suited Patchem. 'Our priority is to locate this thing and prevent it from going bang. I don't care who keeps it afterwards.'

'Exactly, Jack. I'm not getting into a dick-swinging contest with you here. The stakes are too high.'

'I quite agree.'

'Let's keep each other updated. OK, I gotta go now and break the news to my boys.'

'The same here.'

Patchem ended the video call and sat in silence for a moment as he tried to take in the enormity of his task. The internal European intelligence services could be trusted to operate efficiently and professionally, but the Turkish National Intelligence Agency and the intelligence services of Turkey's neighbours could not. In all likelihood the device would slip through Turkey and only be intercepted in the EU, at which point it probably would indeed go 'bang'. Patchem's mouth had become dry and he felt the pressure building at his temples. He desperately needed to get out of Vauxhall Cross and get some air, but that was a luxury he didn't have. A large glass of water and a handful of ibuprofen tablets would have to suffice. He exited his office and made for the staff canteen to find Aidan Snow.

*

In New Jersey, Casey left the secure comms room and returned to the porch. As expected, Harris was lounging against the wall. 'Tell me it's good,' Harris said, flicking his cigarette butt onto the gravel where it joined several others in a haphazard mosaic.

'We need to go to the bubble.'

'That good?'

'Not good and not great. Now come on.' Casey led Harris for a second time through the house and into the bubble. Once the door had hissed shut he spoke. 'Al-Qaeda has acquired an RA-115A.'

Harris's face lost its usual composure. 'Unholy shit…'

Casey briefed Harris on both his conversation with Patchem and, more importantly, the conference call between the UK PM and their own Commander in Chief. 'You need to get your team over to Timisoara airbase by the fastest means.'

Harris took a deep breath. 'I'm on it.'

Chapter 5

Mashhad, Iran

Al-Suri's guests sat with heavy stomachs. He waited for the remnants of the meal to be cleared away before addressing them. Each part of the operation had been compartmentalised; al-Suri knew only of the 'travel arrangements' from Iran to the EU.

'Tomorrow, you shall leave for Turkey. Ahmed will drive you right across Iran to Bazargan. It is a border town and there you shall cross into Turkey. The border guards will not search you. You will each be travelling on these Pakistani passports. So you must speak only in English.' Al-Suri pushed a thick envelope across the table. 'Please study them and learn your names and details. As you will see, they each display your real photograph and have both Schengen and UK visas.'

Tariq passed each passport to its new owner. The men studied the documents wide-eyed.

'What is Schengen?' Lall Mohammad asked.

'It is another name for the European Union. With this visa you can travel from country to country without any delay.' He didn't wish to complicate matters further by explaining that

Schengen was actually the name of a town in Luxembourg where the single visa treaty had been signed.

Impressed by the documents, Tariq asked, 'Are these real?'

'The passports were issued in Pakistan by the correct authorities, as were the visas. We have agents in many agencies.' He smiled at his wordplay. 'To lessen suspicion even further, before you leave you shall receive Western-style clothes, luggage, and your hair and beards will again be trimmed.'

Tariq stroked his stubbly chin and remembered the order to shave off his beard in readiness for the passport photograph. He hadn't been beardless since he was a boy and to him it felt peculiar, effeminate. 'To fight the infidel we must become him?'

'Exactly. No one suspects a man in a suit.'

'I feel so close to the UK now, I can almost see Big Ben!' Ashgollah Ahmadi remarked.

'Once you leave here, even the Queen of England will be proud to invite you in for afternoon tea,' al-Suri indulged him.

'Then we could blow her up.' Sharib Quyeum rubbed his hands together.

'But only after tea,' insisted Ahmadi. 'It would be bad manners to kill her beforehand.'

The group's spirits were high. Tariq caught al-Suri's gaze. Both men were experienced enough to know it was essential to get these nerves out of the way.

'I would rather see David Beckham.' Abdul Shinare was excited.

'He has retired, brother,' Reza Khan added quietly.

Al-Suri cleared his throat. 'On the Turkish side of the border you will be met by two taxis and taken to the town of Dogubeyazit.'

'Taxi?' Tariq raised his eyebrows.

'A taxi is a very common way to travel across Turkey and will not draw any undue attention. At Dogubeyazit you will exchange your taxis for a bus and travel to Istanbul. Your contact is named Orhan.'

'Is he a believer?'

'A believer in profitable business.' Tariq frowned and al-Suri held up his hand. 'Using a non-believer leaves less of a trace and our business dealings have made him much money.'

'A man who is motivated by money cannot be trusted,' Tariq stated.

'Your fears are misplaced. We have used him many times. I have used his services. He is trusted. Besides, we know where his family lives.'

'When will we receive our weapons?' Reza asked.

'No weapons, my brother; travelling businessmen do not carry firearms. It would be another risk. You, Reza, and the rest of you, must leave your knives and anything else you have with me here.'

'Unacceptable.' Reza glared.

'No. It is how it must be,' Tariq stated as he looked at al-Suri.

Al-Suri bowed graciously and then made eye contact with each of the warriors as he continued his briefing. 'On arrival at Istanbul the group shall split into two. Tariq shall lead one team and Reza the other. Reza, your team is to continue from Istanbul into Greece. Tariq, your team is to take the ferry from Derince to Illichevsk in Ukraine. It's a long and indirect voyage, but you are much less likely to get spotted or questioned than if you were to take a smaller private vessel or fishing boat. Your contacts will be waiting for you and shall provide the pre-agreed password.' Al-Suri clasped his hands. 'That is as much as I have been informed of, my brothers. I know your mission is sacred and I know that your targets were chosen by the Lion Sheik himself, peace be upon Him. It is an honour for me to have you in my house, even if only for a fleeting moment.'

Tariq did not want to praise their host but knew he must. 'It is an honour for us to be here and to have been chosen, Yassin. You are a most revered believer and have done much for the cause.'

'My sacrifices have not been great compared to yours. Allah has bestowed on us our own specific strengths and we must use them as his humble servants.'

'*Allahu Akbar!*' Tariq stood.

'*Allahu Akbar!*' the six other men replied.

And then the Al-Qaeda operatives chanted as one. '*Allahu Akbar... Allahu Akbar... Allahu Akbar... Allahu Akbar... Allahu Akbar... Allahu Akbar... Allahu Akbar... Allahu Akbar!*'

*

Abkhazia Region, Georgia

Kishiev studied his reflection. His beard had been removed as part of his indoctrination into Black Dolphin. Two guards had tied him to a steel chair with leather straps, while a third had hacked at his beard with blunt-bladed scissors. When the guard switched to a cut-throat razor, Kishiev had prayed the man would slip, that the blade would penetrate his skin, his arteries, and end his purgatory. The guard knew what he was thinking – Black Dolphin was a final destination prison after all. The guard did, however, inflict several nicks on the Chechen's face for his own sadistic pleasure.

Four years later, Kishiev now stood in front of the mirror at the safe house and studied the unfamiliar reflection as though it was someone else. The face cleanshaven and the once thick mane of black hair now buzzed to the bone. At Dolphin there had been no mirrors. This was the first time he had seen his naked cheeks since he was a boy, but the face that stared back was not that of a boy; it was haggard almost beyond recognition. Kishiev flashed himself a smile and for an instant the fire appeared in his eyes and the boy was back. He grinned wider and his blackened teeth ended the illusion. He would recover. He had been in the darkness, but was now back in the light, as Christian ideology would lead a Russian to believe.

As a Chechen and a true believer he knew it wasn't black and white; his redemption had cost the lives of many noble Muslim warriors. They would be avenged. The FSB had shown Kishiev stills taken from the Moscow metro CCTV cameras of those suspected of carrying out the bombings. He'd recognised two faces; one of these had been martyred in an explosion minutes later. Kishiev had no idea how the FSB had traced the other man he had named, but within two days the international press were being briefed on the successful elimination of the terror cell responsible for the Moscow terrorist attacks. Strelkov had begrudgingly accepted his Director's orders and taken Kishiev out of Black Dolphin and brought him sedated to the safe house. In his room he had found, to his dismay, not a copy of the Koran, but in its place Russian newspapers. He read up on current and world events, as portrayed by the Kremlin-controlled press. For the masses, the Russian sheep, the news as reported within the flimsy paper pages was the truth; but for him it was merely Kremlin propaganda. He read of the Chechen President Kadyrov, perturbed to find the idiot was still alive, and read about the continued joy of the Crimean people in their reunification with Mother Russia. Apparently, the Crimean Tatars were happy to be once again living in a country where their ethnic rights would be respected. He was furious. Like the Chechens, the Tatars had been the victims of Soviet purges; both groups were believers and yet both continued to be abused.

Kishiev turned away from the mirror as he heard a key in the lock. The door to his room opened and a huge FSB commando entered. 'Outside, now.'

Dressed in a cheap pair of jeans, boots, and a thick sweater, Kishiev was met by a second FSB commando in the corridor. The trooper pushed him forward and towards a door at the far end. A third commando opened the door and Kishiev entered.

'Sit.' Kishiev did as Strelkov ordered. 'Your weapon is on the move.'

'How do you know?'

'That is not your concern. Tell me the route and the target.'

'When will I see my family?'

Strelkov's face flushed red. 'There is a portable nuclear device in the hands of terrorists and you dare mention your wife and child?'

Kishiev remained silent. In his prime he could have silenced the Russian in the blink of an eye with his bare hands, but that was before Black Dolphin almost killed him. It was said that after two years at Dolphin the soul died. After this, the human body either decided to shut down or kept on functioning as a life-support machine for the automaton brain. Kishiev's soul was not dead, but his body was weak, for now. 'Your superior agreed my terms. I see my wife and daughter and then I tell you the route of the weapon.'

'I could force the information out of you, Chechen.'

'No, you could not, as I am sure your FSB doctors have explained to you. Black Dolphin has made me weak. You would torture me, I would resist, and then I would die a martyr.'

'There are certain drugs I could use on you.'

'The risk is yours to take. I welcome death and dying defending the faith is the most honourable act of all.'

'Don't you understand? If this device is detonated it will lead to the deaths of thousands. It would be mass murder in the name of your God.'

Kishiev's face tightened. His war had been waged to remove the Russians from his homeland and to herald a return to the true values of the Koran, not to blatantly kill civilians.

'Kishiev, are you listening to me? Men, women, and children – both Christian and Muslim – will die!'

'It will pass through Iran and then into Turkey.'

Strelkov took a deep breath to restore his composure. 'That is the part I know. And from then onwards?'

'Take me to my family.'

'Bring them in,' Strelkov called wearily across the room.

'They are here?' Kishiev felt his heart race.

Strelkov crossed his arms. 'We are where you hid them.'

*

The Iranian-Turkish border crossing was 2,600 metres above sea level and at the foot of Mount Ararat. It was as far as Ahmed was to take Tariq and his team. Ahmed bade goodbye to the men, climbed into his minibus, and headed towards Tehran. Tariq felt a chill of cold air brush his beardless cheek as he watched the driver disappear. The Afghans approached the Iranian emigration counter and in turn each gave their passports to the Iranian official, who with a stamp and a dutiful nod sent them on their way. The Holy Warriors now had a five-minute walk across no-man's land, along a road fenced on both sides, before they reached the Turkish officials, where they would again present their new documents. The Turkish border guard compared the face of each man against his passport and a few minutes later the group were free to enter the Republic of Turkey.

Lall Mohammad looked around. Mount Ararat dominated the landscape to the north with flatlands to the south. In front of them a wide road stretched into the distance. 'So this is Turkey?'

'It reminds me of home,' Abdul Shinare noted.

'We are not tourists,' Reza Khan reminded them all.

'Where is our transport?' Lall Mohammad asked.

Ahead, in a hard-standing waiting area, Tariq could only see one taxi and a battered-looking bus. Both stood with their doors open and several men leant against the taxi smoking. Something didn't feel right; he was carrying a deadly nuclear device, yet had no personal weapon. He swapped a glance with Reza, who was tense. A man who had been sitting on the bottom step of the bus stood up, dropped his cigarette, and ground it into the dirt with his shoe. He was a short, rotund man and gave an enthusiastic wave as he trotted towards them.

'Greetings, brother, I am Orhan Inci.' He spoke in English and held out his hand to Tariq. 'I am driving you.'

Tariq shook his hand; it was not a Muslim custom. 'Greetings. Where is the second taxi?'

'You will be travelling by bus.'

'I was told of no change of plan.'

Inci shrugged. 'A group of foreign men travelling through the town by bus is less suspicious. You understand?'

'Is there no other route?'

'Not for a bus or a taxi. For men on foot, yes, but this is a border area; there are many vehicles moving through. Dogubeyazit is cut in two by the highway.' He made a chopping movement with his hand to emphasise his point. 'A bus will draw no attention, much less than two taxis driving together. We will drive through, directly to Istanbul.'

'How long will the journey take?'

Inci's eyes rolled skywards as he calculated. 'Istanbul is a long way, so all night and all of the day. But this is why we have a large bus, yes? So you can sleep while I drive.'

'You will drive the entire way?'

'No, no. I am not Superman. I have Ferit; he is in the bus. He will take a turn.' Inci mimed holding a steering wheel.

Tariq had no time for flippancy. 'Can we go?'

'Yes, of course. Come, come.'

The Afghans followed Inci towards the bus, each of them carrying their suitcase.

'Do you know those men with the taxi?'

'Yes, yes. They are my friends, they pick up fares from the border,' Inci replied.

At the bus Inci whistled and Ferit appeared. He jumped down and opened up a panel to reveal the luggage hold. One by one the five other warriors handed their cases to the Turk while Tariq kept hold of his.

'We have space, so please put in your case,' Ferit said politely.

'No, I will keep it by my side.'

'You are the chief.' Ferit stood. 'OK, we can go now.'

Once they had chosen their seats the bus grumbled into life and moved off. Reza sat behind Tariq. 'This does not feel right, brother.'

Tariq did not turn around. 'I agree, brother, but I am sure it is just our unease at being closer to our target.'

'I wish I had my knife.'

As the aging bus travelled deeper into Turkey, Tariq was ever mindful that, unlike Iran, the Turkish government was a friend of the West, and that, as such, he and his men were very unwelcome guests.

*

Camp Bastion, Helmand Province, Afghanistan

Mike Webster's orders were classified and unequivocal. The Russian known as Mikhail was to be immediately flown back to the UK to be questioned further. His eyes wandered around his soon-to-be-vacated office; the orders made sense. Camp Bastion was about to be handed over to the Afghan National Army as the UK finally left Afghanistan. At its peak the Camp had been home to ten thousand British soldiers, but in recent weeks it had become a ghost town. Webster's Military Intelligence team were becoming demob-happy, counting the minutes almost until they escaped. He wouldn't be sad to leave 'The Stan', or 'Asscrackistan' as the Americans more colourfully put it; he didn't know if his presence had done any good, or achieved anything, up until now that was. Mikhail's appearance had changed something in him, though; it had made him see that what had started in Helmand province could end back home with the deaths of thousands. A nuclear device was on its way to Europe, of that he now had no doubt, and the man he had been ordered to send to the UK was potentially the key to stopping it. He left his office and felt the mixture of hot air and sand blast his face – no, he wouldn't miss this at all. He proceeded to the glorified cell that had been assigned to the Russian. He returned the guard's salute and then, as a courtesy, knocked on the door before nodding at the guard to open it.

Mikhail stood in the centre of the room facing him. Webster was still unnerved by the hardness of his eyes. 'I have some good news for you.'

'Go ahead.'

'You'll be leaving for the UK today.'

'So the British Government has decided to give me a passport?'

'That I don't know, but they've certainly agreed to have you in the UK to help with the current threat.'

'I see.' The Russian's eyes narrowed. 'And then what is to be done with me?'

'I'm sorry, but that I don't know; it's above my pay grade.'

Mikhail shrugged. There was nothing for him now in Afghanistan, and if going to the UK, albeit to be interrogated by the British, prevented the bomb from being detonated, then go he would. 'Very well, I accept.'

'Good. You'll be leaving within the hour.'

*

Abkhazia Region, Georgia

'I am going to ask you once again, Kishiev. Are you certain that this man knows the terrorists' plans?'

'He will collect them at the border and transport them to Istanbul to await further instructions.'

'You are aware that if you are deceiving me the lives of both your wife and daughter are forfeit?'

102

Kishiev had been given half an hour to reacquaint himself with his family before they had been taken away. 'I led your FSB to the Moscow bombers, for which you let me see my family. Why would I lie to you now?'

'Because you are a convicted Islamic terrorist and have the blood of many Russians on your hands.'

'You have my word, you have my family. What more do you want?'

'Tell me exactly where this man can be found.' Strelkov's eyes were hard.

'As I told you, he is the owner of a taxi and excursion company.' Kishiev placed his finger on a map of Turkey. 'It operates from here in Istanbul. He has been in the pay of Al-Qaeda for many years and is a trusted conduit for believers. The Holy Warriors will stay with him here.'

'Warriors? Terrorists, Kishiev, like you.'

'Of course.'

'And they will have the device with them?'

'Wouldn't you?'

Strelkov slammed his fist onto the desk. 'Will they have the device with them? Yes or no?'

'Yes. They will have instructions not to let it out of their sight.'

Strelkov took a breath and sat back in his chair. 'Then my team shall go to Turkey, liquidate the terrorists, and reclaim the weapon. You shall remain here until we decide what is to be done with you.' Kishiev didn't speak but gradually let a smile appear on his lips as Strelkov scowled at him. 'What is it, Chechen?'

'You do not know what the target is or where it is.'

'True, but that will become irrelevant once we have recovered the device.'

'Don't you want to trace the Al-Qaeda network? What if there are other attacks planned?'

'Are you saying there are more nuclear devices?' Strelkov felt his mouth go dry. The idea that there might be more active terror cells hadn't occurred to him.

'That I do not know, but you should.' Kishiev made his gambit. 'It would be pertinent to know who planned the attack, and who the cell's next contact is. If I travelled to Istanbul I could confirm Inci's identity and the presence of the device.'

'How is that?'

'I have used Inci's services before. I will recognise him and he will recognise me. The cell will trust me.'

'You have been to Turkey?' Strelkov was incredulous that a known Chechen terrorist had been able to travel so easily before finally being brought to justice by the Russian legal system.

'It is fertile ground for Western recruits.'

Strelkov wasn't at all happy that his only lead on the location of the rogue nuclear device came from the terrorist who sat opposite him, but Kishiev's words made sense and Strelkov's orders were to reacquire the device at all costs. He was nonetheless suspicious. 'You could have kept quiet. Why are you now willing to help me? What is it that you want, Kishiev?'

'What I want is to prevent the murder of innocent people in the name of Islam.'

Strelkov sneered. 'Were not the Russians you murdered in Chechnya innocents?'

'They were an invading army and I was at war.'

'Invaders? Chechnya is an integral part of the Russian Federation! You led a terrorist group with the sole purpose of murdering Russian patriots. Remember, it was I who stopped you then. I was there!' Strelkov took a breath to regain his calm; Kishiev angered him in a way no other adversary ever had. 'Very well, you shall come with my team to Istanbul; but remember, we still have your family.'

Chapter 6

Kryvyi Rih, Ukraine

The ground was difficult to dig, hard from the early frosts, but he knew he must. Eliso had received good news from her sister: the man had agreed his terms and they were soon coming with the device. The components he needed to make it active lay buried in the garden of his *dacha*. He had acquired them in his last days at the plant as the Soviet Union crumbled. He grinned; his cabbages had protected what would make him some real cabbage. At first it had just been about the money and helping Eliso's mother, but now it was more than this. The money wouldn't make up for the bitter years since his wife's betrayal with his former supervisor. The device, however, would. It would enable him, albeit via the hands of others, to hit back and at the same time implicate his wife's second husband, as at best a thief and at worst a supporter of terrorism. His eight million dollars was enough to escape for ever if he wished, even buy a new face. He could screw the world's most expensive whores and drink its most exquisite liquor. But no. Now he had Eliso and wanted to share the rest of his life with her. A thought struck him. Would his wife want him back when her husband was hauled away in chains as a traitor? He wiped his brow. She would of course have to beg; he would be a hot commodity, an eligible bachelor. But did he really want her back, a woman in her sixties? Of course not. He was attached to Eliso, their relationship cemented by the components he was now unearthing.

He looked around. Not a single light shone from his neighbours' windows in pre-dawn Kryvyi Rih. He wouldn't miss the place. Any good memories he had of his work had been tarnished by the manner in which he had been let go, the chaos which ensued after August 1991 when Ukraine declared itself independent. When the robber-barons took over that was it; only the Director and a few of his favourites remained to grow wealthy by selling off state assets, state secrets. Kozalov had the knowledge, he had the experience, he had designed one of the most deadly weapons mankind had not yet seen, and he had been given a measly pension! What was more, it hadn't been paid until almost a year later when the new Ukrainian government finally caught up with its obligations! He chose to overlook the fact that the state had given him his *dacha* and apartment. In his mind these were his by right as compensation for twenty years of toil. At the time, paranoia and fear had prevented him from capitalising on his skills, unlike others across the former USSR who found themselves employed in Pakistan, North Korea, or Iran. He had been too conditioned; he had taken the news and gone home. Then the next day, after a night of drinking, he had returned to work with a bag to collect what was his, and what rightfully should be his, and then left. His wife left him soon after. Kozalov found himself unemployed, unloved, and unkempt. He retreated into his *dacha* and his drink, which luckily enough remained dirt cheap.

His spade hit something hard. He scraped away the earth and finally exhumed his treasure. It didn't look like much, but that didn't matter. It was what it would do that counted. He would take it inside, check the contents, and then rebury it once again for safety until the buyers arrived.

*

RAF Brize Norton, UK

The flight from Camp Bastion had left Mikhail drained, but any fatigue he had felt was instantly lifted upon stepping onto English soil. His welcoming party had consisted of one man who introduced himself in perfect, Moscow-accented Russian as Aidan Snow. The gates of the base grew smaller behind them; Mikhail rubbed his leather armrest with a coarse palm. 'This is a very nice vehicle.'

'It's not bad,' replied Snow, sticking to Russian as he concentrated on the road ahead, 'for a company car.'

'My father had a Volga. It, too, was comfortable, but of course the seat coverings were not made from dead cows.'

'What did he do, your father?'

'He was a lecturer of English literature, and also taught English language.'

'In Moscow?'

'Yes, but the family were originally from Tula. It is not far from Moscow and to the south. Of course, in Soviet times the majority of students he taught English to would never have had the opportunity to use it in front of a native speaker.' Snow didn't ask any more questions and Mikhail became silent, lost in thought as he took in the passing English landscape through the Audi's front passenger window. When he had entered Afghanistan, travelling to the West had been a fanciful dream only diplomats, sportsmen, actors, and spies could aspire to, but here he was in the land of Shakespeare and Elton John. The countryside outside was verdant, compared to the barren wastes he had left. Grassy fields watched over by the occasional half-naked tree, leaves turned crimson in death, lined either side of the motorway. The countryside eventually fell away to be replaced by the urban landscape of the London suburbs. Mikhail realised he had been quiet for most of the journey; it was time to break the silence. 'I have seen more cars and people in the last hour than I have in the last twenty-five years.'

'London is a bit different to Kabul.'

'It is a lot different, Aidan.'

They slowed as they came to a roundabout, the motorway petering out to become a London artery. Snow waited for a food delivery van to pass before he pulled out.

'What is Tesco?'

'It's a supermarket, a grocery shop.'

'Ah, like a Gastronom?'

'Yes.'

'And that truck was taking produce to the shop?'

'No, that one was delivering food to the customers.'

'They come to you?'

'Yes. The customer can go to the shop or place an order via the internet.'

'And the shopkeeper does not worry that he will not get paid?'

'They are paid by credit cards.'

'I see.' Mikhail shook his head. 'I have been living on another planet.'

'Everyone should get a chance to.'

'May I ask you a question?'

'Go ahead.'

'Your name is Irish, yet you are an Englishman and speak fluent Russian?'

Snow knew he shouldn't be sharing his personal details, but they were so removed from the operation that it would do no harm, and building trust with Mikhail was essential. 'It's my father's fault; he was in the diplomatic service and a bit of a comedian. I was conceived while he was serving at the British Embassy in Aden, South Yemen. Hence my name; and the Russian comes from following him to Moscow when I was a kid.'

'Is your father James Bond?'

Snow laughed. 'I'll ask him next time I see him.'

'Moscow is not that bad; I enjoyed it as a child. I especially liked the Ferris wheel at Gorky Park.'

'There's a big one in London called The Eye.'

'That I would like to see, if I am allowed. Where does your father work now?'

'On a farm.'

Mikhail frowned. 'I do not understand.'

'My parents own a place in the South of France. They keep a few chickens.'

'Ah, I see.' Mikhail was thoughtful for a moment. 'What will happen to me now?'

'I'll hand you over to our team at the safe house and they'll look after you.'

'And then?'

'And then they'll question you about the missing bomb.'

Mikhail sighed. 'That device must not be allowed to detonate, anywhere. It is a thing of pure evil.'

'I agree.'

'Do you know what the target is?'

'No.'

'Do you have any idea where it is?'

'None.'

'I hope you find it.'

'Me too.'

Snow brought the Audi to a halt in a smart London street. 'Here we are.'

'This is the safe house?'

'Yes. I'm going to lock you in the car for a moment, while I let them know you've arrived. OK?'

'OK.'

Snow turned off the ignition, climbed out of the A4, and clicked the remote locking button. He walked up the two steps to the front door of the SIS-owned townhouse and pressed the buzzer. A discreetly hidden camera verified his identity and the door clicked open.

'Aidan Snow!' The cheery-faced woman with immaculate hair and nails beamed at him.

'Hello, Karen. Are you ready for him?'

'Is he dishy? I had visions of him looking like Omar Sharif in *Doctor Zhivago*.'

'Karen Campbell, you keep your mind on your work.'

'Always, Aidan.'

Snow turned back to the car, unlocked it, and led Mikhail into the safe house.

Mikhail held out his hand and spoke in English. 'Thank you, Aidan. I hope we can chat again sometime.'

Snow shook. 'I'm sure we will.'

As Karen introduced herself, Snow started the Audi and drove away. Once clear of the street he pressed the phone button on his steering wheel and called Patchem. 'Just confirming that our asset is in place.'

'What did you make of him?'

'I spoke Russian the entire time and as far as I can tell he's from Moscow – well, a town near enough to share the same accent. I let him tell me a bit about himself. It checks out with what he said before.'

'Gut feeling?'

'I trust him, I think he's genuine.'

'I sincerely hope so.'

*

110

Inside the hot, cramped, windowless room, James Brocklehurst yawned as he reviewed the take from the digital video and audio recorders. Officially based out of the British Embassy in Ankara, SIS had now tasked him with placing electronic recording devices in several locations around Turkey's largest city, Istanbul. The cameras were to monitor targets intel had identified as being used to facilitate the transportation of radicalised British Muslims into neighbouring Syria to fight for Islamic State, or IS, as the British government called it. 'Hegira', as Vauxhall Cross had inappropriately named the covert operation, referred to the flight of the Prophet Muhammad from Mecca to Medina to escape persecution. To Brocklehurst, however, the name sounded more like an Italian supercar.

As a proud Yorkshireman, Brocklehurst had strong ideas on what the UK government should have done about the deluded British jihadis, and letting them leave the country in the first place wasn't one of them. But as an SIS officer his views remained unspoken. Brocklehurst continued reviewing the last tape, which had already been remotely beamed back to the UK to be run through facial recognition software. 'Belt and braces' was his mantra; he'd manually check the tapes in Istanbul while analysts with computers did their work in the UK. The problem with the software was that it didn't read a face in the same way as the human eye-brain combination, but rather compared measurements and position of facial features. Brocklehurst had a file with images of 'persons of interest' and was primarily looking for those, as well as anything else out of the ordinary. That morning he had been alerted to the latest 'persons of interest': three teenage British Muslim girls who had taken direct flights from Gatwick to Turkey the day before. Although their families had heard nothing from them, it was presumed by both police and the British security services that they were attempting to join IS as 'jihadi brides'. It was beyond his understanding why any person, let alone a sixteen-year-old girl, would want to join a terrorist organisation as a sexual plaything, yet that was exactly what they would become if they reached Syria. An old joke popped into his head: 'What do you call a goat tethered to a post in an IS camp? – A leisure centre.' These deluded girls were about to become the goat.

Brocklehurst was disgusted by IS and anyone who tried to join it. Even the name annoyed him. To refer to the terrorist group as a state of Islam was utter nonsense, an utter perversion of the Muslim religion and the concept of statehood. It was not an Islamic state; it was a 'coterie of cretins' hellbent on murdering anyone and everyone who was a non-believer. He and others in the global intelligence community had started to call IS by another name, one the group itself hated: 'Daesh'. Daesh was an acronym formed from the Arabic spelling of IS's full name – al-Dawla al-Islamiya fi Iraq wa al-Sham. Unfortunately for IS, Daesh in Arabic sounded like the word meaning 'monstrous'. Yep, thought Brocklehurst, Daesh was something monstrous.

He stretched to relieve his aching back. This part of the operation hadn't taxed his abilities. At the moment he was little more than a glorified security guard as he studied footage, but getting the cameras in place had proved harder. Although Turkey was a so-called friendly state, SIS hadn't informed the Turkish authorities about Operation Hegira for fear of compromising operational security. With the spectral hands of Al-Qaeda and the newly empowered fists of Daesh banging on their borders, Turkey had become another frontline in the war on terror. In addition to the usual staff in Ankara, two SIS officers were now stationed in Istanbul: Brocklehurst and his new boss, Simon Scarborough, who, despite his name, was actually a southerner.

He took a gulp of tepid coffee and continued to inspect the newest tape. The camera that had taken it was positioned on the balcony of a flat directly across the road from a coach tour company. The taxi rank and two-storey building behind were owned by a local man. He had a steady stream of business, which included contracts to provide sightseeing tours and excursions to some of Istanbul's tourist-class hotels. He had been flagged up by the Turkish National Intelligence Agency (NIA) and placed on a watch list for suspected links to Al-Qaeda and Daesh, although, thus far, no actionable intel had been gathered that would confirm the NIA's suspicions. The digital device recording him had been in place for several weeks already, giving Brocklehurst the chance to understand his normal pattern of business. Four days a week, subcontracted coaches arrived to exchange paperwork before leaving to collect Western tourists. In addition to these, three or four minibuses each week took tourists further afield. And then there were the taxis that came and went at all hours of the day and night, and lastly the foot traffic. As Brocklehurst watched the newest tape he saw the target pull up in a coach. He was in the driver's seat. He had passengers. They did not look like tourists, but they also did not look like jihadis. Six men, cleanshaven and dressed in business suits, stepped down from the coach. On tape the target looked around furtively while he ushered them inside his office building. Then, while he stood in the street, outside the front door, one of the passengers reappeared. Brocklehurst pressed pause and made a still from a frame of the men speaking. It was a departure from the established norm, and the new arrivals were interesting, but the whole event was unremarkable. Brocklehurst yawned again. He glanced at his wristwatch – once he'd finished this tape he'd switch off for the day.

*

Officially it was the remit of the Russian Foreign Intelligence Service (SVR) to carry out intelligence and espionage activities outside the borders of the Russian Federation, but neither Strelkov nor his boss, Director Nevsky, were willing to share this operation. The acclaim for averting an act of nuclear terrorism and retrieving the rogue device would be theirs alone. From his observation point in the commandeered apartment Strelkov studied the target building. It was a flat-roofed, two-storey structure, with the dispatch office on the ground floor and an apartment above. Three beaten-up yellow Hyundai taxis were parked outside. A litter-strewn piece of scrubland, impersonating a square, lay between his observation point and the target and was home to a pack of homeless dogs that slept fitfully. During daylight hours a steady stream of customers came and went, many of them Western tourists carrying large packs. Strelkov turned from the window and addressed the Chechen. 'Is that the man?'

Kishiev peered through the viewfinder at the squat Turk who was busy checking his front tyres. 'Yes.'

'You are certain?'

'Yes, that is Orhan.'

'Orhan Inci?'

Kishiev removed his eye from the viewfinder. 'That is the man.'

'Tell me about him,' Strelkov ordered.

'I have told you already all I know. What more is there to say?'

'I am in no mood to play games. Tell me about Orhan Inci.'

Kishiev slowly moved away from the scope. 'As I told you, he runs a taxi and excursion company, but his real business comes from believers wishing to transit Turkey. He has transported many to and from Iran and to and from Syria.'

'A good Muslim,' Strelkov mocked.

'On the contrary, he is a non-believer but a good businessman.'

'So what are you saying to me?'

'I don't understand.'

Strelkov paused a moment to check his rising anger. 'Is Orhan Inci the terror cell's contact in Turkey?'

'He is responsible for facilitating their transportation, but has nothing to do with the plan.'

'And will he believe your story?'

'I doubt he will be much concerned by my unexpected appearance. The deciding factor for him will be how much I offer to pay for his services.'

Strelkov didn't know how many terrorists were in the building or if indeed they actually had the device. His requested feed from the nearest Persona-class Russian reconnaissance satellite had proved inconclusive. The IR images had shown bodies on both the upper and lower floors of the building; the issue was that they were difficult to distinguish from each other. Added to this, the constant stream of customers and drivers confused matters further. Strelkov had decided that the only way to confirm the presence of the device and the terrorists was to send Kishiev in. He addressed a bearded commando. 'Boroda, you will accompany Kishiev into the target building to confirm the Turk's identity.'

'Yes, sir,' Artur Khalidov aka 'Boroda' (beard) replied, snapping to attention.

Strelkov continued. 'You also need to confirm the number of terrorists in the building and if they have the device. Boroda, get a visual on the device.' He pointed at Boroda but spoke to Kishiev. 'This is what a real Chechen looks like, Kishiev. This is how a real Chechen acts.'

Kishiev shrugged. 'He is a fine example of a Kadyrov dog.'

Boroda grunted and took a step towards his countryman. 'Traitor scum!'

'Enough!' Strelkov barked. Both Chechens faced each other, the air thick between them. One paid to be on Moscow's side and the other coerced. 'Just so this is clear, Kishiev, if Boroda has any reason to believe that you are warning Inci he will kill you on the spot.'

Kishiev let a smile split his lips. 'I would like to see the little man try.'

Boroda's eyes showed contempt but he remained silent.

'Go. I shall be watching,' Strelkov ordered.

Boroda guided Kishiev down the stairs to the ground-floor foyer by nudging him in the back with a silenced 9mm pistol. Both men were dressed in scruffy civilian clothes that gave the impression they had been sleeping rough. Another member of Strelkov's team was leaning against the wall in the far corner, keeping eyes on the street outside.

'Make a run for it, I dare you, Kishiev!' Boroda said through gritted teeth.

'Your father must be very proud of his son for abandoning his faith,' Kishiev replied without irony as he stepped into the bright Istanbul sunlight. Boroda followed Kishiev a beat later and they crossed the road.

'Stop!' Boroda ordered as they reached the edge of the litter-strewn square. 'The Turk may have lookouts. We cannot just walk into the building – it is too obvious. Turn and face me. Pretend we are having a friendly conversation.'

'So, we shall converse.' Kishiev looked his younger countryman in the eyes. 'Do you enjoy being a Russian slave? Does it not offend your faith to serve those who have destroyed our motherland?'

'You are a terrorist, Kishiev. You have killed innocent women and children.'

Kishiev shrugged his shoulders. 'I killed Russian soldiers who invaded my land; it was the Kremlin who planted the bombs that murdered our people. Or do you not believe this? Has that goat molester Kadyrov brainwashed you?'

Boroda's right arm shook as he suppressed the urge to strike Kishiev. 'Ramzan Akhmadovich is a great man, a true servant of the faith. As President of Chechnya he had led our nation out of the darkness!'

Unlike Boroda, Kishiev had learnt to hide his anger, a necessary skill at Black Dolphin. 'He is a Russian puppet like you, but a rich one.'

'Move,' Boroda growled, nodding at the target building.

They exited the square and walked up the couple of steps into Inci's office. It took a moment for their eyes to adjust once more to the darkness within the building, but as they did so they were greeted by a youth speaking Turkish.

'*Iyi ak amlar.*' 'Good afternoon,' the boy said in Turkish. 'My name is Ferit. How may I help you?'

Kishiev replied in Arabic. 'Good afternoon. I would like to speak with Orhan.'

Without missing a beat, the youth switched languages. 'Of course, he is upstairs. May I enquire who is asking?'

'Two weary travellers who need nothing more than his hospitality.'

'Please be seated.'

'Thank you.'

The two Chechens sat on a threadbare green settee and watched Ferit disappear through a beaded curtain which hung at the bottom of a flight of stairs. Kishiev took in his surroundings; nothing had changed since his last visit. The settee and desk were the only two pieces of furniture in the room, and both had seen better days. An asthmatic fan moved above them, swirling the warm city air, and a radio quietly played Turk-pop. 'You do speak Arabic, I presume?'

'Do not attempt to insult me further, Kishiev. I am Chechen.'

'A real one, according to your master.'

'Correct,' Boroda grunted, the insult sailing above his head.

They heard the short, rotund Turk before they saw him, his feet sounding a surprisingly light pitter-patter on the steps, like a child. As he pushed through the curtain, accompanied by Ferit, his eyes widened. '*Ahlan sadiqi.*' 'Hello my friend,' Inci said in Arabic.

Kishiev and Boroda stood. Kishiev held out his arms. 'Hello, Orhan, may peace be upon you.'

Inci took Kishiev's hand and then examined him quizzically, staring at his bristly scalp and stubbly face. 'Of course I had heard you were held by the Russians?'

'No longer. The will of Allah is greater than the walls of any prison.'

'Of course.' Inci turned to Boroda. 'You are one of his men?'

'He is,' Kishiev confirmed with a smile.

'I am Orhan. I am happy to be of assistance to you.'

Boroda did not take the man's hand. The Turk's protruding belly and choppy Arabic disgusted him.

'I understand that several of my brothers now stay with you.' It wasn't a question from Kishiev but a statement of fact. 'I must speak with them.'

Inci was surprised, not wary. As a smuggler for hire, operational details weren't his concern and he had received payment from Al-Qaeda for many years. There was no reason for him to believe his business was in jeopardy. He'd been paid to move Kishiev and, later, men sent by Kishiev, and the paymasters for his current guests were the same. 'I will ask if they wish to see you.'

'That is most kind, Orhan, but we have our orders. I hope you understand?'

'Of course, but please just wait a moment.'

Inci retraced his steps back through the beaded curtain.

Boroda spoke quietly in Russian. 'Kishiev, if you have in any way warned Inci, your family will be slaughtered like lambs.'

'One day, Boroda, you shall die. I will kill you and, at that moment, Allah shall pass judgement upon you.'

'You have already been judged, Kishiev, and you have failed.'

Inci reappeared. 'Follow me up the stairs.'

The stairway was narrow, the walls a grimy green, giving way to a landing with two doors. A skylight above, in contrast to the dirty interior, gave a glimpse of crisp, vivid-blue sky. The door on the right had the word 'Tuvalet' stencilled on it, and the door on the left was open. Through it several beds were visible. Four men stood in the room, well dressed, their business suits at odds with their intense eyes.

'These are the two men who wanted to see you,' Inci said before backing out of the room. He had no interest in learning more about their business.

'Who are you?' Mohammed Tariq was the closest to the door. His arms were loose by his sides and he stood on the balls of his feet.

'Brother, my name is Kishiev. I am, just like you, a humble servant of Allah, peace be upon Him. I have come to aid you in this most noble of missions.'

Tariq's eyes narrowed. 'What mission is that?'

Kishiev heard footsteps from the corridor and fought the urge to turn. Boroda snapped around to face the remaining two members of Tariq's team, who had concealed themselves in the toilet.

Kishiev held up his open palms and smiled in a manner he hoped would put the men at ease. 'Of course you are wary, and you should be, for the device you carry is the most potent weapon we have ever possessed.'

'What device is that, brother?'

'The portable nuclear device you have transported through Iran with the aid of Yassin al-Suri.' Kishiev now spoke to each man in turn. 'Many years ago, I was one of those who sat with the Lion Sheik and planned your mission, brother.'

Tariq was suspicious that this man knew of their connection to al-Suri. 'Is that so?'

'It is, my brother. You are the chosen warriors who will use the Hand of Allah against the infidels!'

'Insha'Allah.' Tariq let himself relax a fraction at the name of the weapon. His visitor knew of the device, but what did he know of the mission, and who was he? 'Search them.'

'I have nothing to hide,' Kishiev said.

'And neither do I, brother,' Boroda stated with an even tone.

The two Chechens held their arms away from their bodies as they were frisked. Kishiev locked eyes with Boroda and waited for the right time to make his move, but as the search concluded he became confused as he saw a faint smile form under the Chechen's beard. Satisfied that neither Chechen was carrying a weapon, the Afghans stepped away.

'So, brothers...' Tariq's tone was now much relaxed. 'Explain who you are and why you are here.'

Kishiev quickly recalculated – the best lies contained the seeds of truth. 'We are Chechen. Like you, our lands have been invaded, our crops poisoned, our women raped, and our faith defiled by the infidels. Together we shall strike back. We are here to guide you on the next stage of your journey.'

'To guide us where?'

'Your team shall be split into two groups. Half of you shall head for Greece where you will be assigned your target by another true believer, while your team,' Kishiev said, pointing at Tariq, 'shall accompany us to Ukraine with the nuclear device. That is why you will need our Russian-language skills.'

Boroda tried to hide his surprise – his thick eyebrows and beard helped.

'Understood, brother.' Tariq now accepted that the men before him were Al-Qaeda, as they spoke of operational details no one outside the management council would know of, such as the splitting of his team into two and mentioning Ukraine. 'Why the change of plan?'

'The Russians, my brother. They have invaded some parts of Ukraine and now all ports of entry to the south of the country are heavily monitored. You would be questioned, and without our linguistic abilities they will detain you. We may enter together, however. I have the necessary contacts.'

Tariq was satisfied. 'Please accept my hospitality and have tea with us.' He waved his hand at a small table.

Kishiev placed his hand on his chest. 'Alas, time is short. We are to leave tomorrow at sunrise so you must be ready.'

'Before we leave, may I see the Hand of Allah?' Boroda asked.

Tariq addressed Reza Khan in Pashtun. 'Show him the device.'

'Is that wise?'

'Do not question me, Reza.'

Khan said no more. He knelt beside one of the beds, removed a case from underneath, and then held it at arm's length. 'Here.'

Boroda felt his heart start to beat faster and a bead of sweat appeared on his brow. It was true; the bomb was in the hands of the terrorists. He had to act, to retrieve it, but he was one man against six – seven if he counted Kishiev. Could he grab it and, if so, could he make it safe? Would they not just detonate it right here and now? He took a step forward. Tariq blocked his path. 'I need to see the markings on the case, that is all.'

'OK,' Tariq agreed, 'but do not attempt to touch the device.'

'I understand, brother.' Boroda took three more steps and leant forward slightly to study the metal case. The heavy clasps were identical to the photographs he had been shown, as was the design of the corners, but he realised there was no way he could take it alone. He made a show of being satisfied and walked back to Kishiev. 'Be ready to leave at sunrise. Until tomorrow.'

'Until tomorrow,' Tariq repeated, as the Chechens left the room.

Boroda hustled Kishiev towards the stairs, almost colliding with Inci as he exited the toilet, still buttoning up his fly. 'We need transportation north.'

'Ah,' Inci sighed. 'Transportation is no problem, it is what I do. When do you need to travel?'

'At sunrise,' Boroda grunted.

'You know that prices have changed? I have much demand now.'

'We can pay,' Boroda bristled. 'Be here at sunrise.'

'So it shall be.'

Holding his arm with a vice-like grip, Boroda took Kishiev down the stairs, across the office, and out into the street. 'You set us up, Kishiev.'

'True, I was expecting them to find your gun.'

'You think I would have been so foolish as to take it in there? I left it in the foyer of our apartment block.'

'You believe you are safe with me unarmed?'

Boroda growled. 'Try me.'

Strelkov watched the two Chechens exit the target building and take a snaking route towards the OP. Minutes later they were back in the Russian-commandeered flat and Boroda had explained what had transpired.

'You can confirm that the device is present?' Strelkov asked almost mechanically.

'Yes.' Boroda wasted no time with rank. 'The case is of the type used on an RA-115A.'

Strelkov folded his arms. It was too soon to feel elated. His anger at Kishiev had started to rise and soon it would boil over unless he channelled it. 'You lied to us, Kishiev.'

'Yes,' Kishiev admitted without emotion.

'You knew all along where the device was headed.'

'No. I made it up.'

Strelkov shook his head. 'What is the target?'

'Which one?'

Strelkov's eyes flashed with anger. 'The target of the bomb!'

'I do not know.'

'But you do know that the team will split into two?'

'Yes. I know the outline of the plan, which is why we are here. I have led you to the bomb, as we agreed.'

Strelkov laughed mirthlessly. 'You think you are able to play us? To outwit the FSB?'

Kishiev became indignant. 'I have handed you the device; now you must keep your end of the bargain, Strelkov.'

'I will. You have proven that you know more about the inner workings of Al-Qaeda than you have disclosed to us. Our interrogation wing shall now be responsible for your safekeeping just as soon as they arrive. In the meantime, Boroda shall take you away.'

'Where?'

'Not the circus, if that was what you were expecting,' Strelkov sneered.

'I have seen enough performing dogs here.'

'That's it; carry on with your inane remarks now, because when the interrogators arrive you'll have little breath to speak.'

*

The target building was quiet and the streets outside were still. Strelkov studied the building yet again for anything he might have missed, but it was unremarkable in its ordinariness. Two of the three tatty Hyundai taxis had left in the small hours of the morning with their drivers and, as far as Strelkov could make out, were not expected back until midday. The last remaining yellow saloon belonged to Inci and its presence was a sign that he had slept on the premises. Strelkov studied the scrubby square. The dogs were sleeping and the benches were tramp-free. Moving away from the window he gave his hand-picked assault team the ready signal and said 'Go! Go!' in Russian. '*Davai! Davai!*'

With the sun still an hour away, the Russians advanced to target. Dressed in full assault coveralls, body armour, helmets, and respirators, they were aliens in the urban environment. They skirted the square and then lined up against the side wall of the building, unsighted by the windows directly across the room.

The Russians then split into two subteams. The first used a grappling hook to get onto the roof while the second took up position by the front door. The lead man of the second team placed a frame charge against the front door, before trailing out the det cord and retreating away from the rest of the assaulters to the opposite side of the doorway. A second later the door imploded and a pair of flashbangs were tossed into the void. They exploded and were immediately followed by the Russians in snake formation. A further pair of flashbangs were dropped through the skylight and followed a second later by the roof team.

As Strelkov continued to look on he saw flashes in a first-floor window before everything for a moment became calm. Then the sound of dogs howling and the neighbourhood complaining at being woken up took over. Strelkov left the apartment, and its owner, who lay drugged up in his empty bath. He jogged across the street and through the square towards the target. The assault had lasted no more than a minute and they had a further five before the local authorities would arrive and start to ask questions.

*

The Russians had drugged Kishiev before transporting him to the flat that acted as a safe house, injecting just enough sedative to make him compliant, but now it had worn off. Kishiev sat on the cold, laminate floor, handcuffed by the left wrist to a radiator. His FSB guard was a huge man, completely ill-suited to covert operations. He was the muscle, the man they used to intimidate and suppress. And now, as the rest of the Strelkov's team, led by Boroda, assaulted Inci's building, the guard was attempting to intimidate and suppress Kishiev. He hadn't spoken a word to Kishiev, merely watched him with a cold anger that suggested deep hatred. Meanwhile, Kishiev stared at the wall, and retreated into a meditative state in an attempt to clear the remnants of the drug-induced fog from his mind. His years at Black Dolphin had taught him patience and how to channel his mental strength, an unexpected gift from Mother Russia.

A shrill ringtone reverberated around the sparsely furnished flat. The Russian answered. '*Da?*'

There was a pause while the guard received his instructions and before he moved towards Kishiev. As he bent, off balance, arm extended, to hand Kishiev the phone, the doorbell rang. The Russian hesitated, and then walked away, speaking into the phone. Kishiev saw his chance and acted. He wrenched his arm and felt the wall mount give slightly. As he heaved again he heard a heavy thud come from the hallway, like a large book landing flat on a wooden floor. Kishiev turned his head towards the door and that was when he heard a whistle. A whistle he recognised. He heard it again and this time he replied with one of his own; it was a signal he hadn't used for many years.

From outside the room a familiar voice asked in Arabic, 'Are you alone?'

'Yes, brother, I am,' Kishiev replied.

'I'm coming in,' the voice said. A figure emerged from behind the door. He was carrying a suppressed Glock 19. Even though they hadn't stood face to face since Afghanistan, more than a decade before, the man known within Al-Qaeda as the 'White Eagle' was unmistakable. '*Ahlan sadiqi*,' he said, a smile forming on his lips.

'Hello, my brother,' Kishiev replied. 'It has been a long time.'

'And a hard time for you, or so I hear.'

Kishiev let his lips curl into a smile. He pulled his left arm, the radiator wall mounting snapped, and the handcuff slipped free. 'The Russians thought they could break me. They were wrong.'

'The Russians are wrong about most things, Aslan.'

Kishiev stood. 'How did you find me?'

'It wasn't that difficult. Strelkov let the cat out of the bag when he came to see you at Black Dolphin. Then I just had to follow him.'

Kishiev grunted his agreement. The White Eagle was one of Al-Qaeda's deepest cover agents. 'So you have finally decided to use the nuclear device?'

The White Eagle shook his head. 'This is not the same bomb you knew of. This one was discovered in Afghanistan.'

Kishiev was surprised. 'This is not the Hand of Allah?'

'It is his other hand. His right hand is too well guarded.'

'By the management council?'

'No, by the CIA. I had to let them have it; they had got too close.'

Kishiev trusted the Al-Qaeda operative. 'But the plans have remained the same?'

'They have changed. The EU is too hard a target and would not best serve our cause.'

'I am confused. Was it not the purpose of the late Lion Sheik to strike terror into the hearts of the infidels, as punishment for murdering our Muslim brothers and invading our lands?'

'It remains so, my brother, but the battlefield has moved. Many things have happened during your incarceration. We have a new target, one that no one suspects and one that will catch the aggressor completely unaware. It will also please you immensely.'

'What is the target, my brother?' Kishiev scratched his stubbly chin.

The White Eagle quickly explained and the Chechen allowed himself to smile. The dead guard's mobile phone started to ring. 'Your Russians cannot be too far behind me. We need to go.'

'Not before we leave them a parting present,' Kishiev said.

Chapter 7

Istanbul, Turkey

Pushing and barging their way through the first of Istanbul's morning traffic, it took Strelkov and his team half an hour to reach the Russian safe house. There had been no reply from the mobile phones of the men left to guard the Chechen. Strelkov cursed himself for moving Kishiev as they crested a small rise and the entrance to the apartment block came into view.

'Stop,' Strelkov ordered Boroda. The VW transporter came to an immediate halt. As Strelkov looked on, the scene became clearer. A police car, an ambulance, and a small crowd had gathered outside the building. 'Take us into the car park at the back.'

Boroda steered the van forward before turning and bumping up over the pavement and into the cracked, concrete parking lot. Strelkov pointed to three of his team. 'You come with me. The rest of you secure the van and be prepared to move when I give the order.' The men nodded their assent. Strelkov removed his MP-443 Grach from its pancake holster and stepped out of the van. Weapons held flat against their thighs to minimise the profile, the three assaulters followed him quickly towards the apartment building's rear entrance. Unbidden, they took up positions either side of the door before bursting in, weapons ready. They cleared the small lobby and sandwiched Strelkov as they took the stairs, reaching the sixth floor soundlessly. The lead man lay flat on the top step and peered round the corner into the hallway. Empty. He paused for half a minute, tuning in to the heartbeat of the building, before moving forward at a crouch. He placed his ear at the apartment door and listened for any signs of life. He beckoned the remainder of the team over. Once ready they kicked the door open and bomb-burst inside. Two men went left to clear the hall, bathroom and kitchen, while Strelkov and the other moved right to the bedroom and living room. The apartment was empty. Strelkov looked down and saw a trail of blood on the tiled floor, leading from the middle of the living room towards the balcony. The doors were open and the sound of the city wafted in. Two team members headed for the balcony. Strelkov's eyes now saw something new by the threshold. A wire! His eyes widened. As he opened his mouth to yell a warning an explosion erupted inside the apartment.

*

British Consulate, Istanbul, Turkey

Simon Scarborough, 'Scarby' to his drinking buddies, bit into a bacon sandwich and closed his eyes with satisfaction. He loved bacon and couldn't understand how Muslims did without it. Why did a religion forbid its followers from eating specific foods? Narcotics he could understand, even alcohol at a push, but bacon? Seriously? Bacon? Still, it didn't matter to him. He had bacon and that was all that mattered. Breakfast was his favourite meal of the day and it was his habit to eat it slowly at his desk as he checked his overnight emails. In his opinion, bacon and tomato wrapped in two doorsteps of granary bread, with a squirt of Heinz tomato ketchup, and washed down with a mug of milky, sugary PG Tips, couldn't be beaten. He took another bite just as there was a knock at his door.

'Come in,' he mumbled through his mouthful of meat.

'Scarby!' Brocklehurst pointed an accusative finger at his boss's sandwich. 'That's haram.'

'No, it's bacon.'

'You ever tried beef bacon?' Scarborough shook his head. 'Had it in Saudi. All we could get when the consulate ran out, but it weren't bad with a dash of brown sauce.'

'Thank you, Jamie Oliver. Now, what do you want?'

'Your spy is here.'

'Ah.' Scarborough put his sandwich back on his plate and stood. His "spy" was Ekrim Keser, a former Deputy Director of the Turkish NIA and long-time friend to the British. Keser would only speak to Scarborough, a fact that irritated Brocklehurst.

'I've put him in interview room two; he's quite animated.'

'Thanks.'

Scarborough followed Brocklehurst out of his office, along a corridor, and entered the interview room. Brocklehurst shut the door on the pair and went back to work. Keser was immaculately dressed as per usual, giving the impression that he was en route to a wedding. He came straight to the point. 'Simon, I have some very alarming news. There have been two separate terrorist attacks this morning.'

Scarborough's eyes became wide. 'What? Where?'

'Perhaps I exaggerate, a little.' Keser shrugged. 'An address the NIA has on a watch list was attacked today by armed men. They gained entry to the building with explosives. Local residents saw flashes and heard gunfire.'

'When was this? I've heard nothing.'

'Just over three hours ago, and you won't, because the NIA are trying to keep it quiet. I only know because… well… you know.'

'I do.' The elderly former intelligence officer had innumerable contacts.

'Inside, the police found four bodies. One taxi driver and three others who appeared to be from the Indian subcontinent. A Pakistani passport was found on one of them.'

Scarborough sat back in his chair and pursed his lips. 'Why were the NIA watching the address?'

Keser leant forward in his seat conspiratorially. 'They were suspects in a people-trafficking ring.'

'Oh, really.' This was a little too close to home. 'But who attacked them?'

'Ah!' Keser held up his index finger. 'That's where all this gets, how does one say, "cloak and dagger"? Two hours ago there was a call from an apartment block known to the NIA as containing a Russian safe house. The call was made by a neighbour. He's a jogger and was setting off for a run when he found a body on the pavement. It looked as though it had fallen from a balcony. It was a huge man, like a bodybuilder, but that is not the end of it. No. A matter of some twenty minutes later there was an explosion in the apartment block, in the Russian safe house.'

'Were there any casualties?'

'Only a lot of blood; the casualties, bodies, appear to have been dragged away!'

Scarborough blinked; there was only one possible conclusion. 'A Russian black op?'

'That is what my thinking is. The police have been told to leave it alone, the NIA have taken over. I want to know what a Russian team was doing there. What was their target? Were they after someone, or something? You know, Simon, I have heard some rumours.'

Scarborough started to hear alarm bells in his head. 'What about?'

'You and your American friends are looking for something, perhaps a terror cell? I do know that something is in the air.'

'Ekrim, I need to make a phone call. I hope you understand.' The veteran intelligence officer stood and extended his hand.

'Yes, I do. Good luck, Simon. You know where I am if you need me. And I would like to know, eventually, what this was all about.'

'Of course.' Scarborough shook his spy's hand and left the room. Less than a minute later he was back in his office, eating the last piece of his, now cold, bacon sandwich. If anything, stress made him hungrier. His desk phone rang. 'Yes?'

'I take it your spy has left?'

'Yes.'

'I need to come to your office immediately.'

'OK.' Scarborough ended the call and barely had time to wipe his mouth and finish his mug of tepid tea before Brocklehurst walked into the room and sat. 'What's so urgent?' he asked, but he had a feeling he already knew.

'One of the Hegira locations has been hit,' Brocklehurst said, shutting the door.

He did know. 'I know.'

'How?'

Scarborough quickly explained his meeting.

'GCHQ got onto me after I left you with Keser. The camera shows an assault team going in. Explosive entry, flashbangs, and then, two minutes later, someone else joining them before they bug-out.'

'OK. I've got to call Jack Patchem.' Scarborough reached for his plate and then remembered he'd finished his sandwich.

'You think this could be related to that other thing?' Even though both men were SIS officers, they had refrained from using the terms 'nuclear', 'nuke', or 'bomb' within the consulate.

'It seems too much of a coincidence.'

'Shouldn't we call Harry first?' Brocklehurst referred to their London-based head of section Harry Slinger-Thompson.

'No, this is time-sensitive. Jack can have someone tell Harry.' Scarborough pressed a button on his desk phone to put it on speaker and then dialled Vauxhall Cross. He was connected on the second ring to Patchem's PA and a moment later to Patchem himself. 'Jack, this is Simon Scarborough, here in Istanbul. I've got James Brocklehurst with me. You're on speakerphone.'

'Hello, Simon, what do you have for me?' Patchem sounded tired but affable.

Scarborough explained once more his meeting with Keser and then let Brocklehurst add to the mix the news from GCHQ.

Patchem hadn't been briefed on Operation Hegira as Turkey didn't come within the remit of his desk, but now he would request and be granted full access to their electronic take. When he spoke again the fatigue had left his voice. 'James, for how long had this camera been in place prior to the attack?'

'Just over three weeks – twenty-four days to be exact.'

'Good. I'll have the techies run the tapes again through their facial recognition software. Is there anything else you can tell me about Orhan Inci?'

'His business seemed brisk. There were always tourists coming and going.' Brocklehurst frowned. 'Actually, I did see a group arrive two days ago who seemed unusual.'

'In what way?' Patchem prompted.

'There were six of them and they were wearing suits.'

'Did they look like Afghans?'

'They were Asian; to be honest, if it hadn't been for the way they were dressed, I'd have said they were Brits abroad.'

'Simon, I need you to ask Keser to use his contacts to get photos of the bodies; it'll be faster than a request via official channels. I don't care how you do it, but we need to know who the Russians took out and who they took away.' More importantly, Patchem thought to himself, we need to know if they're now in possession of the bomb.

'Are we sure it was the Russians?' Scarborough asked.

'I'm going to watch the tapes myself, but if it walks like a bear and moves like a bear, the chances are it's Russian.' If the Russians had retrieved the device the immediate threat was over, and the attack averted. But how in hell was he to verify that the Russians had the device? He couldn't very well ask them. 'Simon, do we have anyone monitoring the Russian Consulate?'

'No.'

'James, are any of your cameras near the Russian Consulate?'

'No.'

Patchem wasn't surprised. Until events of the past year, Russia hadn't been an enemy of the West, merely an antagonist masquerading as a partner. Their aggression in Ukraine, however, had changed all that. He was certain the US had eyes on the consulate and could run up a list of who had passed through its large, ornate gates, but that was probably reason enough to discount the consulate as a destination for the assault team and any prize they might have. 'I'll ask the Americans if they've seen anything. The Russian safe house where the explosion happened – was this place on our radar?'

'No,' Scarborough replied shamefaced. 'Keser told us about it.'

Patchem said nothing. He wasn't one for the blame game; he had bigger fish to fry. 'In that case, also ask Keser if there are any other Russian assets the NIA knows of.'

'Will do.'

'Stay on top of this, you two, and if you need anything whatsoever, call me.'

The line went dead and Brocklehurst raised his eyebrows at Scarborough. 'Bloody hell!'

In London, Patchem quickly left his office. His first stop would be the desk of Harry Slinger-Thompson and then he had a phone call to make to his favourite American. He hoped to hell the Russians had the device and he could call off his search, but life was rarely ever that easy, however it seemed at the time.

*

Mikhail was having the dream again, reliving the day that had defined his existence for the last quarter of a century. He was once again a young Spetsnaz officer. It was a nightmare, but the most frightening part was that it had been real...

The chill of the Afghan night had all but disappeared, to be replaced by the weak warmth of dawn. In the half-light, poppy fields stretched ahead of them and westwards on the valley floor. It was a beautiful flower to some, but to others as deadly as any bomb. To the east, the unnamed village, with its ramshackle mud huts. A few feet away he saw his commanding officer, Bull Pashinski, lower his binos and rub his eyes. Their Spetsnaz assault group had been given specific orders: attack the village, eliminate all Mujahideen, burn the poppy crop. His comrades, the true elite of the Red Army, were ready. They lay prone on the ridge, waiting.

To their left and hidden in a dip, Captain Lesukov's fire support team had the mortars ready; to Bull's right Sergeant Zukauskas and the rest of the Brigada. The plan was simple, brutal, and effective: Lesukov's men would shell the village; then their team would move from house to house, picking off anyone and everyone that survived. Intelligence supplied by a local informer had said the village was a sham, nothing more than a base for Mujahideen fighters and Arab Islamic mercenaries to grow and distribute the death that came from the poppy in the field. The Red Army could not let this continue in a partner state. Hence the unequivocal orders.

Bull looked at Lesukov. 'Start firing your mortars in two minutes.'

Lesukov saluted. 'Good luck.'

Bull returned the salute. 'Ivan, we are Spetsnaz, we make our own luck.'

Mikhail, Bull, and the rest of the team moved silently over the ridge and into the valley.

Thumph... thumph...

Mortar shells whistled through the sky. There was sudden movement from the village. A robed figure appeared and gazed directly at the ridge. He yelled, raised his rifle, and fired into the sky. As he did so an explosion tore the very earth from under his feet. More shells landed, flattening the Afghan houses and destroying the beauty of the new day. Then, as abruptly as they had started, they stopped. The Soviets now swept through the carnage before them. The dead and dying littered the village; many had been asleep, others in the process of grabbing weapons. Several fled to the fields and were chased down by rounds, which not even the fastest could outrun. Mikhail and Bull reached the building they believed housed the village elder. The roof was intact, even though part of one wall was now missing. The old man was sitting on a crimson rug in the corner, his henna-red beard specked with dust. His eyes displayed anger, not fear. He waited until Mikhail had entered the room behind Bull before speaking with venom-laced words.

Mikhail translated. The old man jabbed at them with a bony finger. 'He says it is a trap, that we have all been tricked... we are infidels, not men of our word, not men of honour.'

'Enough.' Bull stepped forward and crouched. 'We are men of honour. We did not break our agreement.' Bull stood, drew his Makarov, and shot the elder point-blank between the eyes.

Shocked, Mikhail stared down at his captain. 'Why?'

Pashinski stared at the young officer, his eyes angry but his face dismissive. 'He was Mujahideen; that is all you need know.'

An explosion sounded behind them, then another. Bull turned as Mikhail backed out of the house. On the ridge above, the fire support team were under attack. Gathering up his men, Bull charged back towards Lesukov's squad. Reaching the ridge, wild rounds whistled past them. Lesukov's men had been taken by surprise; a group of fighters numbering more than twenty had flanked them from the west. Lesukov fired controlled bursts from his Kalashnikov at the Afghan hordes. Of Lesukov's eight men,

Mikhail could see that only Lesukov and two others were left. The colossal Lithuanian, Zukauskas, grabbed a mortar and turned it around to face the oncoming threat; one-handed he dropped a shell into the tube and fired. Unsighted, the shell flew over the Mujahideen and exploded without causing a casualty. Securing the tube on the ground he sighted it while Mikhail dropped in a new shell. This time the explosion landed just to the left of the advancing fighters. Some stopped, others carried on. Bull joined Lesukov. There was a grin on Lesukov's face. 'We make our own luck!'

'No. We make it unlucky for them!'

Listening to instructions shouted by Zukauskas, Mikhail adjusted the mortar. They launched shell after shell until their ordinance ran out. Meanwhile, Lesukov and the rest of the remaining Russians fired well-aimed rounds at the approaching fighters. Eventually the sun banished the last shadows of night and the gunfire stopped. Mikhail looked around. Lesukov's team was all but wiped out, and his own team had lost many members, too, yet Zukauskas had a smile on his swine-like face. He slapped Mikhail heavily on the back. 'We showed those goat fuckers!'

Unable to speak with exhaustion, Mikhail heard solitary rounds ring out from the Spetsnaz as they made sure the fallen Mujahideen remained so. Bull and Lesukov approached. Bull spoke to Zukauskas in Lithuanian. The big man slammed his fist into the side of Mikhail's head, causing him to fall to the ground. Caught by surprise he rolled onto his back and attempted to stand. Suddenly the boots of the three men rained down upon him. Unable to move away, Mikhail curled into a foetal position.

'Stop.' Bull looked down at the lieutenant. 'The old man said it was a trap. You betrayed us. You have spoken to the locals; you have become one.'

'That is not true.' Mikhail tried to sit but a heavy boot pushed his chest back into the ground.

'You have betrayed us, your Spetsnaz brothers, you have betrayed the Red Army, but most of all you have betrayed the

Soviet Union.' Bull spoke again in his native Lithuanian to Zukauskas, who grunted and heaved Mikhail to his feet.

Bull brandished a knife. 'You have led us to be slaughtered like animals so you will now be slaughtered as one.' With a sudden thrust the knife ripped through Mikhail's shirt and into his stomach.

'No, please!' The pain was momentarily unbearable, then a wave of cold flooded his body. He felt himself fall.

'Captain Pashinski. Report,' Nevsky ordered.

Bull turned and met the eye of the KGB Political Officer. 'As ordered we have completed our mission. As instructed I am about to execute the traitor.'

Nevsky peered down at Mikhail, but addressed Bull. 'There can be no record of this, Pashinski. Do I make myself clear?'

'Yes, Comrade.' Bull saluted.

'What this man has done has brought dishonour to the KGB and the Spetsnaz. Finish him off and then leave his body for the Mujahideen. It may entertain them.' There was a distant whoop of rotor blades and a Mi-17 troop carrier flanked by a smaller but deadly Hind gunship appeared above the horizon. Over the sound of the Mi-17's rotors Nevsky shouted at the assassins, 'Time to leave.'

*

Mikhail awoke, and lay still, wondering where he was. The feel of the mattress was alien to him, as was the sound of the London night on the street below. He clambered out of bed and moved to the window; the bars permitted it to open only a couple of finger widths, but it was enough to let the cold air of England fill his lungs and reassure him that he still lived. Mikhail had not had the dream for years, but two weeks ago it had returned. It now haunted him every night and left him feeling raw. Had there been any meaning to it? That day heralded the death of Mikhail the soldier and the birth of Mikhail the believer. He had no idea how he had survived, but survive he had. Taken by Afghan fighters, he had babbled away in Pashtun, renouncing his Soviet masters and embracing Islam. The Afghans had seen a chance to use him. It took months for the physical wounds to heal and years for the psychological ones to do likewise. A local tribal leader took him under his roof as a guest and granted his protection, as was dictated by the Koran. Mikhail was not trusted, yet it was hoped that, as one of the 'devils in red', he would aid the locals in their fight against the invaders. One night, months after his rescue, Mujahideen fighters came for him with murder in mind. It was then that he played his last card. He took them to the location of his weapons cache.

He had no love for the Soviet Union – how could they even think of using such a devastating weapon on a defenceless nation? He had removed the RA-115A from his base, hidden it with other weapons, and replaced it with a rock-filled metal case. He created a cache of weapons and supplies that would sustain him when he made good his desertion. He lied about the nuke to the Mujahideen, saying it was a worthless box of electrical components, some sort of transmitter, and the simple fighters had accepted this, but what they had taken had won him their trust.

Mikhail was now a Muslim, but swore an oath to himself that he would remain near the weapon to ensure it would never be used by either side. He returned later to the cache, retrieved the device, and hid it. He took for his wife a woman who had been widowed by a Soviet shell and grew to love her and her two daughters. Without any sons she had been of little worth to anyone else. Although she could bear him no further children he became content as time and wars passed. He was referred to less and less as 'the Russian', and when the Taliban took over where the Soviets had left off, he was just another simple man living in a simple village. All the while his nuclear device lay buried beneath his home, until a man from Pakistan discovered it. He was Al-Qaeda and checking out 'the Russian', once more to gauge his loyalty. He became very interested indeed in the box. He tried to take it; Mikhail wouldn't let him have it until, at gunpoint, the man threatened his family. Mikhail crumbled. Now, the shame was harder than ever to live with. Terrorists had the weapon. And then, a matter of months ago, more fighters had brought another Pakistani to the village. This one demanded that Mikhail make the device work and hauled him off to a camp where he saw, firsthand, men training. Some of them were known to him as local fighters.

Mikhail eventually drew up the same plans he had given to Captain Webster. He lied to the Pakistani and persuaded him he wasn't just a believer but a true believer in jihad. The man placed Mikhail in a hut with a guard outside, where he was to stay until he had no further use for him. Mikhail had been contemplating escape when an explosion had reduced the camp to rubble. Unlike the assault he had been in a quarter of a century before, this attack by ISAF involved no men on the ground, just a drone high above them. With the walls broken and the terrorists in disarray, he took his chance and ran. Without transport it was a long and dangerous journey home. The fighters arrived there first. They slaughtered his family and burnt his house. All that he had been, for the last two and a half decades, was ripped out of him and turned to ashes. But the fire burnt Mikhail too; it burnt away the man, uncovering the warrior within. He vowed revenge. With every ounce of his being, until his last breath, he would fight the men who had murdered his family, who had murdered him, and who planned to murder innocents in Europe. Now, in London, he had answered many questions from serious men and women in suits about the weapon, its history, and his. He had sat next to a man at a computer terminal who had taken his handwritten schematics and turned them into what looked to him like the original documents. He didn't know what fate awaited him after the weapon was either found or detonated, and he did not care. His sole purpose was to guard the innocents who were undoubtedly the targets of the bomb – his bomb.

British Consulate, Istanbul, Turkey

Keser proudly handed Scarborough a thumb drive. 'The photographs you requested are on this little disc.'

'Thank you, Ekrim. I don't know how you managed to get these so quickly, but I owe you one.'

With a flick of his hand Keser waved away the thanks. 'Add it to your tab. When the national security of my country is at stake, I am more than happy to help.'

'Thank you all the same,' Brocklehurst added.

Scarborough plugged the device into his laptop and opened up the images. He repositioned the screen so that he, Keser, and Brocklehurst could see the display. The photographs had been taken by the NIA and showed the bodies lying where they had fallen.

'As you will see, each man has been shot by a professional. Look at the entry wounds; they are from a 9mm. One in the chest and one in each head. It is a clinical "controlled pair" to make certain of death.'

'You've seen these?'

'Oh, yes,' Keser confessed. 'I thought you might want my expert opinion.'

'Thank you.' Scarborough clicked on to the next image. Brocklehurst shuddered as he saw the face of the man he knew as Orhan Inci devoid of any life. 'So, who does the NIA feel is responsible for this?'

'You don't really need to ask me that, do you, Simon?' Keser folded his arms.

'Thank you for bringing these to us, Director Keser.'

Keser acknowledged Brocklehurst, but spoke to Scarborough. 'So, can I take it that these men were part of some sort of terror cell?'

Scarborough nodded. Keser had been quick to get the images

and now a titbit of information would keep him sweet. 'Yes, and with these photographs we may well be able to find out who they were and, equally as important, where they were going.'

'When I met with my contact, he said the coroner had not as yet confirmed the time of death, but that is of little importance – we know who shot them and when.'

The remaining photographs scrolled in a slide show until an image of a passport appeared on the screen. The next image showed its interior. 'Pause that one,' Brocklehurst requested. All three men stared at the image. It showed a Schengen visa.

'So he was going to the EU?' Keser asked.

'It now looks that way.'

'Not to the UK?'

'A UK visa is much harder to get.'

'They are an Al-Qaeda terror cell or Islamic State, perhaps?'

Scarborough lied. 'We don't know for certain they were Muslim extremists.'

'Of course, but that is the most likely scenario, unless...'

'Unless what?'

'No, no, just ignore me, I am thinking aloud,' Keser said with a smile.

Brocklehurst frowned. 'I don't understand why this single passport has been left behind? Where are the passports of the other men in suits? Why leave this one at all? Is it misdirection or does someone want us to know the group was heading for the EU?'

Brocklehurst had impressed the veteran intelligence officer. 'You have raised good points. Why indeed?'

Scarborough closed down the image. 'I need to get these off to London, pronto.' He opened up his email and sent the photographs directly to Patchem. He was sure they would be of interest, but perhaps the biggest lead would come from the passport. Dates and numbers could be checked from the photos and both it and the visa's origin traced, even if the original document was safely in the hands of the Turkish Intelligence Service.

'Have the Russians claimed the body that fell from the balcony?' Brocklehurst asked Keser.

'No, and how could they without admitting it was one of their men?'

'Perhaps he was on holiday, or got lost,' Scarborough said.

'This isn't Ukraine,' Brocklehurst replied.

Keser held up his index finger. 'Ah, but we are near Ukraine and that is what I had begun to think about. What do we have here that they also have in Ukraine?' Both Brits remained silent. 'Tatars.'

'Tatars?'

'Yes, and Tatars are also Muslims.'

The two SIS men exchanged glances. Scarborough spoke first. 'Do you think this terror cell is somehow related to the Crimean Tatars?'

Keser shrugged. 'I have no idea, but you have seen how the Tatars in Ankara have created large demonstrations at the Russian Embassy? And I am sure you will have read about the mass intimidation of Tatars in Crimea by the occupying Russians?'

Scarborough leant back in his chair and clasped his hands. 'As far as I'm aware there is no radical Tatar movement. Are the Tatars militant?'

'No, they are a very peaceful group and mostly secular – if one can use that term to refer to a Muslim – but surely if one is provoked enough, one will fight back?'

'That's certainly a point to consider.'

'We'll pass it on to London,' Brocklehurst added.

Keser stood. 'Gentlemen, I must now go. As always, you know where to find me.'

The retired intelligence director shook Scarborough's hand before Brocklehurst escorted him out of the room and towards reception. Returning, Brocklehurst found his boss slumped back in his chair.

'What do you think of his Tatar hypothesis?'

'I think I could murder a bacon sandwich,' Scarborough replied.

Chapter 8

The cold hit him first, then the muscular pain, which seemed to come from all over his body. As Tariq opened his eyes he realised he was lying on the floor, naked. The room was dimly lit and stank of bleach. With effort Tariq shuffled backwards until he was lolling against the wall.

'I am speaking to you in English because I know you can understand me.'

A desk lamp switched on and Tariq saw, sitting at a table in the middle of the room, a white man in a pair of jeans and a leather bomber jacket. There were two tin mugs in front of him and a second chair. 'Join me – we are not savages. My name is Boris.'

'Where am I?'

'Don't you worry. Mother Russia has you tucked up nice and safe.'

Tariq felt a fiery rage surge through him. He snarled at the infidel. 'You have lost, Russian.'

'Maybe, maybe not.' Boris drank from one of the mugs. 'Tea or perhaps a coffee? Mine is Irish, but I don't believe you'd want the same, being a good Muslim. Or perhaps you are not a good Muslim?'

Tariq felt a twinge of anger at the affront to his faith. 'You would offer me tea laced with drugs to get me to talk?'

'No, just tea.' Boris held up a plastic package. 'We burnt your old clothes. They were covered in shit and piss. You had an accident when we captured you. Here are some clean ones.'

Tariq felt his blood boil. 'You are very generous.'

'Catch.' Boris threw the bag.

Tariq struggled to get out of the way but was too slow. The package hit him on the head.

Boris laughed uncontrollably. 'Are you the best that Al-Qaeda has? A man who is scared to get dressed?'

'And you are the best the KGB has to offer me?' Tariq hesitantly stood, and used his fury to rip open the plastic wrapping. He was suddenly aware of a dull but growing pain in his temples. He swayed as he started to dress.

'The KGB no longer exists. I am FSB.'

'You are a fat man in cheap clothes.'

'Oh, please, please – your jokes are killing me. I know you would in reality like to, but, well, here is the thing, my friend. We have you in a facility that is so secure and so secret that even I didn't know about it until my boss in Moscow told me. Now you, not Allah – peace be upon Him, etc. – are the master of your own destiny. You can decide to talk to me and live, or not talk and die.'

'I shall never talk, I shall die a martyr!'

'You really should do stand-up comedy; you have the perfect delivery.'

Tariq frowned, he didn't understand. 'I shall die a martyr.'

'You shall die a comedian.'

Tariq, now fully dressed in dark-blue sweats, pointed a bony finger. 'You have underestimated the soldiers of Islam. Do you think that by capturing me it is all over? Fool. Our attacks cannot and will not be stopped by you infidels, with your feeble minds and fat bodies!'

'I see that your head has started to hurt. Do not worry, that is a mere side effect of the drugs we gave you to make you talk. You see I already know quite a lot about you, Mohammed Tariq.'

Tariq's mouth opened for a moment before he could find his words. How did the Russian know his name? 'But I... I do not remember. No! You lie to me!'

Boris shrugged and then, without warning, hurled his metal coffee mug. Catching Tariq off-guard it hit him on the temple and he stumbled. Boris lurched across the room and grabbed the prisoner by the neck before swinging a right hook into his jaw. Tariq went limp. Boris let go and the Afghan fell to the floor. Boris opened his flies and urinated. Tariq jerked awake as the warm liquid hit his face. He flailed his arms and rolled onto his stomach.

'Coffee makes me piss like a Moscow circus elephant.'

The light snapped off and the Russian left the room. Alone and covered in the waste of an infidel, Tariq spat blood and planned how he would escape and kill the man who had disgraced him in such a manner.

*

Consulate General of the Russian Federation, Istanbul, Turkey

'Four of our men dead, an escaped prisoner, and still no bomb!' Director Nevsky's rage was little tempered by the video-link. 'Are these the types of results I can expect from you? That the President can expect from you, that the motherland can expect of you?'

Strelkov's anger at being spoken to in such a manner was temporarily masking the pain. Twin grenades had been set off by the tripwire on the balcony, grenades taken from his dead men's webbing. He had suffered a concussion and lacerations to his face and chest. The two men nearer the balcony had no chance... their bloody bodies, and those of the dead guards used as bait, had been cleared away by the remainder of his team. But it had been too late for them to secure their comrade on the street. 'I do not know what to say, Valentin Romanovich.'

'Explain to me again what has happened.'

'When we entered the target address we found that the place had already been hit. The Al-Qaeda courier, Orhan Inci, had been executed along with three men, whom we presumed to be members of the Al-Qaeda cell. All had been shot with 9mm rounds. The device was nowhere to be seen. It was a standard six-man cell, therefore we can deduce that the three remaining terrorists have the weapon.'

'You deduce, Strelkov! You must not presume. You must find the device. Was there any hard intelligence that it had been there in the first place?'

'We found trace levels of radiation in the building.'

'So the weapon is leaking? Is that what you are saying?'

'Yes.'

'How hard is it to follow a trace radiation signal?'

'It is impossible. They have a twelve-hour head start on us and the level is not enough to be picked up by our satellites. The casing of the device was designed to shield the radiation signature for this very reason and the leak is minimal.'

Director Nevsky fell silent, took a sip of tea from an ornate china cup, which appeared minute in his large paw, and then, albeit digitally, looked Strelkov in the eye. 'Tell me about the Chechen. How did he escape?'

'He overpowered the man guarding him. He then threw him out of the balcony window. After that he booby-trapped the apartment.'

'Do you realise how ridiculous you sound?'

'Yes, Valentin Romanovich.'

'How could he do all this? You said he was weak.'

'He was.'

'Yet he overpowered a younger, stronger FSB operative?'

'He did.'

'He had help. Who knew of the safe house?'

'No one.'

Nevsky drank more tea. 'We can safely say that if the safe house was not compromised before this incident, it is now. Do you have any idea whatsoever about where the device might have been taken? Where Kishiev might go?'

'Mainland Europe was always their target.'

'Red Square is in Europe.' Nevsky's rage had been replaced by sarcasm.

'We recovered Pakistani passports from the bodies of two of the terrorists. They were issued in the same place and had Schengen visas commencing on the same date.'

'So, you are saying our missing terrorists are heading for the EU?'

'Yes, Valentin Romanovich.'

'Their target?'

Strelkov took a deep breath. 'Any of the major capital cities. London, Paris, Berlin.'

'We need more than guesses. I have alerted our embassy teams. Do you at least still have Kishiev's wife and child?'

'We do. What shall we do with them?'

'Keep them for now; they may come in useful. This is really no good, no good at all.' Nevsky hammered his desk, making his cup jump. 'It would have been better for us not to have known about this weapon's reappearance. The only small comfort I can take in all this is that the device will not be used against us or on our soil. But you have still lost it!'

'I swear, Valentin Romanovich, that I will retrieve it.'

'Use all available methods. You understand me?'

Strelkov bobbed his head, but Nevsky had already ended the call.

London, Undisclosed Location, Secret Intelligence Service Safe House

The new clothes felt fresh against his skin; they were soft, smooth, and warm. The quality was far superior to anything he had worn before he joined the Red Army and beyond comparison with what he had owned since. Mikhail was puzzled – was this the result of capitalism, or was it the British monarchy he should thank? He was, after all, in the UK at the behest of Her Majesty's Government. He added milk to the tea, the way Karen Campbell had shown him; he had found he liked it the English way. His visitor, a man he had not met before, sat facing him and placed a cardboard box file on the table. The right wall of the room contained a huge mirror which Mikhail had little doubt concealed a viewing room and another guest.

'It's nice to meet you, Mikhail. My name is Jack,' the guest in the room said.

'Nice to meet you, Jack.'

'Likewise. I'm hoping you can help me. I have some surveillance photographs taken in Istanbul that I'd like you to look at.'

'I have never been to Turkey.'

'But there may be a chance that you know these men who have.' Patchem opened the file, removed a pile of 10x8 photographic prints, and pushed them towards the Russian.

'Then I shall take a look.' He put his china cup down and picked up the nearest image. It was a close-up of one of the bodies left in Inci's apartment.

'He was executed?'

'Yes.'

'Good. I knew this man. He was twisted by the Taliban's rhetoric and then recruited by Al-Qaeda.'

There was a rushing in Patchem's ears as his heart started to pump faster. 'Really?'

'Yes. He is from a village several valleys away from my home.' Mikhail paused as his wife and family swam into his memory. 'His group controlled the local market. The last time I saw him he was with an Al-Qaeda man from Pakistan.' He tapped the print. 'But then, of course, he had a beard, and was not wearing Western clothes.'

'You have a very good memory.'

'Photographic.'

'The correct term is *eidetic* memory.'

'Oh? I did not know that word. I shall use it.'

'Do you remember the man's name?'

'Abdul Shinare. His father had only one leg and blamed the Soviets for his loss. He did not like me.'

'Can you look at the rest of the photographs and tell me if you know anyone else?'

'Of course.' Mikhail picked up the next and placed it beside the previous one. It was also taken postmortem. 'He, I also met at the camp. His first name was Sharib – I did not hear his family name. He was younger than the others. He told me that he wanted to go to London one day and blow up the Queen.'

This was the first time the UK had been mentioned as a possible target. Patchem managed to hide his concern, his right fist clenched under the table. 'That's not on any tour I've seen.'

'British humour is like Russian humour.' Mikhail grunted and a thin smile split his lips. 'The only difference is that British humour is funny.'

'So, you had a conversation with this man?' Patchem's hands were now clasped tightly together as he subconsciously leant forward in his seat.

Mikhail shrugged. 'A few words. He brought me my meals. They kept me shut in a hut for several days.'

'Did these men say anything about a target or an attack?'

'No.' He went on to the next two images, both of corpses. 'This man I do not know, but he looks to be Pakistani, or Afghan, and this one looks different.'

'His name is Orhan Inci. He's the owner of the building.'

'That name means nothing to me.' Mikhail's hand hovered over the next photo. With its visible grain, which was actual pixels, and muted colours, it looked to him exactly like a colour print from the Eighties. 'What is this?'

'It's a still from a surveillance video.' Patchem searched the Russian's face for any trace of recognition as he studied the photograph of a group of six suited men being ushered inside by Inci.

'Ah. This is Inci and these two other men I have identified, but I cannot see the faces of these four.'

'Look at the next photograph.' It showed Inci with one of the six men.

'Only one man? What of the other three?'

'We don't have any photographs of their faces.'

'I see. Yes, this man I recognise.'

'Who is he?' Patchem's chest felt tight.

'He is the leader of the dead men you have shown me. His name is Mohammed Tariq.'

'How do you know?'

Mikhail folded his arms. He had told the story initially to Webster in Afghanistan and then to Karen Campbell, who had been the first to question him in the UK. No doubt 'Jack' knew this, but it wouldn't hurt to tell it again. 'When I was taken to the training camp I saw many fighters, but the group containing the men I have identified drew my attention. That was because they were with the man from Al-Qaeda who had stolen my bomb. They were present when I explained how the device worked to the Pakistani and studied the diagram I had drawn. One of the fighters especially was interested in the plans.' He tapped the photograph again, 'This man, Mohammed Tariq.'

'The men at this base, were they Taliban, Al-Qaeda, or local fighters?'

'They were a mixture. The Pakistani was Al-Qaeda; he told

me so proudly. I think that Mohammed Tariq was from the borderlands, the Tehrik-e-Taliban perhaps? But these fanatical groups are interchangeable.'

'I see. Were you a fanatic, Mikhail?'

'I was fanatical in not wanting either the Soviet Union or the terrorists to possess my bomb.' Mikhail fanned the photographs across the table. 'So I can name two of the dead. But what of Mohammed Tariq? Is he not dead?'

'We believe he escaped.'

'That is very serious. Of the group of six fighters I showed the bomb to, three are missing.'

Patchem knew as much. 'Do you know their names?'

'Alas, no, but I do know their faces.' He tapped the side of his face. 'I have an *eidetic* memory. If you get me a sketch artist I can provide you with drawings of their faces.'

'I shall do that, but we use computers now.'

'Ah, the world continues to move on.' Mikhail looked down. He felt an uncontrollable wave of remorse hit him. The loss of his family was a seeping wound that refused to heal. If only he had forgotten about the bomb, taken his family and left the village... but he hadn't. He had made a vow with his life to keep the bomb out of the hands of all enemies. The vow had been broken and it had cost him his family.

There was a knock on the door and Snow stepped into the room. He made eye contact with Mikhail, who gave him a friendly nod, before speaking to Patchem. 'Development.'

'If you'll excuse me, Mikhail.'

The Russian bowed his head as both SIS men left.

Snow shut the door behind his boss and held up his iPhone. 'Neill, I'm handing you over to Jack. Can you repeat what you said to me about the passport?'

'Hello, Jack.' The voice of Neill Plato, the Russian desk's technical officer, was jovial in Patchem's ear. 'Good news. The Schengen visa in the dead man's passport was one of sixty-five

151

issued by the Italian Embassy in Islamabad on the same day two months ago. I was also able to get a match for the two other dead gentlemen. That means three to find. I've discounted twenty for being female – we know the terrorists to be male – and a further fifteen due to their age. So that leaves us with twenty-seven possible suspects. Unfortunately, none of the surveillance tapes we have catch the suspects' faces.'

'Send the pictures over here.'

'Already done and as a precaution I've updated the Schengen Information System with the passport numbers tied to the visas. If anyone on this mini-watchlist does attempt to enter the EU, they'll get pinged.'

'Good.' If the Russians had the terrorists, Patchem saw them travelling only one way, and that was six feet down. 'Is that all?'

'Yes. It did take me a while to get the visa information; the Italians are quite slow.'

'I was being flippant, Neill. Thank you.' Patchem handed the phone back to Snow. 'So we now have more photos to show Mikhail. Get the computer while I go back in.'

'Boss,' Snow said, adopting SAS-trooper mode.

Patchem rolled his eyes and opened the door. 'I'm sorry about that.'

Mikhail considered Jack with mild amusement as the Englishman retook his seat. 'That is not a problem; I have no other meetings scheduled for today.'

Patchem smiled politely before once again becoming serious. 'One thing I don't entirely understand, and forgive me for asking, is this: why did you stay in Afghanistan?'

Mikhail was thoughtful; his eyes flickered. 'To prevent the RA-115A from ever being used. The KGB wanted it to be deployed against the Mujahideen, so I stole it. I did not want the KGB or the Afghans to possess it. And there was no way that I could destroy it. It is an abomination.'

'You sound like a pacifist.'

'Perhaps I am? As I am sure you are well aware, the KGB controlled my life in Russia and they controlled the life of my entire extended family. In Afghanistan I was attacked and left for dead on the orders of a KGB political officer, by my own commanding officer. This was before they knew of my deception. I was meant to disappear; perhaps the entire nuclear programme I was a part of was supposed to vanish? So I did. There was no route I could take back to Moscow, and even if I had miraculously managed to arrive home, how would I have explained myself? I was a conscientious objector to nuclear weapons, not a traitor. How could I have told my parents the truth without in turn implicating them? And what if I were to be seen by a neighbour or acquaintance?' Mikhail drank his tea.

'You could have tried to return to Russia after 1991.'

'What would I have seen? The same KGB but now wearing different hats? It was best for all that I remained dead and forgotten in Afghanistan, and I was until Al-Qaeda took my bomb and murdered my family.'

Patchem saw fire in the Russian's eyes so chose his words carefully. 'Would you like to know what became of your relatives in Moscow?'

'What good would that do? It has been a quarter of a century; they may very well be dead.'

'Or they may not. Your father was an English teacher?'

'That, as you may have guessed, is the reason I can speak English. He was also an idealist, which is probably the reason I am the way I am.'

Another knock and Snow entered. He placed a Dell tablet computer on the table in front of their guest. 'Mikhail, we have some more photographs for you to look at.'

'Then I shall.' Mikhail became baffled. 'How do I work it?'

'It's touchscreen.'

'Ah, of course it is. Where do I touch?'

Snow explained.

'The photographs you are looking at are taken from visa application forms. I need you to tell me if you recognise anyone,' Patchem said.

'A terrorist must now apply for a visa to detonate a bomb in Europe?'

'Yes. It's Health & Safety gone mad,' Snow quipped as he exited.

Patchem moved his chair so he could see the screen as Mikhail swiped for the next jpeg. Eight passport photos in, Mikhail said: 'That is one of the missing men.'

'It is?' Patchem's chest tightened again.

'That is what I said.'

Patchem made a note of the image. 'Please continue.'

Five more swipes and the remaining men had been found. Patchem leant forward and took the computer, as he did so getting a waft of coal tar soap from the Russian. 'You have been very helpful.'

'What will you do now?'

'Issue a European-wide border alert.'

'I have a question.'

'Please.'

'Who has the bomb?'

Patchem frowned. 'I'm not sure I understand.'

Mikhail folded his arms. 'The cell was attacked and three members were assassinated. The killers now have the remaining men and the bomb. Yes?'

'That is our belief.'

'So my question is, who has the bomb?'

'I can't tell you that.'

'Can't or won't, Jack?'

'Can't,' Patchem bluffed. 'We don't know for sure.'

'OK, I understand. But, for all our sakes, I do hope it isn't a rival terrorist organisation that has taken it. Since leaving Afghanistan I have heard many things about the Islamic State and I know they are active in Turkey.'

154

'I've been thinking the same.' Patchem felt a chill. 'Before I leave, is there anything I can do for you?'

'Can you get me a razor?'

'Isn't it haram for a Muslim to shave?'

'It is forbidden, yes, but as well as losing my family, I have lost my faith. So I wish to lose my beard.'

Patchem wasn't a religious man and said calmly, 'I can't give you a razor, but I can arrange for a barber to pay you a visit.'

'A barber for a barbarian?' Mikhail stated humourlessly. 'Thank you.'

*

Snow closed down the monitoring equipment in the viewing room and met his boss in the entrance hall. 'What's your take on his point about IS?'

'I bloody well hope the Russians have the bomb, Aidan. If they do we can just go home and forget about it.'

'It's a shame we can't just ask them.'

'That's a fact, especially now their President has gone mad.'

'Is that the official view of the Secret Intelligence Service?' Snow asked drolly.

Patchem shook his head. 'You know it's not.'

'All done for the today, Jack?' Karen Campbell asked, appearing from a side door.

'Yes.' Patchem noticed her nails had been painted black with intricate white paisley droplets. 'Thank you, Karen.'

'I'll let you out.' Campbell signalled to the guard at the front door to release the electronic lock.

Patchem's car was parked immediately across the road from the townhouse, the driver waiting at the wheel. To a casual observer the pair had just left the London office of a small export company, the building's façade itself a façade for the SIS safe house. Patchem and Snow slipped into the backseats. Snow looked out of the window as the Jaguar joined the flow of London traffic. They stopped at a set of lights and two motorcycle couriers drew up alongside them. Wearing the liveries of competing companies, they jostled to be first when red turned to green. 'Something's not right.'

Patchem glanced over. 'Like what?'

'It's too easy, too simple.'

'Aidan, sometimes you forget that, even though I am a section chief for the Secret Intelligence Service, I'm not a mind reader.'

'How did the Russians know the location of the Al-Qaeda team?'

'Kishiev.'

'Assuming the Russians have him and he's being cooperative, wasn't he locked up in Black Dolphin for, what, three years?'

'So, the attack was planned before he was arrested.'

'Mikhail said the bomb had only been taken by Al-Qaeda three months ago. How did Kishiev know about the Hand of Allah? Did Al-Qaeda take the bomb earlier than he led us to believe?'

'We know from the NSA intercept of Strelkov's call that the name the Hand of Allah relates specifically to the RA-115A we're tracking. Mikhail must have lied to us or become confused. I don't think his memory would have failed him. Karen's team will be questioning him further; they'll get the truth out of him, but that's not an issue now. What is an issue is confirming that the Russians have the bloody thing!'

The Jag purred onwards towards Vauxhall Cross. 'Why did the Russians leave a passport behind? Even they aren't that slapdash.'

Patchem shrugged. 'They got interrupted or simply didn't see it.'

'Or they wanted it to be found by whoever discovered the bodies?'

'You think it's a red herring?'

'I don't know what I think.'

'But something is fishy?'

'I'm glad you said that. What about the falling man?' Snow referred to the body found on the pavement outside the Russian-owned apartment. 'What about the explosion? Two attacks within, what, an hour of each other involving Russian spec ops in Istanbul? I just don't understand what was going on.'

There was a shrill ringing from Patchem's suit pocket. He reached inside, produced his phone, and answered it. 'Patchem.' He pressed the speaker button. 'Please repeat that, Simon. You're now on speaker with me and Aidan Snow from my Russian desk.'

'Yes, OK,' the tinny voice said from Turkey. 'I've just had a call with Keser. The Turkish NIA coroner has confirmed the time of death for the suspected terrorists as being somewhere between 9 p.m. and 2 a.m. The Russians hit the building at dawn, around 5.45 a.m.'

Snow and Patchem swapped looks. Patchem felt a rushing in his ears. 'How sure is the coroner of this timing?'

'I asked Keser that question and he told me the man is very professional and has been doing his job for years. He one hundred per cent stands by the times he's given.'

'Simon, can you get someone into the building with a Geiger counter?' Snow asked. 'I want to know if this thing was leaking, or if it was actually there at all.'

'We could try, but I don't know how tightly the Turkish NIA has the place sewn up.'

'Can't you check your camera?' Patchem asked thinly.

'No. the camera's gone offline.'

'Simon, get James Brocklehurst over there to check the building and the camera immediately.'

'Yes, Jack.'

Patchem ended the call. 'So the Russians didn't take the bomb?'

'Not the team we have on film, but that doesn't mean there wasn't an earlier team.'

'One that we didn't see enter or leave… or did we?' Patchem

dialled Plato's direct line. 'Neill, drop everything else you're doing. I need you to make a list of everyone who entered Inci's building on the day before the assault… Yes, of course we want to see their faces.' He looked at Snow and took a deep, calming breath. 'He'll have them ready by the time we get back to the office.'

*

New Jersey, USA

The curtains were drawn to allow the fall sunlight into the room. Casey sat in an armchair next to the unlit open fire. A man Gorodetski hadn't met before leant against the fireplace with his arms folded. His hair hung loosely on his shoulders and he wore a tan-coloured field jacket over jeans and a T-shirt.

'You wanted to see me?' Gorodetski asked.

Casey pointed Gorodetski to a chair and, after he'd sat, said, 'Congratulations. You're in.'

Gorodetski took a moment to understand Casey's words. 'Thanks.'

'We have a fastball in your part of the world. This is Michael Parnell, one of my specialists. You'll be travelling with him and both of you will be working under Harris. Is that an issue?'

'No.' It made no difference to Gorodetski who he worked with, just as long as he was working.

'That's what I thought. He wanted you in on this. Harris, Needham, and Beck are already in Europe. You and Mike will leave immediately. There's a company jet standing by at Newark to take you to Timisoara airbase in Romania where Harris will give you further instructions. Any questions?'

'What's the mission?'

'An Al-Qaeda cell is planning an attack within the EU. We're hunting them.' Casey omitted the small fact that the cell possessed

158

a suitcase nuke; if Harris wanted Gorodetski briefed in, he'd do it himself. He leant back in the chair and collected an envelope from the floor. 'Catch.'

'Thanks.' Inside was a US passport and credit cards in the name of James East, as well as three thousand dollars in cash.

'You're on probation and if anything goes wrong, if you even look at any of the team funny, you'll find yourself sitting in an Interpol cell. *Rozamish?*'. Casey asked Gorodetski in Russian if he understood.

'*Da.*'

'I don't mind telling you I'm taking a huge risk on you. Good luck and good hunting.'

*

Vauxhall Cross, London, UK

Neill Plato was already standing by Patchem's door as the two SIS officers stepped from the lift. He had a file under his arm and was rocking slightly on the balls of his feet, which were encased in a pair of cherry-red Dr Martens. 'I've got something for you,' he said as they approached. 'I don't know how the folks at GCHQ missed it.'

'Let's have it.' Patchem unlocked his office.

'After pulling up the images from the surveillance tape I spotted several very odd-looking visitors.' Plato plonked the file on the desk as Patchem and Snow removed their jackets, Patchem's jacket being part of a made-to-measure suit, Snow's being made of leather. The three men sat. 'I've sent you electronic copies but also taken the liberty of printing out the shots – I know you prefer paper to pixels.'

'Thanks.' Patchem opened the file and took out the photographs.

'They're in chronological order, starting at 10 a.m. when the building opened for business.'

Patchem gazed down and studied the prints. Plato fell silent and Snow remained so. A minute later their boss looked up. 'Kishiev.'

'Yes,' Plato said.

'And two shooters.'

'Yes,' Plato said again.

'Here.' Patchem handed Snow four of the prints.

'Were the Russians in Istanbul with Kishiev?' Snow queried as he took in the first two prints, which showed a dishevelled Kishiev and another equally grubby-looking figure entering the building and then facing the camera as they left. 'Who's the other man, Neill?'

'Haven't found him yet, but if there's a digitised image of him on the interweb I will. Until then let's call him *Vladimir*.'

'Vladimir's beard makes him look Chechen to me. Is he part of Kishiev's escape story, or is Kishiev really at large with his old group?'

'We can't discount either possibility,' Patchem conceded. 'But if he's there without the Russians, it's a hell of a coincidence, and that opens up a whole new set of targets.'

Snow felt as though he'd been punched in the stomach. 'Moscow.'

Patchem became pale. The Russians would never accept the detonation of a nuclear device as being the act of terrorists. Regardless of any evidence, the Kremlin's fingers would be pointing at the US, shortly followed by their own nuclear warheads. 'We'd better start praying he doesn't have the bomb.'

Snow now moved on to the next images; they were taken at dusk and showed two men with backpacks entering the premises. Both men were white and wore baseball caps. Plato anticipated Snow's question. 'With the exception of Kishiev and Vladimir, those were the only two individuals to pay Inci a visit that day whom we hadn't seen before on the surveillance tapes.'

'I see.' The men looked unremarkable, like any other Western tourists, but the fact that they were the only tourists that day made them remarkable. Their perfect cover had been blown by imperfect timing. 'Where are the photographs of them leaving?'

'There aren't any.'

'Just a minute, Neill.' Patchem sat forward. 'Are you saying these two men didn't leave?'

'That's correct, at least not by the front door.'

Snow shook his head. 'The camera only covers the front.'

'It does indeed,' Plato confirmed.

'Can you ID them?'

Plato seemed unfazed by the magnitude of the threat hanging over them all. 'Well, that's trickier because of the lighting conditions. I won't be able to get as high a percentage match as I'd like. Feature extraction will be harder to do, as will getting a reference set for each face. But again, if their photos appear anywhere on the web, I'll find 'em.'

'You're already searching, aren't you?' Patchem asked as he sat back and folded his arms.

'That's what you pay me for,' Plato replied.

'We need to focus on our only concrete lead, the passports.' Patchem pushed the photographs into a neat pile. 'Can you now check the Schengen Information System again to confirm a European-wide border alert has been issued for the three men?'

'Yes, I'll do that.' Plato nimbly got to his feet and went back to his own office.

Patchem took a deep breath and then exhaled. 'Gut reaction?'

'The Russians don't have the device, the shooters do,' said Snow.

'And?'

'They're going to use it.'

'Shit!' Patchem was immediately embarrassed. 'I'm sorry,

Aidan. I've not been feeling myself recently and having a bloody rogue nuclear device to find isn't helping.'

'We'll find it,' Snow said, with more certainty than he felt.

'Right. You're right. I've got to call Vince.' Snow started to get up. 'No, please sit in. I need your cool head.'

It took five minutes to find and connect with the American, but after that Casey was gurning at the duo from the video screen. 'Good afternoon, gentlemen, what's up?' Patchem explained and Casey's mood changed. 'So we don't know who has the nuke, where they are, or what they're going to attack?'

'In a nutshell.'

'How long will it be until your guy gets a hit on the faces?'

'He's one of the best, so I'd say a couple of hours.'

'I'll inform my team of the development.'

'Have your satellites picked up anything?'

Casey shook his head. 'Nope, not a thing. We were too late to spot them at the border and now too late to track anyone after the attack. There's been a bit of chatter over the Echelon system about how swell it is that Kishiev has escaped from the Russians, but it's nothing of any worth.'

'Our best bet is still the EU. That's where they'll head for the maximum impact.'

Snow shifted in his seat. 'Why would the terrorists risk entering the EU?'

'Where else would they go?' Patchem frowned.

'South to Syria, north to Ukraine?'

'OK, I'm listening,' Casey said via the screen. 'I know you've got a theory somewhere, Aidan.'

'If Kishiev hasn't got the device, we're assuming the target of any attack is going to be in the EU, correct?'

'Correct.'

'Why?'

'Because the West and her allies,' Patchem said, jutting his chin at Casey, 'like America, are the traditional target of Al-Qaeda.'

'Exactly. It would make the most sense to attack a traditional enemy now they have their hands on their deadliest weapon ever, but...'

'But what?' Patchem became impatient.

'But what if the device doesn't work? Our assessment is that, in its current state, the chances are very high that it won't detonate.'

'Yes, we've had this discussion.' Patchem clasped his hands together. 'The radioactive material inside would still produce a highly effective dirty bomb.'

'I understand that, but I think we're missing something. If I were an Al-Qaeda planner, why would I waste my time and people by deploying a faulty weapon?'

A kernel of an idea formed in Casey's mind. 'What would you do if you had this faulty bomb, Aidan?'

'I'd fix it.'

'You'd also have to run diagnostics and, let me tell you, on a small, experimental device that takes an awful lot of time and money. We're the CIA and we couldn't get ours to work.'

'But,' Snow countered, 'this bomb is a tactical multiplier that can be taken without a second glance into the heart of any capital city. If I were launching an attack, I'd want to secure the best possible chance of success.'

'So make it a small dirty bomb,' Patchem said flatly.

'No, hang on,' Casey noted with a wry look. 'Aidan, I'm going to ask you again: what would you do if you had this faulty bomb?'

'I'd get the original schematics, or find the designer, or, failing that, I'd go to the place that produced it, locate the people who made it, and get them to fix it.'

'A quarter of a century later? Aidan, you've read my report on the RA-115A and the research centre in Kryvyi Rih. There's no trace left,' Patchem stated.

'Vince, why doesn't the CIA bomb function?'

Casey sighed. 'It's in the info I gave Jack, but essentially it's something to do with the firing unit decoder.'

'So you find the person who designed the firing unit decoder, who may have failsafe codes for it, or perhaps even a new decoder.'

Casey stroked his chin. 'OK, I'm warming to your idea.'

'Jack, have the scientists from Kryvyi Rih ever been traced or questioned by a Western intelligence agency?'

'Not as far as I'm aware.'

Casey shrugged. 'We haven't.'

'The way I see it,' Snow said, 'is that back in '91 the workers had the Soviet mentality of staying shtum; the KGB had sworn them to secrecy on pain of death. But who's going to threaten them now if they talk? The facility, the country, and their KGB don't exist. If I've come up with this idea over the course of a morning, you can bet whoever's running this Al-Qaeda operation has had more than enough time to come to the same conclusion.'

'He has a point, Jack. The weapon's effectiveness lies in its size and the punch it packs. Sure, you could make a dirty bomb, we all agree on this; and heck, Al-Q probably has the means to reuse the components and pack 'em into a bigger case. But this device is portable and all but untraceable. It's the ultimate stealth weapon and that's the whole point of it. And if Kishiev does have the device, the easiest way for him to get back into Russia is via its rebel-held borders with Ukraine. He'd be just another Chechen fighter.'

'Terrorist,' Snow said.

'It's also not that hard to get into Poland from Ukraine, if you pay the right people,' Patchem noted, as he steepled his fingers and thought about his next action. The Ukrainian Security Service was already on high alert and in May had intercepted a group of six men travelling from Moldova's disputed autonomous region of Transdniester with 1.5 kg of a radiation-emitting substance, later confirmed as uranium-235. The fact that the SBU had successfully tracked, intercepted, and stopped a potential dirty bomb was noteworthy, but could the SBU be trusted with full disclosure? Patchem couldn't rule out any possibility at this point, yet it still sounded like a wild-goose chase, and bringing in another foreign intelligence service, especially the SBU, had huge risks. With Crimea annexed by Russia, the Red Army shelling in the East, and an untold number of Russian sleepers in the SBU, Ukraine was a country where friends in power had to be chosen carefully. In short, there was a significant and palpable hazard that information shared with the SBU could end up in the hands of Russia's FSB. But Knight had told him to pull out all the stops to locate the device. If Snow's theory was correct, if there was anything to be found in Ukraine, then Aidan Snow was the man to find it. And it was better to have Snow working on a hunch than sitting twiddling his thumbs. 'Aidan, do you trust the SBU?'

'No, I trust Director Dudka and his team.'

'Jack, I ain't running your show, but I'd say we've got nothing to lose and everything to gain.'

Patchem nodded, decision made. 'Aidan, contact Dudka now. Make him get to a secure line. Tell him we need to trace any scientists who might have worked at the Kryvyi Rih plant. But even Dudka mustn't know what we're looking for; say we've had a tipoff that someone is trying to sell old classified documents to the Iranians.'

'Iranians?'

'Yes, blame them – difficult to prove otherwise.'

'OK.' Snow nodded at Casey. Casey in turn flashed Snow a salute as he exited.

'Who do you have in Ukraine?' Patchem asked the American.

'The usual embassy team, and a few military advisers training the Ukrainian army.'

'What about your team?'

'As I told you before, Jack, they're on standby in Romania. Harris is directing them, and he's very hands-on.'

'As opposed to you?'

'Ha!' Neither Casey nor Patchem were well-suited for desk jobs. 'But he's a regular MacGyver.'

'Perhaps, then, whoever has the bomb should ask Harris to fix it?'

'I'm glad you still have your sense of humour, Jack.'

*

Detention Centre, Location Classified

Tariq readied himself for the woman to enter his cell. He'd watched her the last two times she'd brought him food and she'd made the same mistake. She would approach him and place the metal tray on the table, then turn away, and that would be when he would strike. He had heard but not seen the guard at the door; he knew there must be at least one.

'Food.' The door opened and the woman entered. 'Stand facing the wall, with your legs apart and your palms against it.'

'Of course.' Tariq still found it hard to speak after the hammer blow the fat Russian had delivered to his jaw.

'Lamb.' The woman placed the food on the table and turned away, as predicted.

Now was Tariq's chance. He pivoted, took two quick steps, collected the tray, and brought it down over her head. The woman dropped with a faint murmur. He grabbed the sidearm attached to her waist and hit her again on the back of the head. She made no sound. He checked the clip: full. Switching off the safety, he moved stealthily for the open door. Then he took a deep breath and mouthed '*Allahu Akbar!*' before springing into the corridor. He looked left, nothing but a dead end. Right, one sentry, and then a door to daylight. Tariq charged at the man, bare feet slapping against the concrete floor, Makarov 9mm trained at the target's unprotected head. The man turned, a cigarette fell from his open mouth, and his arms moved for the short-stock AK hanging across his body. Too late. Tariq fired; the retort reverberated like thunder in the confined space. Not stopping to assess his victim, he ran towards the exit. A door burst open in front of him and to the left. Tariq sent two rounds at a figure that had started to move. The glass shattered and the figure stumbled backwards. Tariq hurtled past the door and sent a further round into the gloom within. He reached the exit and exploded into the daylight. His bare feet hit gravel. Eyes darting frantically, assessing his options and ignoring the pain of the rough stones underfoot, he darted towards the nearest vehicle. He tried the door. Locked. Rounds erupted around him. He ducked and, using the car for cover, sprinted immediately left and towards the tree-line. Crashing into the wood, he kept running as undergrowth tore at his ankles. His breathing had become laboured, not due to his lack of cardiovascular fitness but because of the drugs that still circulated in his system. His limbs felt heavy and his lungs burnt, but he refused to give up, refused to let the Russians stop him again.

*

'Goddamn it!' Harris shouted at the ceiling. 'You mean to tell me someone hit our fucking terrorists before we could?'

Via secure video-link at the New Jersey facility, Casey nodded. 'The Turkish NIA found four bodies. One was a taxi driver and the other three are believed to be Pakistani nationals.'

'Pakis?'

'One had a Pakistani passport on him. Obviously they're legends but I'm having them checked out at the moment.'

Harris shook his head and pursed his lips ruefully. 'Shit in a goddamn fucking hat and punch it.'

'Whoever took them out has almost twelve hours' head start. The location of the hit was on the edge of the NSA bird's splash, so they're backtracking their video feed to see if they can find 'em. They could be in mainland Europe by now.' Casey paused to take a swig of Coke; he appeared exhausted. 'SIS had a theory that the device might surface in Ukraine, but now that looks unlikely.'

'That's pissing distance from Istanbul. Where in Ukraine?'

'The place where it was designed, Kryvyi Rih. Their logic being that the nuke would need a service at the very least to make it go bang, and where better to do it?'

'Anywhere? No, I mean it. The plant's been, what, closed for a quarter of a century, yet the Brits think it's an auto-shop?'

Patchem shrugged. 'Stay on it. We have to find this nuke.'

'I'll shake some trees here, but if you find any apples before me, Vince, do share.'

Casey ended the call without another word. He was too tired for Harris's humour.

*

Tariq didn't know how long he had run for, or how far, but he knew he could run no further. Chest heaving and lungs burning, he collapsed onto the damp forest floor. Immediately, the cold soil sapped away his warmth and gnawed at his bones. Darkness had started to fall and with it the temperature. As he lay looking at the stars through the forest canopy, he realised he had no idea where he was or even if he was still in Turkey. A dog barked in the distance; he raised his head and tried to pinpoint the direction.

Rising to his haunches, he steadied his breathing; the dog barked again, then a voice silenced it. Slowly he moved towards the sound, and then, through the trees, saw the dim lights of a building. He relaxed slightly as he realised it was nothing more than a domestic pet and not part of a pack sent to track him.

He drew nearer to the building and noted that it was a wooden shack. In the ever-diminishing light he could just make out a wisp of smoke rising from a chimney. Tariq shivered and imagined the warmth to be found inside, and the food. He edged nearer, his feet numb with pain and cold, until he reached the perimeter of the small garden. As quietly as he could, he straddled a low fence and landed on the wet earth. Certain he hadn't been spotted, he moved nearer to the house until he was close enough to peer through the window.

In the gloomy interior he saw a fire burning happily in the hearth and a figure slumped in an armchair beside it. A large, sand-coloured dog – he didn't know the breed – lay at its master's feet. Tariq stayed motionless and assessed the situation. He needed the warmth, he needed to get inside, but that would mean killing both man and dog. This wasn't something he was averse to, but something that would leave a trail. He searched around on the dark ground and found a large stone; it was ornamental and had been placed to strengthen the side of a flowerbed. He made sure he had a firm grip on it before he banged on the wall, just next to the window. Instantly the dog barked and then he heard the protestations of its master, who rose from his seat. Hiding to one side of the window, he banged again, and this time heard the lock on the front door rattle. Crouching in the darkness as the door opened, he hurled himself at the figure. The man was elderly and stumbled. Tariq brought the stone down on his head, instantly rendering him unconscious. The dog yelped and tried to bite him with half-toothless jaws. Tariq grabbed the animal by the throat and slammed its head against the doorframe. He stood, panting, and kicked the dog before stamping on its neck.

Both master and dog lay dead, or dying; he cared not which. They were silent; that was all he needed. He shut the door and made for the fire. As the heat hit him he felt dizzy and fell into the fireside chair. As his eyes closed heavily he realised the FSB drugs were still in his system.

Chapter 9

Timisoara, Romania

Sergey Gorodetski stood across the road from the hotel and stared at the receptionist. She was unaware of his presence as she checked in an elderly couple for their weekend in Vienna. Her hair was up in a bun and her black-framed glasses were squarely in place, but her uniform was too tight across her ample breasts. Sergey felt his heart pound. He wasn't meant to be there or to see her again, but he hadn't been able to stop himself. She cast a glance out of the window and he felt himself shudder as, for the briefest moment, their eyes met. She turned back to her guests and when she looked up again, with a wrinkled brow, he had gone.

Gorodetski balled his right fist and swore as he marched away across the square. This was the one thing he couldn't control: his heart. He was dead to her and must remain so, but he couldn't stop, couldn't pretend anymore – she was the only woman he had ever loved and she was standing less than fifty yards away... He felt himself start to shake and then realised someone was shaking him.

'Hey, Wee Willie Winkie! It's time to open your eyes!'

For a second Gorodetski was confused by the face that confronted him. 'Where am I?'

Michael Parnell cocked his head and looked out of the cabin window. 'I'd say we're about ten minutes out of Timisoara. Hell of a view, you should take a look – if you can keep your eyes open.' Parnell punched Gorodetski playfully on the arm.

Gorodetski rubbed his eyes and sat up. So she was still in his mind, and now he was in Romania she was nearer to him than ever. Would she leave him or was she for ever to be a ghost, haunting his dreams but vanishing as soon as he opened he eyes? Sergey could see distant mountains through the window. He had to focus. This was his only chance; if he blew it, what would he do? What could he do? He'd hidden from Interpol and various police forces but he couldn't hide from the CIA. Parnell threw him a bottle of water, sat in the seat facing him, and buckled up. Several minutes later the CIA Gulfstream G550 landed smoothly on the former Romanian Air Force runway and taxied to a hanger used exclusively, but unofficially, by the CIA.

Once the hanger was securely closed, the pilot popped the cabin door release and Parnell got to his feet. 'Ah, Romania, birthplace of Vlad the Impaler.'

The doors gently lowered and Parnell held out his arm. 'Age before beauty my friend.'

'Are you saying I'm not attractive?'

'Ha, ha, not to me. I'm looking forward to those Romanian Gypsy women. For now we've got to settle in and await further instructions.'

The crew joined them at the bottom and someone started up the coffee machine.

'Where's Harris?'

Parnell shrugged. 'I never know. He's a law unto himself, but he gets results. And that's why Casey trusts him.'

'Do you trust him?'

Parnell's eyes narrowed. 'Now trust is a tricky thing, James. I only trust myself.'

'Casey seems big on trust.'

Parnell squinted. 'Don't tell me; he pulled his "loaded Glock trick" on you?'

'He did. I was in a hospital bed at the time.'

Parnell made a gun shape with his hand. 'You do realise he was bluffing?'

'It was loaded. I checked.'

'He'd removed the firing pin.'

Gorodetski shook his head; a crew member appeared with a sat phone and handed it to Parnell. 'It's Harris for you.'

Gorodetski took a step away and collected a plastic cup; the coffee machine had started to make gurgling noises. He walked over to it and, after a couple of attempts, managed to get a half-full cup of brown sludge.

'Well, shoot, we're off again,' Parnell sighed as he placed his own cup next to the machine.

'Where are we going?'

'Harris has ordered me to liaise with the Turkish border guards. Apparently he got some new flash intel and couldn't reach us in the air. There's a full intel package waiting for me at the consulate in Istanbul. And as for you…' Parnell handed Gorodetski the sat phone. 'He wants you to call him. Just press redial.'

'Thanks.' Gorodetski pressed the button and put the handset to his ear.

'James.' Harris answered on the first ring. 'I'm glad you made it back to Europe safely.'

'So am I.'

'Now listen, I have a situation here. We have verified intel that an Al-Qaeda cell is attempting to buy classified military hardware from a Ukrainian buyer. You and Beck are going to stop the buy from taking place. You'll take out the buyers and grab the seller. This is going to happen in a Ukrainian industrial town called

Kryvyi Rih. There's an airport not too far away. Beck will meet you with a full briefing and tactical package.'

'What are you and Needham going to be doing?'

'Son, that's need to know – and you don't – but we are contactable should you need us. The trade, we think, is happening within the next forty-eight hours.' Before Gorodetski could ask any more questions, the line went dead.

Parnell raised his coffee cup. 'Welcome to the Agency; we are here, there, and everywhere, and all at the same time.'

'Yippee.' Gorodetski took his own cup and sipped his coffee.

Parnell checked his watch. 'OK, we've got an hour while they refuel the bird to get some chow.' He slapped Gorodetski's shoulder. 'Let's go meet some entrancing Gypsy beauties!'

'Copy that.' A woman had bewitched him, thought Gorodetski, but she was Austrian.

*

Vauxhall Cross, London, UK

'Aidan.'

'Yes?' Snow looked up from his screen.

'Artur Khalidov.'

'And the same to you.'

'No.' Plato folded his arms. 'Artur Khalidov is the name of the man with Kishiev. I've just told Jack. I got a positive ID on him. He's Russian Intelligence.'

Snow sat upright in his seat. 'SVR or FSB?'

'That part is unclear, but do you want to know how I found him?' Snow nodded. 'It was on VKontakte. He was tagged in the background of a photograph taken in 2008 in Georgia. Then I found some more of him at a military parade in Moscow this year.'

'Unbelievable.' Whoever was running the world of special operations in Russia hadn't yet latched onto the fact that soldiers liked to show off. 'So Kishiev was with the Russians in Istanbul?'

'It does look like it.'

'Great. What about the shooters?'

'Nothing on them yet. It seems they knew what they were doing but I haven't given up hope. I'm going to try to look again at the tapes and check for gait recognition.'

'Gait recognition? You can do that?'

'Walk this way and I'll show you.' Plato suddenly laughed. 'That was not intended.'

'I don't believe you, Neill.' Snow followed the computer whiz to his office. A bank of monitors faced the desk and a row of large servers took up most of the floor space to the left. The only thing in the room that wasn't cutting-edge technology was a teapot. It wore a stripy woollen cosy and stood in a cramped corner of the desk next to a half-eaten packet of fig rolls.

'Right.' Plato sat swiftly in his swivel chair. 'Let's first bring up the tape of the day in question, M'lud.'

'Come on, Rumpole.'

'Who?'

'Rumpole of the Bailey.'

Plato shrugged, none the wiser. 'So, here is the tape and there are the two gents we're interested in. Now what I do is drop this quite nifty program over them and it maps the way they move. See?'

'Yep, the green lines and dots.'

'Exactly. So now I export this biometric reference set and can apply it to any other surveillance footage I watch.'

Snow was unconvinced. 'How good is this?'

'It wouldn't, on its own, stand up in a court of law, but what it can do is lead us to a potential face match, which I can then play about with.'

'How do you know where to look for the video?'

'I don't. It would be a lot easier in the UK, say, because of the huge amount of CCTV cameras, but in this instance I'll start by pulling it up from the nearest airport and see what happens.'

'You can get access to footage from Istanbul Airport?'

'Istanbul Atatürk Airport, yes. And you can thank the Americans for this.'

'I won't ask how.'

'Better you don't,' Plato said as he started to type. 'As soon as I have anything I'll let you know.'

'Thanks.'

'Oh, and one other thing: I also found some pictures of you on VKontakte and Facebook.'

As an SIS operative, Snow wasn't allowed social media, and regular searches took place to ensure his face didn't appear. 'Who posted them?'

'It was a British journalist who works for the Russian broadcaster 'ON'.'

'Darren bloody Weller!' Snow shook his head. He had tried to persuade Darren to leave the conflict zone, but the young Moscow-based correspondent was determined to become the next Kate Adie. 'Have you deleted them?'

'Oh, yes, and now both of his accounts are merrily posting anti-Kremlin cartoons and videos of cats.'

'Good.' Snow walked along the corridor to Patchem's office and knocked on the door.

'Come in.'

Snow found Patchem standing and facing the window that overlooked the Thames. 'Jack, I've spoken to Dudka.'

'And what has he got to say?'

'He doesn't have the records for the Kryvyi Rih plant, but can take me to the place they're stored if I meet him in Kyiv. He says there's no other way, due to the sensitivity of the material and the current political climate.'

Patchem turned and leant against the windowsill. 'Then get

on the next plane. We need to follow up anything and every-thing.'

'OK. Neill told me about identifying the Russian.'

'Looks like the Russians were equally as eager to find the device. Aidan, watch your step. They may be looking in Kryvyi Rih too.'

'The more the merrier.'

*

Undisclosed Location, Turkey

'Good morning, beautiful.'

Eyes snapping open, Tariq saw the barrel of a handgun pointing at him. 'You!'

'Yes, me,' replied Harris.

'You may have found me, Russian, but you will never find the device or my men! We shall triumph!'

'Yes, I know you will.' Harris was sitting in an armchair oppo-site the one Tariq had slept in. He had a plastic package on his lap. It served his purpose that the man believed he was Russian. 'I know you will succeed because I am here to help you.'

'What?' Tariq did not understand.

'I'm your contact, dumbass.'

Tariq squinted at the man as brilliant sunlight flooded in through the open door. 'You expect me to believe this?'

Harris shrugged. 'I don't give a shit what you believe, Tariq – it's the truth. I am your contact. I'm the guy who's going to get you and the rest of your team out of the country.'

Tariq frowned. He still couldn't accept it. 'You urinated on me, you drugged me!'

'I had to know what you knew, Tariq. You might have been an informer; I had to confirm you knew nothing about me or the target. I was present at the development, trialling, and field usage of the stuff we pumped into you. Believe me, you've told me all you know.'

'But you are an infidel!'

'True, but I also ain't no Christian. I met your Lion Sheik, twenty-five years ago in Kabul. A group of us infidels were helping him rid your country of the Soviets. Since then I've kept in contact with my Muslim brothers, some of them very high up within your movement. I even have a name; Osama gave it to me for all my help.'

Tariq shook his head. 'It is all lies. You are trying to trick me.'

'I let you escape, boy. I let you kill one of my hired thugs with this...' He held up the Makarov Tariq had taken. '...And you put a woman in a coma. Now why didn't I just shoot you in your sleep, or tie you up? Because I'm your contact. You get it?'

Tariq was still wary. 'Where is the device?'

'The nuke is being guarded in a safe house by Reza Khan. Lall Mohammad is outside waiting for you.'

'Enough! You are lying to me!'

Harris sighed theatrically before he stood, put the Makarov in his pocket, and pointed his Glock at Tariq's head. 'We could have done this the easy way. I like the easy way. Get up, get dressed.' Harris threw the package at Tariq. This time the Afghan caught it and slowly rose to his feet before changing into the new clothes and shoes. Harris looked around the room. 'I can understand the old guy, but seriously, did you have to kill the dog?'

'They are noisy.'

'Get outside.'

Tariq moved slowly away from the man and through the front door. As he shielded his eyes from the daylight he saw that a small track ran in front of the house. On this a Toyota Land Cruiser was parked and a figure he recognised was leaning against it. 'Brother?'

Lall Mohammad pushed himself away from the 4x4. 'It is I, brother.'

Tariq kissed him on both cheeks. 'How did you survive the attack?'

'The White Eagle saved me.'

Tariq stiffened at the name. The Al-Qaeda operative known as the White Eagle was the stuff of legend, a foreigner who operated under the very noses of his own people to ensure the success of Al-Qaeda attacks. Most dismissed the agent as a myth, but Tariq knew of elders who had met the man and spoke highly of his actions when he had fought with them against the Soviets. 'But the White Eagle is American.'

'No, my brother, that is why the Americans could not catch him. The White Eagle is Russian!'

Tariq was still confused. 'Where is the device?'

'Reza has it. All is well, we are safe.'

'Now do you believe me, brother?'

Tariq turned around on hearing the man speak Pashtun. 'I meant no disrespect, Sheik.'

'White Eagle will do.' The White Eagle pointed his Glock at the Toyota. 'Get in, we have to hustle.'

With Lall in the back and Tariq sitting next to him in the front, Harris guided the 4x4 out of the forest and onto a metalled road.

'So what happened?' Tariq's brain was struggling to recollect the attack.

'I knew to expect you, but the problem was that someone else was also waiting for you.'

'Who?' he asked the White Eagle.

'The Russians; and I have no idea how they found out about your little group.'

'Our men died as martyrs.' Lall became solemn.

'Peace be upon them, brother.' Tariq looked out of the window at the dark trees and his brain found the few images his eyes had seen before he had been rendered unconscious. A light sleeper, he had awoken just as two masked men with silenced weapons entered the room. Sharib had been first to his feet but his fists were no match for lead. Two precise rounds had finished him and then, as Tariq had tried to get up, unseen, something had hit him and the world had gone black.

'Do you not remember, brother? They cuffed us and put sacks over our heads.'

Harris inwardly congratulated himself on the false memory implanted in Lall. 'And then my team took out the Russians; they never saw us coming. We stopped them once, but they'll keep searching until they find you and that case.'

Tariq realised he had no idea where they were. 'Are we in Turkey?'

'Yes, and the mission is still a go. The Sheik will brief you fully.'

'Sheik?'

'The Sheik is a worthy warrior,' Lall confided to his friend. 'He is the only man ever to escape from the Russian Black Dolphin prison!'

'Who?' Tariq did not understand.

Lall explained, 'Do you not remember? He is the brother who came to see us while we stayed at the Turk's apartment. His companion was martyred by the Russians as they attempted to prevent the attack on us.'

'His name is Aslan Kishiev and he is one of my men,' Harris stated.

Chapter 10

Kryvyi Rih, Ukraine

Inside her jeans pocket, the Samsung Vanya had given her bleeped. Eliso finished serving her customer and then asked Tatyana Vladimirovna, the portly woman who ran the meat counter, if she could watch her position for a couple of minutes.

Even though it was mid-afternoon and custom was slow, Tatyana made a show of sighing and rolling her eyes before replying in her deep voice, 'Yes, OK.'

Eliso thanked her, slipped out of the back door of the Gastronom, and retrieved her phone. Unlocking the screen, she read the message: *See you tomorrow tonight. Will be with two friends. Make sure you are ready to party*! She was shaky and took several deep breaths of frigid air to calm herself. It would finally be all over. God, she needed a drink. She closed the screen and quickly put the phone away. Stepping back inside the shop she saw that Tatyana was engrossed in selling sausages to a regular customer. Quickly, and checking again that she wasn't being watched, she poured herself a shot of vodka from the one they sold by the plastic cup. She shuddered as it slipped down, but it made her feel better. By the time her next customer had appeared, her face again displayed its usual warmth.

*

Istanbul, Turkey

The room was dank, sparsely furnished, and hadn't been redecorated since the time of Mustafa Kemal, but none of the Afghans noticed this; their attention was focused on Kishiev, whom they now called Sheik, as befitted the leader of the Islamic International Brigade.

'The infidels will not know what has hit them! For they will not be able to comprehend how we have penetrated their weak defences. It will be a pair of killing blows that will destroy Western resolve. It will be a victory for almighty Allah!'

The three warriors spontaneously started to chant, '*Allahu Akbar... Allahu Akbar... Allahu Akbar!*'

Kishiev let the chanting continue for a while before he raised his hands and signalled for silence. 'We have suffered a defeat at the hands of the infidel Russians. Our numbers have been depleted, but you who are left have been spared for a purpose. The reason is to take our holy mission to the very heart of Europe!' He pointed at Reza Khan and then Lall Mohammad. 'You two warriors will be the vanguard of our attack. In Berlin the infidels dared to defile a scared site, the Ahmadiyya Mosque, so you shall go there and destroy what they hold holy! Your target is the Kaufhaus des Westens department store!'

'What is a department store?' Lall Mohammad frowned.

'It is like a market, but the stalls are all under one roof,' Reza Khan explained.

Lall was underwhelmed. 'Sheik, we are to attack a market?'

Kishiev's eyes flashed with anger but he kept it from his voice as he replied. 'This market, brother, is the largest in continental Europe. Tens of thousands attend it each week; but, much more than that, it is a monument to the infidels' false god, Mammon! They will live in fear for ever, wondering each time they leave their infidel homes and families if it will be their last. Germany will provide you with a lush hunting ground.'

'How are we to attack?' Reza asked in a voice that betrayed no emotion.

'On arrival in Germany you will be met by a believer who will furnish you with automatic weapons, explosives, and hand grenades.'

Lall felt his chest swell with pride; he was one step nearer to striking the infidels and one step closer to becoming a *shahid*. 'When can we go?'

'Today, my brother. You both shall go today!'

'And what of the Hand of Allah?' Tariq asked. 'When shall this be used?'

Kishiev placed his hand on Tariq's shoulder and looked him in the eyes. 'Your sacred mission will commence at the same time. There are to be two targets.'

'One in Germany and the other in Ukraine?'

'No, brother, Ukraine was never the target destination: it was a transit point. You will be striking at the heart of Russia.'

'Moscow?'

'Not only Moscow, but the very heart of Moscow: the Kremlin itself! It shall be glorious. We shall destroy their senate building and, after the explosion, Russia will never be able to use it again! All of Europe shall live in fear of Allah's wrath!'

The three warriors again started to chant. As it died down the door opened and Harris entered, a smoking cigarette in his hand. 'Lall and Reza, it is all confirmed. You have an hour before you are to leave. You must bathe, shave, and dress in the new clothes we have purchased for you.' He flicked the cigarette onto the threadbare carpet and ground it out with his foot. 'You shall be travelling to Greece by luxury coach.' Lall grinned and Khan jiggled his head. 'From there to Italy by ferry, before striking at Germany. An executive room has been booked for you in Berlin. Tomorrow you shall meet your next contact and then Allah's work will commence!'

*

Zankovetskaya Street, Kyiv, Ukraine

The flat was in the very centre of Kyiv on Zankovetskaya street, a place Snow knew well. The old Soviet shops that had satisfied the needs of the original residents, including a bakery, a cobbler's, and a dressmaker's, had vanished, to be replaced by those pandering to the wants of the new inhabitants. Boutiques selling fur coats and diamonds for pampered wives, watches for oligarchs, and underwear for supermodels dotted the street. The Maidan movement and the subsequent overthrow of the old President had seen some swanky shops close, in many cases commandeered by the protesters. Now, however, it was back to business as usual.

'Knightsbridge-ski,' Snow muttered as he stepped between a parked Porsche Cayenne and a Bentley Flying Spur before climbing the steps to Dudka's building. The lobby was unlocked. Snow rode the lift and pressed the bell for flat 28. The double-height door opened a moment later to reveal Director Dudka of the SBU's Anti-Corruption and Organised Crime Directorate. Once Snow was across the threshold, Dudka extended his hand.

'Does British Intelligence have only one agent?'

'Seven, but they thought a friendly face would be appreciated.'

'It is, Aidan.' Dudka ushered Snow into the flat and pointed at a pair of slippers. Once suitably attired, Dudka directed him along the high-ceilinged hallway towards the kitchen. The room was warm and clean but smelled of cabbage, boiled meat, and fresh bread. Dudka motioned at a chair by the kitchen table and Snow sat. Dudka produced a bottle of Ukrainian vodka and two shot glasses from a cupboard and sat across the table from his guest. He filled both and gestured for Snow to take one. 'Let us drink to friendly faces.'

Snow let the alcohol warm his throat before speaking. 'Gennady Stepanovich, I'm glad you've come through recent events unscathed.'

'So am I, Aidan. What has happened and continues to happen to my country is shocking; it is unthinkable and unforgivable. But we are trying to rebuild. The dead and rotten wood must be removed from the government, the judiciary, the militia, and my SBU. The Russians made a grave mistake in believing that Ukraine would ever accept being subjugated by them again.'

Snow agreed. It had been a tumultuous time for the nation, with the fall of a corrupt President and Russia's aggressive actions forging in blood a new European path for Ukraine.

'Thank you for agreeing to personally help HM Government with this issue. I understand that our request has put you in a difficult position.'

'Not at all. It is my former President – that filthy goat from Donetsk – who has placed us all in an extremely difficult position!' Dudka took a large breath to relax and then continued. 'The night before he ran away to his masters in Moscow, our beloved President ordered the SBU headquarters to be looted. SBU officers, whom I can no longer bring myself to name, who were loyal to his Party of Regions, destroyed countless computer hard drives, and stole thousands of flash drives and data pertaining to over twenty-two thousand SBU officers and official informers! Men I had worked with for years vanished, only to turn up several days later in Russia. In total, two deputy directors, a further two of their deputies, and twelve of their subordinates defected to Russia.' Dudka refilled the shot glasses, moved his hand to pick his up, but then instead raised his index finger. 'As of today over two hundred SBU officers have been arrested, and twenty-five of these are being investigated for high treason! This resulted in all SBU regional directors and half of their deputies being replaced! However, Aidan, the most worrying aspect is that investigation reports on all the active cases up to February 2014 were given to Russia's FSB!'

Snow hadn't seen Dudka this animated before. He was speechless at the scale of the damage done to the SBU. It was far more serious than he had imagined.

Dudka shook his head and sighed before clasping his glass and holding it aloft. 'Glory to Ukraine.'

Both men drank.

'But life must go on.' Dudka sighed wearily before smiling warmly at the Englishman he considered a friend. 'So, you think someone wishes to sell our old secrets to terrorists?'

'Yes.' Snow could see the Ukrainian didn't completely believe the story. He didn't like deceiving Dudka. 'Your directorate is the best chance we have of finding anyone who used to work at the Kryvyi Rih facility.'

'One would think so,' Dudka said as he folded his arms. 'But that is not quite the case.'

Snow frowned. 'Oh?'

'I am sorry that I could not be more specific on the telephone, but even with a secure line nowadays, as you understand, there are great risks. You know what happened when the Soviet Union collapsed? Of course you do. State-owned plants and facilities were ceded to the directors, who stripped them clean of anything of value. But what you may not know is that there was a short gap between the announcement of Ukrainian independence in August and the Ukrainian Ministry of Defence starting to work in September. No one has admitted exactly what went missing, especially not from the secret facilities, which, of course, were controlled by the KGB in Moscow, not us. Weapons and equipment were stolen, removed, sold. But much of the paperwork was left untouched, destroyed, or simply thrown out like rubbish.'

'So the SBU doesn't have the Soviet-era files?'

'Not for this facility; I've checked.' Dudka refilled the two shot glasses. 'However, there were those among us who believed that the paperwork, the classified paperwork in the case of Kryvyi Rih, was where the real value lay. And so these documents were spirited away from those who would see them fall into the wrong hands. Aidan Snow, I am trusting you with my little secret, one I dare not mention aloud.' Dudka took a scrap of paper from his pocket and pushed it across the kitchen table to Snow. 'Here is the address of my contact. Please memorise it.'

Snow read the Ukrainian text. 'Got it.'

Dudka held out his hand. Snow returned the scrap of paper and Dudka stuffed it back into his pocket. 'His name is Ratanov. He was a KGB records clerk. I have known him a long time; he trusts no one but me, and so you must take him a present.' Dudka tapped the bottle.

'Vodka?'

Dudka shook his head. 'No, he has rather peculiar tastes. Also, you will need to pay him. Two thousand dollars should be enough – he is a pensioner, not a businessman.'

*

Snow asked the taxi to drop him a block away from Ratanov's address, in case either was being watched. It had started to snow heavily and visibility was dreadful. He took refuge in a concrete bus shelter and got eyes on the target address. A bulky, middle-aged woman, in an enormous woollen coat with fur trim, was the only other person in sight. She stood next to Snow and kept looking at her watch and complaining loudly. In this part of Kyiv, the apartment blocks were boxy Eighties' constructions and there were no metro stations or trolleybuses. Locals who didn't own cars had to rely either upon 'Marshrutka' – minibuses – or less frequent, larger city buses. The unforeseen terrible weather conditions had severely delayed both. She continued to complain for several minutes more until a dirty yellow minibus lumbered towards them. The woman got on and mouthed off at the driver; the faces of the other passengers remained impassive. Snow made a show of looking at the number and then shaking his head.

As the Marshrutka pulled away Snow crossed the road and entered Ratanov's apartment block. The address was on the first floor, which in Ukrainian terms made it the second floor. Snow took the steps and found the correct flat. There was a doorbell in the shape of a swallow and, when he pressed it, a peculiar electronic Chinese imitation of a songbird sounded inside. The glass darkened behind the spyhole. As he had been instructed by Dudka, Snow took two paces back and held his right hand aloft with his palm showing. He then slowly reached into the plastic carrier bag he had been holding in his left hand. Snow clasped the bottle by the neck and unhurriedly took it out to display the label. There was a moment's silence before he heard a bolt being undone and a lock turning.

The door opened and a short, elderly man wearing thick glasses asked in a nasally voice, 'Who sent you?'

'Dudka.'

Ratanov accepted the bottle as proof of that. 'Come in.'

Snow stepped inside and the outer door was closed behind him. He noticed that, as had been the case at his own Kyiv flat, there was a second inner door which the owner now duly closed.

'I'll take that.' Ratanov took the bottle before pointing to several pairs of slippers that stood in a row on a rack. 'Choose a pair that fit.'

Snow unlaced his boots and placed them next to the hall telephone table. As he did so Ratanov moved away along the corridor and into the kitchen. Snow chose a dark-brown pair of faux-leather slippers and followed. He took the chance to look around. On his left he saw the lounge, which had a large Soviet rug hanging on the wall that was at odds with an equally large flatscreen television hanging on another, and then the bedroom, which had a second matching rug. Both rooms had balconies that were a mere twelve feet from the pavement below.

Ratanov was already opening the bottle as Snow entered the kitchen. 'Get me a pair of glasses.'

Snow saw a pair of heavy crystal tumblers on the draining board and placed them on the table.

Ratanov picked up each glass in turn, gently blowing into them before filling them with a generous measure of red liquid. 'It has been a while since I have had real Campari.' He raised his glass. 'To old wars and young soldiers.'

Both men drank, and then sat.

'So what is it that Dudka thinks I can help you with, *tovarich*?'

Snow half-smiled at the use of the Russian word meaning 'comrade'. 'I need a list of the research personnel who were stationed at a secret facility.'

Ratanov nodded as though it was an everyday request. 'Which one?'

'Kryvyi Rih.'

'Ah.' Ratanov held out his right hand. Snow understood and handed him a brown envelope, which Ratanov pocketed without opening. 'Wait here.'

The old man stood and left the kitchen. Snow sipped his Campari and pulled a face; he wasn't a fan and doubted this was the sort of setting the drink's manufacturer had envisaged it being enjoyed in. The sound of something heavy being moved, and then the scraping of metal from the room next door, brought Snow back to the present. A minute or so later Ratanov reappeared clutching a yellow-edged cardboard file.

'Here it is. Of course, back then the town was known by its Russian name, "Krivoy Rog".' He sat and studied the papers. It took Ratanov a good five minutes before he raised his eyes triumphantly, having found the list. 'I can't let you take this, but you may photograph it with your smartphone.' Ratanov placed the thin sheet of Soviet-era brownish paper on the table.

'Thank you.' Snow slowly removed his iPhone from his pocket, positioned it so that the sheet fully filled the screen, and clicked off several shots.

'One for the road?' Ratanov tapped the Campari bottle.

'No, thank you. I'm more of a cognac drinker.'

'Very well. I shall see you out.' Ratanov led Snow back towards the front door.

As Snow retrieved his boots he noticed a framed black-and-white photograph on the telephone table. Ratanov followed his gaze. 'That was a long time ago.'

'Is that Dudka?'

'Yes. Dudka and my sister, on their wedding day.'

*

Ipsala-Kipoi Border Crossing, Turkey

Neither Lall Mohammad nor Reza Khan had ever experienced a coach as luxurious as the one they now sat in on the Turkish side of the Ipsala-Kipoi border. But as they were freshly shaven and dressed in casual business attire, they felt as though they did not look out of place. The Sheik's men had dropped them off at Istanbul's Büyük Otogar (main bus terminal), where they had boarded the coach bound for Greece. The coach itself would travel to Athens via Thessaloniki, where the two Al-Qaeda warriors would alight to meet their next contact. As an artery for commercial vehicles between the EU and Turkey, the border crossing was one of the busiest. It was by no means the first border Lall and Reza had crossed, but for them it was the most hostile. Seated in the middle of the coach so as to draw as little attention as possible, the two men stood and joined the line of passengers winding out of the vehicle, down the steps, and towards the emigration counter. The building looked new and consisted mainly of white-rendered concrete walls and large, glass-panelled windows. Reza was amazed each day by what he saw in the West, while Lall was confused to see that one of the emigration officers was a woman. Both Lall and Reza's English-language ability was basic but functional. They had been given intensive lessons in the camp by their Pakistani trainers, and when they spoke it was with an accent that passed for Pakistani. The White Eagle had assured them there would be no problems with either their passports or their visas, and that the English-language abilities of the Turkish border guards were at a similar level to their own.

The woman pointed at Lall and clicked her fingers. He felt his indignation rise and his nostrils flare. How dare she address him in such a manner! His mouth turned down in scorn as he took a step forward and pushed his passport under the ballistic glass. The woman didn't say a word, nor did her face express any emotion as she tapped away at the computer terminal. Lall risked a furtive glance at Reza, who was at the next counter. His indignation had given way to fear, a fear of failing in his mission. To his relief, however, Reza seemed relaxed, and the officer dealing with his passport was nodding and smiling. The woman stamped Lall's passport and pushed it back towards him. She then looked past him and made eye contact with the next traveller. Lall started to walk away, back towards the coach. Out of the corner of his eye he saw Reza do the same. A sense of invulnerability washed over him; they would soon be out of Turkey and would easily enter Greece, their Schengen visas permitting travel across the European Union. Lall climbed back onboard the coach and took his window seat; a moment later Reza was sitting next to him.

'We are on our way, brother,' Lall said in English.

'Yes, we are,' Reza replied.

A scream erupted from the front of the bus. Lall craned his neck to look over the seat in front and came face to face with an armed Turkish police officer. The man pointed his pistol at Lall's forehead and barked commands in Turkish. Beside him, Reza had his hands raised; Lall did likewise. Three more armed men moved past the first; one had a machine pistol pointed at the Afghans while the other two held handcuffs. From the seat behind, Lall was grabbed by a pair of leather-gloved hands and metal cuffs were secured tightly to his wrists. Both he and Reza were hauled out of the coach. Reza slipped on the bottom step and landed awkwardly on his wrists. He let out a grunt of pain. The rest of the coach passengers gawped as the pair were led away to a small, windowless room at the back of the border post. With more barked commands in incomprehensible Turkish, the door was sealed and they were left alone to sit on the bare concrete floor.

Reza listened for a moment before he spoke in English. 'I think I have broken my right wrist.'

Lall saw his brother's hand had started to swell. He asked in Pashtun, 'How did they know? How did they spot us?'

Reza gave him a warning stare and continued to speak in English. 'I do not understand. We are businessmen travelling to Greece, but they have thrown us in here like criminals!'

Lall suddenly understood. 'We have rights,' he said in accented English. 'We have done nothing wrong!'

No one entered the room for what felt like hours; in actual fact, it was less than forty minutes. And then the door opened. Blinding Turkish afternoon sun assaulted their eyes as two police officers entered with a third man. His hair was light-brown and hung below his shoulders. He was dressed in a pair of blue jeans and a tan-coloured field jacket, open to reveal a light-blue T-shirt with the word 'Georgia' stencilled on it.

He spoke to Lall and Reza in Pashtun. 'I know what you are so I will not waste my time asking for your names; they are meaningless. My name I will give you, so that you will always remember me as the person who made you betray your cause. I am Michael Parnell and you two clowns now belong to the Central Intelligence Agency.'

Reza spat. 'You will never learn anything from us, American!'

Lall added, 'We will not talk to a man with the hair of a woman!'

Parnell smirked. 'Said by a man with the body of one.' Parnell switched to English and addressed the policemen. 'OK, boys, can you lift them up one at a time for me, and hold 'em steady?'

'Yessir!' one of the officers replied.

They grabbed Reza first and heaved him upright. He grimaced as one officer yanked his wrists. Each man then held an arm. From a pouch pocket Parnell produced two pen-like autoinjectors. He stepped behind Reza and swiftly stabbed one into his neck. 'Let him go.'

Lall watched as Reza wobbled before falling to the ground. There was a crack as he landed on his wrists for the second time.

'Whoopsy,' Parnell said glibly.

Enraged, Lall sprang to his feet and, head down, charged at Parnell. At the last moment Parnell took a sidestep and kicked out, connecting with Lall's groin. As Lall folded, Parnell stabbed his neck with the second autoinjector. 'Toro!'

Lall fell to his knees as his eyes watered. 'You will die!' he panted through the pain.

'Very true, hopefully between the huge breasts of a *Playboy* bunny, when I'm well over a hundred and ten years old.'

A cool sensation raced around Lall's neck, but before he could comprehend what was happening to him, the sun disappeared from the open door to be replaced by a starless night.

Chapter 11

Dnipropetrovska Oblast, Ukraine

'Are you warm enough?' Blazhevich asked from the driver's seat.

'Toasty,' Snow replied.

Ratanov's document named eight scientists as working at the weapons research centre in Kryvyi Rih. An Interior Ministry database search found that five were dead and one had moved to Russia. The other two were listed as still living in the town. If Snow's theory was correct, the chances had now been vastly improved that they'd be speaking to the right person. The question, however, still remained of whether the terrorists had yet made contact, or if they ever would.

Adverse weather conditions near Kryvyi Rih had ruled out an approach by air, so they had taken an SBU Passat. The car bounced through a slush-filled pothole. Blazhevich's head hit the headrest. 'Bloody roads!'

Snow approved; the Ukrainian's expletives had become decidedly more English over time. Blazhevich continued to moan. 'We should have just used a helo; it would have been a short hop. We could have worn parachutes!'

'And miss all of this beautiful scenery, Vitaly?' The gunmetal-grey sky above them enveloped the treetops lining the highway, while dirty slush covered the bottom of the trunks. Every so often a sheet of black ice emerged from the snow and attempted to tug away the tyres.

'You know, Aidan, I think you are perhaps a bigger Ukrainian patriot than me.'

'If that means enjoying Ukrainian cognac and fancying Yulia Timoshenko, then I must be.'

'Here.' Blazhevich handed Snow his open wallet. 'My wife.'

Through the plastic window, Snow saw a photograph of an almost impossibly beautiful woman. 'Why haven't you shown me this before? Has she got a sister?'

'No, but her mother is single.'

'I like older women; they can't run as fast.'

'I'll give her your number. She's forty-six, but soon to be a grandmother.'

Snow now noticed the woman's bump. 'Oh.'

'Twins.'

'Congratulations.'

'Two boys. We will need a bigger flat.'

Snow handed back the wallet. 'Have you got any ideas for names?'

Blazhevich shook his head. 'We have an American book of fifty thousand names; there aren't many Ukrainian ones there, though.'

'What about Bill and Ben?'

Blazhevich frowned. 'After William Shakespeare and Benjamin Franklin?'

'No, the Flower Pot Men.'

'What?'

'It was a children's television programme.'

'So, you are suggesting that I call my kids something like Mickey and Pluto?'

Snow burst out laughing as Blazhevich's phone burst into life. '*Tak?*'

Blazhevich guided the car into a petrol station as he spoke and motioned for the attendant to fill the tank. When he disconnected the call his tone had changed. He now wore his 'mission face'. 'Nedilko reports that suspect one's Lada is outside his *dacha*. No definite sighting of him, though. It looks like he hasn't left the house yet today, but he will later, to go to the local Gastronom.'

'How do you know?'

'Know what?'

'That he'll go to the Gastronom?'

'You do surprise me; you must have been living back in England for too long. It's a Friday. Who doesn't go out to buy bread and vodka for the weekend?'

'True, let's go to the Gastronom.'

Blazhevich frowned. 'What's your plan?'

Snow shrugged. 'I just want to get an eyeball on him, see if I can learn anything. However cool a customer he is, you can bet if he's aiding foreign terrorists, he won't be behaving normally. Stay in the car if it bothers you – besides, there's less chance of one of us getting compromised than two.'

'OK, I agree. But you won't do anything, will you?'

'Vitaly, do you honestly think I'll sneak up on the old bugger and double-tap him?'

'No, but I know what you old SAS men are like; remember, I've seen you in action.'

Snow switched to his Moscow-accented Russian. 'Everything will be OK, *tovarich*. I promise I'll ask questions first and shoot second.'

'Thank you, Comrade. Now I really feel relieved.'

*

The ice had started to melt as Kozalov stepped from his car. The usual Mafiosi were outside the Gastronom, propping up their BMWs, staring at him, and eating poppy seeds, seemingly oblivious to the cold. He ignored them and, entering the store, headed straight towards the drinks counter and Eliso. As he neared her a shard of sunlight hit the counter, momentarily illuminating her like a seraph. He felt young again. 'Good morning, Eliso.'

She turned and beamed. 'Hello, Yuriy, what can I get for you today?'

He loved her smile. 'Need you ask, my dear?'

She turned her back to reach for his 'usual'. His gaze was instantly drawn to her backside, which was framed perfectly by her tight-fitting jeans. He asked, 'What are your plans for the weekend?'

She placed his bottles in a carrier bag; he now no longer had to pay extra for one. 'I was going into town, but now I will stay at home. And you?'

'I was hoping to invite you over for a drink?'

She glanced around furtively, her hands paused suggestively on the neck of the last bottle. 'You are naughty, Yuriy.'

'At my age, my dear, that is almost impossible.'

On the other side of the shop, Pavel sneered. 'Look at the old fool. He's, what, seventy-five and thinks he has a chance with her?'

'She talks to him more than she does to you,' Kirill goaded.

'Ah, shut up. If he touches her I'll see to it that he doesn't reach seventy-six!'

Snow stood within earshot of both conversations. After waiting for just over an hour and a half, Kozalov's Lada had approached the Gastronom. Snow had left Blazhevich and entered the shop. He now listened as he took his time choosing a packet of crisps. The local lads were unaware of his presence just behind them, and by their posturing showed themselves to be little more than thugs. Snow moved to the counter as Kozalov handed the assistant several notes.

'Keep the change.'

'But Yuriy, this is too much…'

'Then use it to get something nice for yourself, or to help your mother. How is she?'

Snow quickly stepped forward to block Kozalov as he saw the larger of the two thugs moving nearer the counter. 'A bottle of Alexx VSOP, if you have it?'

'Yes, of course.' Eliso removed her hand from Kozalov's and went back to work.

Kozalov stood patiently and gazed up at the new customer. He was tall and cleanshaven, unlike the local Mafiosi, who seemed only to shave as often as they washed: weekly. 'You have expensive tastes.'

'Just taste.'

'Then you are in the wrong place.'

'Old man!' Pavel pointed at Kozalov. 'Give me your bottles!'

'No, I won't!' Kozalov held his head up defiantly.

'Then I shall make you. Outside! Now!'

'Are you afraid to kiss him in front of your boyfriend?' Snow asked.

Pavel stared at Snow. 'What the…'

Snow snapped his right arm forward and landed a heavy palm strike to Pavel's jaw, sending him back against the counter. 'If you want to fight, choose someone who can fight back.' Snow turned and easily ducked an ill-timed haymaker from Kirill, grabbing the leather-clad arm and using the attacker's own momentum to throw him to the ground.

Kirill attempted to scrabble to his feet as Pavel rubbed his face, hatred in his eyes. 'I'm going to kill you!'

'Please try.'

'Please, stop!' Eliso screamed.

'Enough. I'm leaving!' Kozalov collected his shopping and left the store.

Pavel took a step towards Snow. 'Who the fuck are you?'

'Mind your language. Did your mother not tell you to be respectful in a lady's presence?'

'Lady? She's a Georgian whore who likes…' Snow's fist ended Pavel's sentence.

As Pavel fell, Kirill came at Snow again. Snow sidestepped the first punch, grabbed Kirill's arm, twisted it, and forced him to the floor. Kirill lay in a pressure hold, facedown, with his right arm behind his back.

'Who the… who are you?' the thug grunted.

'I'm just a customer.' Snow tugged the trapped arm. 'Now will you let me pay or do I have to really hurt you?'

'OK… OK!'

Snow let go and took a step back. Kirill slowly got to his feet and started to massage his wrist. He looked at Pavel, who was out cold. The woman from the meat counter arrived with a metal bucket. She poured its contents over the bandit, who spluttered and jerked awake. Snow handed Eliso a handful of notes, took his bottle, and left the shop. He saw three other lads outside, smoking, and ignoring the freezing conditions. He saluted them as he walked down the street towards the Passat and climbed in.

Blazhevich saw a look on Snow's face he'd seen before. 'What did you do?'

Snow shrugged. 'I just spared our target a beating.'

Blazhevich manoeuvred the car back onto the main road as Snow explained further.

'So what do you think?' Blazhevich asked.

'He seemed normal enough, but he was buying several bottles of booze, so maybe he's expecting company? Where's the OP?'

'Nedilko is in a nearby house; it overlooks the empty plot at the back of Kozalov's place. It's empty, half-built – you know the score.'

He did. 'I hope they have a roof.' Snow looked skywards; the clouds had become dark and ominous.

'We've placed a camera in a tree opposite his *dacha* and another on a telegraph pole a few houses along.'

'OK, so let's see our second candidate.'

'We'll go to his office. It's not far.'

After twenty minutes of travelling down Kryvyi Rih's central drag, Snow was starting to get a feel for the place, which, at over one hundred and twenty-six kilometres in length, was Europe's longest, and possibly thinnest, town. Soviet-style apartment blocks lined each side, some with garish, neon-fronted stores on the ground floor. Yellow buses and trolleybuses trundled in both directions through the grimy-looking slush. Blazhevich parked the VW side-on to the kerb outside a newish, square building and showed his SBU ID as he and Snow pushed their way into the local council headquarters. Much to the consternation of a heavily made-up, peroxide-blonde secretary, the pair walked into the top-floor corner office. Taken by surprise, Mayor Kantorovich snatched a napkin away from his shirt collar and slowly got to his feet.

'Can I help you?' he demanded, with crumbs falling from his fleshy face.

'SBU. Please, sit, Leonid Ruslanovich.'

'I was having my lunch!' Kantorovich was indignant as he retook his seat. 'What is it that the SBU wants from me?'

Blazhevich and Snow sat. Blazhevich spoke. 'We understand that you were the director of the Kryvyi Rih weapons research centre?'

'You know as well as I do that I cannot discuss anything about my former work.'

'Oh, come on, the plant closed over twenty years ago and your employer no longer exists.'

Kantorovich frowned. 'I will not talk of my previous employment. I was a successful businessman for many years before I became the representative of the people of this town in the nation's parliament.' He pointed to a photograph on the wall showing him standing outside Kyiv's parliament building, the Verkhovna Rada.

Blazhevich motioned to another photograph, this one on the desk, which showed the Mayor and his wife standing outside a grand house. 'You have a beautiful home. What we'd like to know is how you paid for the land it sits on and how you funded its construction?'

Kantorovich looked at both, his eyes narrowing. 'What is it you really want to know?'

Snow now spoke for the first time, using his accented Russian. 'Have you been contacted in the last year by anyone else asking about your work at the facility?'

Kantorovich jabbed with his forefinger at Blazhevich and then Snow. 'He's SBU. What are you?'

'Someone you don't lie to. Answer my question.'

Kantorovich stiffened. 'No one has asked me about my facility for many years. It is old news around here. History. Now, what is this about?'

'Someone may be selling state secrets,' Blazhevich said.

'The secrets of a state that, as you pointed out, no longer exists?'

'Yes.'

'There are only myself and that alcoholic, Kozalov, left; the others are dead.' Kantorovich raised his right hand like a policeman stopping traffic. 'And no, I haven't spoken to him for years, before you ask me. I mean, why would I? He is nothing to me.' Kantorovich stared at Snow. 'What is it that is being sold?'

'I can't say.'

'Everything was destroyed; I should know. Anything that was of importance was…' Kantorovich stopped abruptly, realising he had said too much.

'Stolen by you and sold on?' Blazhevich asked.

'How dare you!' Kantorovich bristled. 'I am the duly elected

Mayor of Kryvyi Rih, yet you accuse me of being a common criminal!'

'Yes,' Snow confirmed.

Kantorovich shook and his face reddened. His mouth opened and closed but he was unable to form any words.

'Thank you,' Blazhevich said. 'That is all for the moment.'

There was a commotion at the door as two heavily built men appeared. Snow and Blazhevich rose to face them. The nearest 'heavy' spoke. 'Is everything OK, Leonid Ruslanovich?'

Kantorovich regained his power of speech. 'Sasha, where were you?'

'At lunch.'

'Thank you for your time, Mayor Kantorovich,' Snow said.

'My pleasure,' Kantorovich muttered.

The men at the door parted and the intelligence operatives left the mayoral office. Snow started to smile as they took the steps down to the ground floor.

'What's funny?'

'I've just realised who the Mayor reminds me of.'

'Who?' Blazhevich asked.

'Christopher Biggins.'

Blazhevich was puzzled as Snow sniggered. 'I'll never get British humour.'

They exited the building and got back into the car. Blazhevich drummed his fingers on the steering wheel. 'So?'

'I don't think Kantorovich is our man; he's as crooked as they come. If he'd got his hands on anything he'd have sold it years ago, and now he likes his status too much to jeopardise it.'

'True,' agreed Blazhevich. 'However, he was a member of the Party of Regions; his feeding trough is not as full as it used to be.' The political party of the former Ukrainian President had been notorious for its endemic corruption, nepotism, and ties with Russia. Now ousted from power, without their 'presidential protection' and under scrutiny in the wake of recently passed lustration laws, its members were watching their backs and scrambling to cover their tracks. 'Would he really say no to a few million?'

'That's true as well, but my gut tells me Kozalov is our man. He's alone and got nothing to lose. OK, here's the plan. Drop me off at his *dacha* and then double back here and keep an eye on Mayor Kantorovich.'

'You want to see him alone?'

'I don't want to spook the old goat; besides, he's met me already.'

'Agreed. What are you going to tell him?'

'I'll tell him I'm a Russian journalist writing a piece for an American science magazine, and that his knowledge would be invaluable.'

'I see. Old men like to talk?'

'Especially after a drink.' Snow held up the cognac he'd bought at the Gastronom. 'And then, once we've had a few, I'll start to question him properly.'

'Just don't waterboard him.'

'I can see why Dudka chose you.'

'Seriously, you won't do anything, will you, Aidan?'

'It'll be a friendly chat.' Snow winked. 'I'm a friendly guy. Start the car.'

*

British Consulate, Istanbul, Turkey

'I'm Simon Scarborough. It's nice to meet you.' He shook Casey's hand nervously. The news of the apprehension of the two terror suspects at the border that afternoon had been swiftly followed by a direct call from Patchem telling him to expect a senior CIA officer and to set up a video conference call.

'Good to meet you.' Casey sat. 'Is Jack ready?'

'Yes, yes.' Scarborough scooted around his desk and pressed a few buttons on his computer. 'Sorry, I don't use this much… ah, that's it.'

'Nice place you have here, small but functional.'

'It is, yes.' Scarborough had always thought the British Consulate to be 'grand', but then Casey sounded as though he was from Texas, and he seemed to remember that everything was bigger in Texas.

'Sorry I couldn't get here sooner.' Brocklehurst came to a stop in the doorway. 'Oh.'

Casey waved him in. 'Join the party but shut the door.'

Scarborough looked up from his desktop. 'Mr Casey is from the CIA.'

'It's Vince. My father is Mr Casey. Now have a seat or you'll fall over when you hear the news.'

Perplexed, Brocklehurst took a seat as a video screen sprang to life on the wall opposite. It briefly displayed the FCO screensaver before Patchem appeared. 'Vince, I see you're in Istanbul already?'

'That's right. Now listen. The Turkish police have handed both suspects over to my specialist and, after we asked them nicely, they became very helpful.'

Patchem knew what 'asked them nicely' was a euphemism for. 'Where is the device?'

'We still don't know, but we know what the target is. Moscow.'

In London, Patchem felt as though the air had been sucked out of the room. 'Where and when?'

'The when I dunno, but the where is the easy part – the Kremlin.'

'The Kremlin is a big place.'

'They said it's gonna be the senate building. Now I don't think they can get inside it, but any tourist can get near enough if they pay for the guided tour. Capitalism, eh? Lenin was right – it's gonna bite you in the ass!'

Patchem ignored Casey's ill-timed attempt at levity. 'Is it as you surmised? The terrorists will enter Russia via the border with Ukraine held by the DNR?'

'Exactly. No border checks, no Ukrainian control, and no acknowledgement by Moscow that they control the border.'

'Who has the device?'

'That's the kicker. It's Kishiev. It looks like he was playing the Russians and escaped from them.'

Scarborough found his voice. 'It must have been him who was responsible for the deaths at the Russian safe house?'

'I reckon,' Casey agreed. 'But that's not where it ends. Do you remember the rumours about the White Eagle?'

'Fairy tales would be a more appropriate term.' Patchem was brusque.

'Well, apparently he ain't no fairy tale. The Afghans claim the White Eagle is real and working with Kishiev.'

Brocklehurst felt out of his depth and glanced at Scarborough, who seemed equally awkward. 'Who is the White Eagle?'

'He's a ghost, boys,' Casey explained. 'He was meant to be an Al-Qaeda agent inserted into the very heart of US intelligence to spread doom and misery. We took the threat seriously; my department investigated it for a few months after 9/11, but then nothing happened, no chatter, no nothing. But now, and this may make some sense, the cell members are saying he's a Russian.'

'Vince, what are you going to tell the Russians?' Patchem said pointedly.

'Something like this: you know those suitcase nukes you like to pretend you never made? Well, one of them is being trans-ported by a man you claim you have in custody, over a border controlled by Russian soldiers you say are there on vacation, and it's going to destroy your senate building and irradiate the Kremlin.' Casey sighed. 'That's the general gist. Your PM and my President are going to have a joint call in the next hour.

They're going to decide how, what, and when to tell the Russian President.'

'And this intel is confirmed?'

'They can't lie to us, Jack, you know that. I'm sending my team into Ukraine.'

'Snow is already there.'

'Where?'

'Kryvyi Rih.'

'Then I'll have them make contact.' Casey checked his watch. 'I'm flying to Moscow; there's nothing I can do here. Looks like London's off the hook.'

'Only if the Russians believe our leaders.'

'Then may God bless us all.' Casey stood. 'Gentlemen.'

Brocklehurst got up and opened the door. 'I'll see you out.'

'Simon,' Patchem said after Casey had gone, 'I don't need to remind you that this goes no further.'

Scarborough nodded, numb, as what he had heard began to sink in. The FCO screensaver reappeared as Patchem ended the call. Patchem sat in silence for a moment. He didn't know what was wrong with him, but he didn't have time to get it checked out. The world had started to go mad and it was his job to preserve what little sanity he could. He punched in the number for Aidan Snow; he needed to be updated.

*

Black Sea

Tariq had bade farewell to his brothers Lall Mohammad and Reza Khan in central Istanbul, and now sat queasily on the deck of a commercial cargo vessel bound for the Ukrainian port of Odessa. He hadn't been on a ship of any sort before and was embarrassed to admit he wanted to vomit. Around him the crew seemed immune to the bobbing of the boat on the Black Sea's choppy water, but he was suffering. The scent of the air, however, was magnificent, as was the colour of the sky, and the sea, which, fittingly, was turquoise. How he could feel sick to his stomach one moment and invigorated the next was beyond his comprehension but that was the effect the sea, sky, and swell had on him.

'Is it indeed not a beautiful sight?' Kishiev appeared at his side. 'It is, Sheik.'

They leant against the rails in silence, cresting several more waves before Kishiev spoke again. 'I have some disturbing news regarding our brothers. The infidels have them.'

Tariq turned his head. 'They have been captured? I do not understand, Sheik. Were not their passports perfect?'

'They were, my brother, but unfortunately Lall and Reza were not, for it was them who betrayed our glorious mission to the Russians. How else could they have known where you were?'

Tariq shook his head and then paused as another wave of nausea washed over him. 'No. I do not believe it.'

'But, alas, it is a fact.' Kishiev placed his hand on the Afghan's shoulder. 'Think… that is why they were not killed by the Russians. They were meant to survive in order to betray our cause further. We placed them on the coach to carry out their sacred mission, but as soon as we left they stepped off and into a waiting police car. I know this because I had men watching. They are talking to the infidels, working for them. I do not know for how long they have been doing so. That is why we gave them false information.'

'About what?'

'About the attack. The traitors will sing about our plans; they will say that the attack will take place in one direction while we shall attack from another. Tariq, our target is not Moscow; our target is not mainland Russia.'

'What is our target, Sheik?'

Kishiev took a deep breath. It was time to explain.

*

Vauxhall Cross, London, UK

Patchem ate his canteen sandwich without enthusiasm as BBC 24 played on the wall-mounted display. A pair of journalists discussed a US Senate Intelligence Committee report heavily criticising the CIA's interrogation techniques. The screen changed to show footage of a Democrat senator lambasting the CIA for carrying out a programme she alleged was internally known as 'Rendition, Detention, and Interrogation'. Patchem listened sceptically. He wasn't one to condone torture – to give 'enhanced interrogation techniques' their correct name – but unlike the authors of the report, he accepted that it was a necessary evil. In some cases, he had to admit, intel resulting from torture could be unreliable, but in the vast majority of cases it had prevented further terror attacks. Regardless of the report, the rules by which his side played were far more stringent than the opposition. Would the Taliban, Al-Qaeda, or IS stop torturing their captives just because the West had? Did they care about the human rights of their enemies, who, even if they talked, would have their executions broadcast worldwide on YouTube? Patchem rolled his eyes now as the perma-tanned, self-righteous face of another American lawmaker half-filled the screen and stated, in words of few syllables, that the CIA must apologise and repent for the suffering they had caused. Patchem let out a sigh; if these idiots were listened to, the invaluable work carried out by the global intelligence community, including that of Casey's unit and his own, would be greatly hindered or possibly halted altogether. Even Patchem knew little of his friend's group or its make-up, but its mandate was clear: to actively counter the threat of global terrorism. The drugs Casey used on terror suspects were untested by the 'official' US authorities, but they worked and were untraceable. Was it morally right to pump a man full of narcotics to make him incriminate himself? Absolutely. Mistakes were rare, but on those occasions a severe chemical hangover was favourable to broken bones and bruises. The TV footage moved on to sport and showed someone, with what appeared to be an accident at a DIY shop for a haircut, kicking a football. Patchem finished his sandwich and rinsed his mouth with a swig of Irn-Bru, which the canteen manager had ironically started to stock after the Scottish independence 'no vote'. Patchem closed his eyes for a moment, but a knock at his door snapped them open. He waved Plato into the room and pointed to a chair.

'I've had a rather unexpected hit on the gait recognition program.'

Patchem frowned. Plato tapped a tablet he had been carrying under his arm and placed it on the desk. 'I ran the program at Istanbul's Atatürk Airport and came up, as I had expected, with nothing, so I then expanded the search to cover the bus and ferry terminals. I got a hit for the two shooters at Istanbul's main bus terminal.' He touched the screen and footage played of two men watching passengers board a bus. 'This then led me on to their faces and that's where I ran into a wall… well, a firewall to be precise.'

'How so?'

'They're US Special Forces.'

Patchem paused, thought. 'Are you sure of this?'

'One hundred per cent. It's a complete match on the faces and an eighty-nine point six on the gait that led me to the faces.' Plato brought up their official headshots.

'What do you know about them?'

'I retrieved their names, but apart from that nothing more.'

Patchem read the names: Karl Beck and Stephen Needham. 'Can you penetrate the firewall?'

'Jack, are you asking me to hack the Pentagon?'

'No. They'll already have a record of your search, won't they?'

'Yep, sorry, I should have used a false trail.'

'We have nothing to hide.' Unlike the CIA, it appears, he didn't need to add. 'It's best to be transparent. Right, I need to take this upstairs.'

Patchem shut his door and took the steps to the floor above two at a time. Arriving slightly pink in the face he strode past her PA and opened Knight's door without knocking. His boss was midway through a cup of green tea and looking down at a newspaper, aided by a pair of half-moon spectacles.

'It's the CIA!' Patchem blurted out before Knight managed to say a word.

She pointed at a chair. 'Sit. Explain.' Knight didn't interrupt until Patchem had finished. 'What is Vince Casey playing at?'

'I wish I knew.'

Knight frowned. 'So the suspects in the shooting were CIA and they took the bomb, took out half of the Al-Qaeda cell, and also spirited away the two gentlemen apprehended at the border, who happen to be the remainder of the cell.'

'Do you think Vince lied to us about what they said?'

'That would be the easiest explanation, if not the most palatable.'

'Well, anything is preferable to having a rogue nuke detonated in Moscow!'

'If it detonates,' Knight reminded her colleague and old friend. 'If.'

'That could be it!' Patchem suddenly realised. 'It won't detonate; it needs to be fixed.'

Knight pursed her lips. 'Explain to me what you're thinking, Jack.'

'Aidan Snow had this idea that, rather than build a dirty bomb, Al-Qaeda would want to get it fixed. That's where he is now, running down anyone who might be able to do just that.'

'Fix the device?' Knight took another sip of tea. 'OK, we know the CIA already has one RA-115A. Why would they want another?'

'To control the technology, or at least stop others from having it?'

'Is it really that hard to fathom how the thing works?'

'Probably not, but you'd still need to be able to create new parts or adapt the existing device.'

'Which Al-Qaeda hasn't got?'

Patchem shrugged. 'That's something we don't know. Why fix it?'

'Easier than reinventing the wheel?' Knight proffered.

'According to the file, it's something to do with the firing unit decoder that stopped the US bomb from working. The whole device could be replaced and put in a new case, but then that defeats the purpose of the design.'

'So, the gist of what you're saying is that the mention of Moscow as a target is a ruse? And who'd expect a terrorist to be able to get through a warzone lugging a suitcase nuke, anyway? Is that it? The device would simply disappear?'

Patchem nodded. 'The more I think about this, the less sense attacking Moscow makes, let alone the effort of getting there. The conflict zone in Eastern Ukraine would be the perfect place to pretend to lose a bomb.'

'Confront Casey. Put everything on the table, no secrets. We need to end this, either way.'

'What about the PM? He's discussing with the US Commander in Chief about how to tell the Russian President that a nuclear weapon is en route to the Kremlin…'

'I have to inform him.' Knight cut Patchem off mid-sentence. She picked up her desk phone, took a deep breath, and then

pressed a button. 'I need to speak to the Prime Minister, immediately.'

*

Unknown Location

Aslan Kishiev made no attempt to hide his face or conceal his
identity as he stared into the camera lens. Behind him the black
flags of both the Islamic International Brigade and the Mujahideen
of the Caucasus Emirate had been secured to the wall to provide
a backdrop for his statement. Kishiev spoke first in Russian, the
language of his enemy, and then in Arabic, the language of the
prophet. 'For too long the infidels have defiled our lands,
murdered our brothers and sisters, and been shameful in front
of the Prophet Mohammad, peace be upon Him. I am nothing
more than His messenger, and the message to you is this: we will
not stand idly by while you continue to attack our people, our
lands, and our faith. This is not a threat, nor is it a warning. This
is a statement of fact. You shall be driven out of the lands that
you have taken and the price shall be your infidel blood. As I
speak, Holy Warriors under my control prepare to attack. They
have no demands, they are not terrorists; they have the will of
Allah, peace be upon Him, on their side. His will dictates that all
non-believers, all Russians, leave our Muslim lands immediately.
This is but the start of our crusade and it shall not be the end.
We grow now stronger than ever, and have joined our holy
brothers in their Emirate. Allah is merciful, Allah is great.' Kishiev
nodded off camera and a black-clad figure moved behind him
and tore down both flags to reveal beneath one large flag of
Islamic State.

The message, recorded in a Turkish safe house, was uploaded
to several Islamic websites and instantly picked up by Al Jazeera

and then all the major international news channels. Screened by the Kremlin-funded RT channel, it was instantly dismissed as an old and worthless recording. Western news agencies noted, however, that it showed Aslan Kishiev without a beard and looking much older than he had been at the time of his arrest. And they pointed out that Islamic State hadn't existed when he had been captured. The video was screened for the next two hours in news packages until Kishiev's words became true. Making full use of commuter traffic as cover, a convoy of vehicles smashed through the Russian security ring that surrounded the Chechen capital of Grozny. Unexpected and unstoppable, a group of ten fighters reached the city centre where they assaulted local government offices and the FSB building. The Kremlin went into lockdown mode. The Russian President was immediately taken from his *dacha* and transported back to his office by a motorcade over-watched by helicopter gunships, and Moscow airspace was closed to all civilian air traffic.

Chapter 12

Stretched out on the frigid forest floor, Gorodetski ignored the pervading cold and falling snow. He and Beck had watched as Target One's Lada crunched over the frozen dirt track and came to a halt outside the *dacha*; now, an hour later, they were still watching as a VW Passat drew up. A passenger got out and walked towards the *dacha* before the Passat drove away. The *dacha*'s front door opened and Target One emerged onto the highest of the three steps that constituted the veranda. The two men spoke and the new arrival gave the other a bottle.

'Target Two confirmed,' Beck stated as he examined the scene with his field glasses.

Gorodetski slowly readjusted himself, looked down the scope of his Dragunov SVD-M sniper rifle, and awaited the fire command from Beck. But then he blinked and recognised the second man, Target Two, whose face now filled his crosshairs.

'Take Target Two first. Take the shot,' Beck ordered as he kept 'eyes on'.

For the first time since basic training, indecision hit Gorodetski.

213

His trigger finger didn't move as his brain tried to process what he was seeing, who he was seeing.

Beck hissed, 'Take the shot.'

'Target Two is not an X-ray,' Gorodetski replied. 'I recognise him!'

'The target is the target, take the shot.'

Gorodetski inhaled deeply. 'Look, I'm telling you something's not right…'

Beck dropped his binos, letting them swing by their lanyard, and jammed the business end of his silenced Sig Sauer into Gorodetski's neck. 'Pull the fucking trigger or I will. Are we clear?'

'Yes.' He felt the Sig move away and squeezed the Dragunov's trigger. A suppressed round instantly raced towards the *dacha*. Immediately, Gorodetski used the rifle's recoil to start his move. With his hands still clamping the Dragunov he jerked sideways as, a millisecond later, a 9mm round tore through the air where his head had been. Gorodetski thrust the Dragunov's barrel into Beck's chest. The former Navy SEAL opened his mouth to speak but Gorodetski's trigger finger was faster. The 7N14 round tore a hole through Beck, blasting him backwards. He was dead before his body had finished sinking into the fresh snow.

*

'Stay down!' Snow pushed Kozalov inside the house. The flight of the round had been silent; the noise it made as it shattered the kitchen window anything but.

'What the hell are you doing?' Kozalov demanded.

'Keeping you alive! Get away from the door and stay low!'

Snow crouched behind the doorjamb, retrieved his Glock, and scanned the treeline. All was quiet, all was still, save for the falling snowflakes made to dance by a light breeze. He felt his iPhone vibrate and quickly retrieved it.

'Aidan, are you hit?' Nedilko asked in an earnest voice. 'I saw the shot on camera.'

'I'm fine. I need you to work your way into the treeline and see who's out there.'

'Got that.'

Snow now saw movement fifty yards away, in the trees. The shooter spoke, his words in the international language of American-accented English. 'Don't shoot. I'm alone. We need to talk. I'm coming out.'

'Hold your weapon above your head and walk towards me!'

The shooter, rifle held aloft in submission, stepped out of the gloom. Snow tracked the shooter with his Glock. As the man drew level with Kozalov's Lada he spoke again: 'I am alone.'

'Keep moving and keep your hands up.'

The shooter reached the veranda.

'Put the rifle on the top step, then take a pace back and lace your hands together behind your head.'

He did as requested.

'Sidearm?'

'Left pouch pocket.'

'OK. Take it out slowly and remove the magazine.' Snow tried not to tense as the shooter reached for what he saw was a Sig Sauer. He'd have less than a second to react if the shooter drew. 'Now put both pieces on the step.'

'We have to talk.'

Keeping his Glock trained on the shooter's centre mass, Snow ignored the Sig but picked up the rifle he now recognised as a Russian Dragunov fitted with an ugly-looking suppresser. 'Talk.'

'I'm Agency. I was sent to eliminate you and Kozalov.'

'Agency?' Snow's surprise was evident.

'Central Intelligence Agency,' the shooter clarified.

'I didn't think you meant estate agency. Get inside.' Snow stepped back to allow the shooter to enter the hall, quickly shut the door with his foot, and then pushed the shooter left into the kitchen. He could now see that the Dragunov's round had shattered the kitchen window, and then embedded itself into the far wall, where it had finally lost momentum.

'Disgraceful!' Kozalov leant against the worktop, pouring a shot of cognac with a shaky hand.

'Take a seat, my Agency friend.' Snow sounded more relaxed than he felt.

Keeping his hands behind his head, the shooter smoothly sat on a chair at the kitchen table.

Kozalov straightened his back defiantly, tossed back his drink, and wiped his mouth on his sleeve before stabbing his finger angrily at Snow. 'He tried to kill us and you bring him in here?' The language was Russian, the tone outraged. He stamped his foot on the glass shards. 'And who will pay to repair the damage?'

'Please, just let me explain,' the shooter replied, the language also Russian but directed at Snow.

Snow placed the Dragunov on the floor out of reach of both men, and then switched to the same language. 'Speak and speak quickly. You're alone?'

'Yes.'

'Who are you?'

'I'm part of an "Agency" team targeting Kozalov. Intel stated he was in the process of selling classified technology to Islamic terrorists.'

'Fairy tale!' Kozalov roared. 'How dare you make such allegations!'

Snow needed a moment to think. The Americans knew he was in Ukraine; but why would they act unilaterally against a possible lead, and, more importantly, against him? If the shooter was really part of an Agency team, something was wrong in Langley. 'You told me you were alone. Where is the rest of your team?'

'Two, including my field controller, are holed up somewhere in town, and my spotter is in bits back in the forest.' He gestured

216

to the Dragunov with his chin. 'I wasn't meant to miss. When I did he tried to put a bullet in my brain.'

'He's dead?' Snow didn't hide his surprise.

'Yes.'

To Snow this made no sense at all. 'Why didn't you hit either of us? It was an easy shot.'

'I recognised you.'

Snow froze. 'Who am I?'

'My field controller said you were part of a European terror cell.'

'But you knew that wasn't true? How?'

'I'd seen you before, on a roof in Kyiv. You were with Bull Pashinski.'

Snow felt a crushing weight in his chest, as though he'd been kicked by a mule. The memory flooded back… the rooftop chase after the merciless Spetsnaz commando who had killed his friends wounded him and was about to shoot him, before a single round from a sniper had put a dead-stop to Pashinski and his plans. 'Explain.'

'Pashinski murdered my brother. It was my duty to execute him.'

What had happened in Kyiv had been kept secret by Dudka's SBU directorate. No one outside a handful of trusted people knew of Snow's involvement in chasing down Pashinski and his mercenaries, let alone Pashinski's fight with Snow, or how the man had died. Snow now knew without a doubt that the man he was facing had saved his life on that Kyiv morning several years before. But was he Agency? Snow still had doubts. He lowered his Glock and placed it on the table.

'What are you doing?' Kozalov demanded.

'Taking a leap of faith.' Snow addressed the shooter. 'Pashinski killed three of my men.'

'My enemy's enemy is my friend; Pashinski was my enemy,' Gorodetski stated as he slowly lowered his hands and removed his gloves. 'My name is Sergey.' He offered Snow his right hand.

'Aidan.' They shook.

'Irish?'

'No.' It was a common mistake.

'British?' Gorodetski seemed surprised. 'I thought you were SBU? What are you, SIS?'

'Yes.'

'What?' Kozalov spluttered and fell against the sink for support. Even in the watery winter-afternoon light he had clearly turned pale.

Snow ignored the Ukrainian. 'Was this a kill mission?'

'I was ordered to retrieve whatever Kozalov was selling and then eliminate all those involved.'

Was this proof his hunch had been correct, that the RA-115A would be brought to Kozalov for repair, or was Casey just covering his bases? Snow asked: 'And what was he selling?'

'Classified hardware, that's all I was told.'

'I don't know what you are talking about! I've done nothing wrong!' Kozalov prattled rapidly.

Snow again ignored the Ukrainian. It was still a far cry from being proof positive, but Snow was convinced. 'What intel did you have?'

'I have no idea, but I was told it was confirmed.'

'How long until your next check-in?'

'Minutes. My boss is expecting a call.'

'From you?'

'No, my field controller. He's waiting for Beck to call him.' Gorodetski tapped his jacket pocket. 'I've got his sat phone.'

'Beck was your spotter?'

'Yes. Why is the SIS here?'

The fact that 'Sergey' hadn't known of Snow's presence was odd, and the fact that he had the voice of a native Russian speaker odder still. Did he know that Moscow had now been confirmed as the target for the nuke? Snow was circumspect in his reply.

'We've been trying to find the buyers – an Al-Qaeda cell.' Snow thought for a moment as he put the pieces together in his head. 'Do you understand what's happened here?'

Gorodetski shrugged. 'I'm beginning to. The Agency was using me to get rid of its rivals, to get the package, to eliminate Kozalov, and then it gets rid of me?'

Snow was confused; what was the point of securing Kozalov's spare parts without the bomb itself? 'You really weren't meant to miss.'

'I never do.'

'Who's running this?'

'You mean whom do I report to?'

'Yes.'

'My field controller is called Harris.'

'And his boss, the guy who's running the entire operation?'

'I'm sorry, I can't tell you that.'

'Perhaps I can. Vince Casey?' Gorodetski remained silent but Snow noticed a momentary flicker of surprise in his eyes. Snow didn't like to think of himself as expendable, regardless of the stakes involved. 'Something is wrong here.'

Kozalov had no idea how, but these men knew about the bomb, and about him. Did they know about Eliso? He swigged more cognac... and then he realised they had no proof. They would have to find his components first and there was no way he was going to tell them where they were hidden! There was no way on earth they could make him talk! As the last rays of sunlight started to sink behind the wintery trees he glanced at his cabbage patch. The 'package', as the American agent had called it, was safe. Even if it was discovered, the parts were useless unless connected to an RA-115A, and where would they get one of those from? They would have to find his buyers, and even he didn't know who they were or where they were! Emboldened by the cognac, he called out indignantly, 'I'm going to phone the militia! You must leave! You have no right to come bursting in here like this!'

Snow regarded the former KGB colonel. 'Very true, but my friends at the SBU do. You should just count yourself lucky I haven't put a bullet in your greedy old head.'

Kozalov opened his mouth to say something then thought better of it. He grabbed his cognac bottle and drank directly from it.

Snow felt his iPhone vibrate. He removed it from his pocket and pressed the rubberised speaker button on the matte black Otter Box.

'One body. All clear. Are you secure?' Nedilko asked.

'Yes. Come on in.' Snow ended the call.

'Who was that?' Gorodetski asked.

'The cavalry,' Snow replied as Ivan Nedilko appeared from the hall. He had his Glock held in a two-handed grip and trained the business end on Gorodetski.

'You can holster that, he's CIA.'

Nedilko frowned as he put away the sidearm. 'I don't understand.'

'And neither do I, not fully.' Snow turned to Kozalov. 'It's time for you to answer some questions.'

Kozalov, who was now working his way through the last of the cognac, looked up. 'I do not have to tell you anything! What official capacity do you hold here?'

'None.'

'Exactly! You forget I was KGB!' Kozalov stabbed the air with his forefinger. 'It was I who gave orders, who asked questions!'

'Kozalov…' Nedilko sounded stern. 'I am an agent of the SBU, and you will answer our questions.'

'I was giving orders when your parents were still shitting themselves!' Kozalov snapped.

Nedilko nodded slowly. 'Bowel problems run in my family.'

Snow tried to keep a straight face and Kozalov looked confused before he spoke again. 'I will tell you nothing.'

'I know that you worked at the weapons research centre, and

'I know that you produced the RA-115A there,' Snow stated. 'I also know that you have agreed to help foreign terrorists repair their RA-115A.'

Kozalov grabbed at a kitchen chair and sat, his legs trembling. How did these men know so much? Who had told them? Had it all been a charade to trap him? No, it couldn't be. He wasn't going to tell these men anything! 'You have been eating too many of the mushrooms that grow in the forest.'

'What I need to know is, what exactly have you agreed to sell?'

Kozalov folded his arms and shook his head like a petulant child. 'I have agreed to nothing. Now, all of you leave my house!'

'You and I are going to leave together.' Nedilko stared directly into the watery eyes of the inebriated KGB veteran. 'An SBU team will arrive and take you into custody. Tomorrow, when you sober up, we shall officially charge you with treason.'

'Treason!' Kozalov flushed pink. 'My country is dead. Treason to which country?'

'Our country: Ukraine.'

Kozalov reached for the cognac bottle, noticed it was empty, so threw it onto the floor where it smashed, its glass joining that of the window. 'My parents were from Volgograd, I was born in Volgograd, and then in 1991, because the Supreme Soviet could no longer be bothered to work, I suddenly became Ukrainian.'

'What does it say in your internal passport, the one that guarantees your state pension?'

Kozalov stood, on unsteady legs. 'Listen here, Bandera...'

'Officer Nedilko.'

'Where are you from? Lviv?'

'Ivano-Frankivsk.'

Kozalov waved his hand. 'Same difference – Western Ukraine. You may be proud to be Ukrainian, but I am not. I am Russian.'

'Are you selling secrets?' Snow asked.

'Not secrets, no...' Kozalov froze for a second before he realised his mistake. 'What secrets?'

'Sit down, old man, before I knock you down,' Nedilko said.

'I'd like to see you try!'

'No, you wouldn't.'

Snow turned to Nedilko. 'Call Blazhevich. Tell him to park along the road and await my instructions.'

'What about Kozalov?'

'Leave him to me for the moment.'

Nedilko nodded and left the kitchen.

The room became silent as Snow thought back to the CIA report Patchem had shared with him and the reason why the Americans' bomb wouldn't work. 'Where is the firing unit decoder?'

Kozalov said nothing but his jaw tightened and he reeled backwards.

'So that's what you have for them? Where have you hidden it?'

Kozalov remained tight-lipped.

Snow shook his head with frustration. He took a step forward and crouched down in front of the older man. 'Yuriy, I'm speaking to you man to man. Do you honestly want your weapon to end up with terrorists who will kill thousands? Do you want their blood on your hands?'

Kozalov didn't reply.

'The target is Moscow. Do you understand?'

The old man seemed dazed. He opened and then closed his mouth as though he had lost the ability to speak before he replied. 'We built safeguards into the RA-115A. Without the correct decoder for the firing unit an RA-115A will not detonate. How can I be responsible for the deaths of thousands from a device that will not detonate?'

'If you don't give me the decoder, someone less polite than me will come and get it.'

Kozalov shrugged theatrically. 'I do not have any parts for any weapons. Search me, search my house.'

'OK.' It was at times like this that Snow wished he had some of Casey's truth drug, or more time. He reached forward and jerked the front legs of the chair into the air. Taken by surprise, Kozalov fell backwards, arms flailing. His head hit the tiled floor with a crack and he yelped in pain. Snow reached down and picked him up by the lapels of his jacket. 'I'm going to ask you again. Where have you hidden the firing unit decoder?'

'I don't have one!'

Snow dropped Kozalov; he fell like a rag doll.

'Is this about a suitcase nuke?' Gorodetski asked.

'Yes.' Snow now had no reason to lie. 'How did you know?'

'Old Spetsnaz stories,' Gorodetski said. 'They could still use it as a dirty bomb.'

'True, but if these people had wanted a dirty bomb, they would have used it already.'

'Moscow is really the target?'

'Yes, confirmed by your CIA boss to mine at SIS.'

'We need to search the house. I don't know what the decoder looks like, do you?'

'No, and I've read a bloody classified file on the thing.' Snow had an idea. He looked around the room before stepping through the living-room door. A moment later he returned with the remote for the Soviet-era television. 'Where do you keep your knives?'

Kozalov was sitting painfully and massaging his head. 'I won't tell you!'

Gorodetski pointed. 'Try there.'

Snow opened the draw under the worktop, found a knife, and used it to undo the flathead screws on the remote.

'What do you think you're doing? Kozalov demanded.

'Getting a firing unit decoder,' Snow replied, as he opened up the casing and scooped out the innards. 'What do you think?'

Gorodetski examined the electronics. 'It looks old and Soviet, but it won't fool anyone for more than a minute.'

'Langley didn't brief you on what it was you were sent to get?'

Gorodetski shook his head. 'Not at all, but Beck and the others must have known.'

'OK, silly idea.' Snow shook his head. 'Langley or someone at Langley wants what Kozalov is selling and doesn't want anyone to know they've got it. You and I aren't meant to be breathing right now. Plan B it is.'

'What's plan B?' Gorodetski asked.

Snow explained, but switched to English to do so.

Kozalov watched the American pull an odd-looking mobile phone from his coat and make a call. He was now using English, a language Kozalov had never learnt apart from the words to the song 'Happy Birthday', which, inexplicably, everyone in Ukraine seemed to know. Although, he thought bleakly, he was about to lose his biggest birthday present ever – the money. He tried desperately to think of a way out of his predicament.

Gorodetski ended his call. 'He sounded more concerned about the package than Beck.'

'He believed you?'

'Yes.'

'How long have we got?'

'They're in town, that's all I know, but Needham's on his way.'

'He could be here any time starting from now.' Snow thought for a second. 'Why did the Agency use you for this mission?'

'I'm the new boy and I'm not American.'

*

Druzhba Hotel, Kryvyi Rih, Ukraine

A pair of hundred-dollar bills inserted into a passport had bypassed the usual ID checks as Harris booked them into the hotel. With its yellow walls and black-tiled floor, the building resembled a private hospital more than a business-class hotel, but it was clean and functional. On the wall behind the reception desk a flatscreen TV was playing a Ukrainian news channel and Harris fought to suppress a smile as Kishiev's face was seen on split-screen alongside footage reporting the Chechen attack on Grozny. The receptionist seemed unfazed by it all, and after months of similar footage emanating from Donetsk and Lugansk, he couldn't blame her. Harris sent the group to the dining room while he went back outside with his Blackberry. He'd eat later.

Tariq sat nervously in the restaurant. He felt more out of place than ever. Needham had his head in the menu and Kishiev sat tall – almost, it seemed, daring anyone to recognise him.

'Are you OK?' Kishiev asked the Afghan.

'Yes. Are you not worried, Sheik?'

Kishiev's chest swelled with pride. 'No. This is a glorious day; today is the start! What will happen now is beyond my control, it is beyond the control of the Russians, of all men – it is Allah's will.'

Tariq looked around, even though there was no one else within earshot, the only other occupied table being at the end of the room. He was jumpy. 'But what if you are recognised?'

Kishiev was relaxed. 'There is an American phrase, "to hide in plain sight", and that is what I am doing. The Russians are not seeking a well-dressed businessman.' Kishiev shot the cuffs of his shirt with a smile. 'And who in this age does not want to encourage business?' Harris had provided the group with passports, which had enabled them to clear Ukrainian immigration and travel in a hired car directly to Kryvyi Rih. They would appropriate another vehicle for the next part of their mission. 'And what if I am recognised? I shall not be taken without bloodshed. It is the duty of every true Holy Warrior to defend the faith and, if necessary, die a *shahid* in doing so.'

'I could eat a horse,' Needham stated, looking up from the menu.

Tariq frowned. 'Is that a local delicacy?'

Needham laughed. 'Only in Paris.'

The laughter attracted the waitress, who appeared at the table. Needham eyed her up appreciatively, Tariq looked away in disgust, and Kishiev ordered in Russian. When the food arrived some minutes later, Tariq was confused that the meat was neither lamb nor goat. Instead, their celebratory feast started with a red-coloured soup served in a bowl made from a hollowed-out loaf – Kishiev informed him it was called Borscht – a large plate of cut meats and cheeses, followed by a huge piece of beef with vegetables. As Tariq ate, he saw diners at the other occupied table eating what seemed to be pork and drinking alcohol. His hands balled into fists but he managed to let it pass. The infidels with their sinful ways would soon feel the wrath of Allah. They were a small team, but what they would achieve would be colossal.

'You want more?' Needham asked.

'I have had my fill,' Kishiev stated as he cleaned his plate with a piece of flatbread.

Needham signalled for the bill. Kishiev wondered how, unlike Tariq, Needham could be so relaxed while sitting in a foreign country, in public with wanted men, and on the verge of committing an act of nuclear terrorism. Initially he'd thought it was because the American lacked intellect, but he had been wrong about this, as Needham had demonstrated with his rudimentary Russian and fluency in Arabic. Needham spoke with the tongue of the prophet, yet was not a believer. As a man of religious ideals, Kishiev couldn't understand those who fought under the false flag of Mammon. To be without religion was to be without purpose, to be as empty as the Black Dolphin cell he had escaped from. How could a man of intellect exist in a religious void?

Harris, he understood. Harris was a man he had come to know and trust as a fellow warrior of jihad. Harris had a just cause for his actions. It had taken weeks working together in the harsh, inhospitable mountains of the Afghan borderlands for Harris to finally let his mask slip and reveal the true reason for his hatred of the Russians. It was a reason that was so far hidden beneath the tough exterior of the fast-talking American that the CIA's background checks hadn't discovered it. Kishiev had sat amazed as his fellow Al-Qaeda operative had spoken of his origins. Harris had not been born in the United States, and neither had his parents. They were from Yalta, in the Ukrainian Soviet Socialist Republic. His parents were Tatars and victims of the Sürgünlik, the forced deportation of the Tatars from Crimea ordered by Stalin as collective punishment for collaboration with the Nazis. Harris had been born in the Uzbek Soviet Socialist Republic, modern-day Uzbekistan. Harris had no recollection of how his parents had managed, but several years after his birth the family had escaped from the USSR and illegally entered the US. Perhaps they had lied and been granted refugee status? Perhaps... he didn't know the answer to this and probably never would, for shortly afterwards he'd lost both his mother and father to a drunk driver. Sent to a state orphanage, he was adopted by a middle-aged childless couple, and the toddler born Ivan Nabiev became Jon Harris. What had happened next, Kishiev hadn't asked and Harris hadn't talked about, but Harris outlived his foster parents and, after graduating college, joined the CIA. Harris was the most ruthless operator Kishiev had met, but his devotion was to the fight against the Russians and not the protection of the US. As the White Eagle, he'd been responsible for some very high-profile missions. Kishiev felt honoured to be part of his homecoming.

'Beck is dead,' Harris stated quietly in English as he appeared at the table. 'We underestimated the Brit; he put a round in Beck before East took him out.'

'I'd have torn him to pieces.' The venom in Needham's words seeped out slowly.

'Dead is dead, Steve, we can't change that.' Harris sat.

The group went quiet as the waitress placed the bill on the table. Harris handed her a pile of Ukrainian hryvnia and she retreated with a large smile.

'So what does this change?' Kishiev asked.

Ignoring the Chechen's question, Harris reached across the table and took a piece of bread. 'East says he can't get the package from Kozalov. He put a round in the old goat's leg but, can you believe this, Kozalov is hanging out for his cash!'

'Stubborn bastard.'

'Stubborn, but frail too, Steve. I've told East to hold off until we get there. I'll ask him myself.'

'You are going?' Kishiev frowned. 'Is that wise?'

'Hey, it's as wise as any move. We've been sitting around too long. Tariq, you and I will collect the woman – Eliso; Steve, recce the *dacha*, make sure it's secure. Then we go in, recover the package, fix the device, and carry on as per the plan.'

'And East suspects nothing?' Kishiev was doubtful.

'He wouldn't be calling me if he did. He would just have run back to Mother Russia,' Harris conceded. 'But just to be safe, Steve will take East, or whatever his name is, out as planned. And then I'll tip off the SBU so they can close the Choudhry murder case; after all, East is a wanted man.'

Kishiev appreciated how Harris played both sides. 'And then we shall ready the device for our attack.'

'Correct. We head to Crimea and hit the Russians like they've never been hit before.'

'It will be truly glorious.' Tariq felt his chest swell.

*

Vauxhall Cross, London, UK

'Vince, where are you?' Patchem asked pointedly.

'I'm at the US Embassy in Kyiv. The friggin' airspace over Moscow was closed! Looks like Kishiev meant business, eh?'

'Vince, we need to talk.'

'What d'ya call this, Jack?'

Even without the aid of a video screen Patchem knew the American was smiling. 'Look, this is no time for levity. I'm just going to tell you what we've discovered and I need you to explain why we have it.'

'Uh, OK, just let me shut the door.'

The line went dead but before Patchem could redial his laptop showed an incoming call. 'Vince.'

'That's better, Jack, I can see you. What is it?'

'We have positively identified the two men who took out the cell in Turkey. Their names are Karl Beck and Stephen Needham.'

Casey's shock was visible, even though he attempted to keep his poker face. He repeated their names. 'Karl Beck and Stephen Needham?'

'We know they're yours.'

'They are.' Casey shifted in his seat.

'We want to know where the bomb is.'

'Yes, we do.'

'We, as in HM Government, Vince.'

'You think my guys have it? Who knows about this?'

'You and me, the Chief of the Secret Intelligence Service, my analyst, and our PM. We've kept it in house, for the moment.'

'You call that "in house", telling the Prime Minister?'

'Vince, he was about to discuss with your President their strategy for informing the Russians about an imminent nuclear threat!'

'And you couldn't have asked me first?' Casey was offended; Patchem was a friend.

'Not for a nuclear threat.' He could have passed the buck by saying it wasn't his decision, but he didn't.

'I take it your PM hasn't told my President?'

'Not yet. He requested that I speak to you first,' said Patchem, pausing to make his point. 'Because of our "special relationship". I need you to explain the situation to me.'

'Beck and Needham are part of my team. They were in Romania and nowhere near Turkey.'

'Vince, I'm going to ask you again: where is the bomb?'

'Jack, this must be a mistake. This is my team we – you and I – are talking about. I don't know anything about any of this.'

Patchem became angry. 'For God's sake, Vince! Tell me the truth. Did you or did you not know that Beck and Needham attacked the cell in Istanbul and took the nuke?'

'No,' Casey replied in a measured manner. 'I did not and I'd like to see the evidence that they were involved.'

'I take it you have access to your email?' Patchem asked rhetorically. He clicked his mouse and sent a document. 'Look at the photographs and the comments.' He folded his arms and studied his friend's face as the American opened the attachment and examined its contents. He sensed Casey was as shocked as he was, but then Casey had been trained to beat polygraphs. 'So what's happening?' Patchem asked.

'Pinged by the very software the CIA developed?' Casey shook his head. 'I had one extra man in Turkey; he was at the land border with Greece.'

'Michael Parnell.'

'Exactly. He was working with the staff from our consulate to liaise with the Turkish border service. The rest of my team were meant to be at an airbase in Romania.'

'And you didn't check in on them?'

'I don't spy 24/7 on my own men.'

'Maybe you should?' Patchem took a sip of water as he let the criticism sink in. 'So where are they now?'

'Ukraine. At their last check-in they were in country heading for Kryvyi Rih.' Casey started tapping on his computer terminal. 'And according to the GPS locators in their cell phones they're five miles outside Kryvyi Rih and heading north.'

'That's convenient.'

'What?'

'The fact that their phones are still on.' Patchem's sarcasm wasn't lost on Casey.

'It is.' Casey shook his head. 'Shit.'

'Quite. How many are there on the team?'

'Four.'

'Who's running it?'

'Harris.'

'Harris?' Patchem raised his eyebrows.

'Exactly. I trust him one hundred per cent.'

'I see.' Patchem had met Harris a few times. Casey referred to him as 'hardcore CIA'. 'So Beck and Needham have gone rogue with the bomb?'

'Holy shit...' Casey felt his head start to spin. 'The guy's a Russian.'

'Who?'

'The fourth member, the new guy, is former Spetsnaz. He was a friggin' mole!' Casey's face flushed with anger. 'It was all an elaborate play to get him on my team!'

'Explain?'

'He was the guy who stopped the New Jersey attack – remember? He slotted the entire team like it was nothing.'

'You think it was a set-up, an audition?'

'That's the reason the attack happened in New Jersey, not New York! It's got to be. A soft target they could control. They wanted to make sure he was noticed.'

'Vince, that seems too far-fetched, even for you to contemplate.'

'Normally I would agree, but what's the alternative? Beck and Needham suddenly decide to go rogue coincidentally at the same time as a former Spetsnaz officer joins the team?' Casey fell silent as he mulled the situation over in his head.

'OK, we need to look at what we know for sure. Beck and Needham took the bomb. The question is, where are they taking it?'

'Russia.'

'And the alternative?'

'You're talking about a pair of highly trained ex-SF operators. Even if they have crossed to the dark side, there's no way they'd attack innocent civilians. Never.'

Patchem didn't share Casey's conviction. Human nature was hard to explain, and harder to predict. 'We still don't have a target.'

Casey rubbed his face, 'Never mind a friggin' target. We've gotta find my team and stop whatever it is they have planned. Snow's in the area, correct?'

'You know he is.'

'Alone?'

'He's working with the SBU.'

'And you know we can't rely on them.'

'Can't we?' Patchem paused. 'They have their own antiterror commando group – Alfa. I could ask Dudka to send them in?'

'No! We can't risk it – we don't know who we can trust.'

'I know.'

'Jack, that is not helpful. What about your special SIS group, the Increment?'

'It's now called E-Squadron.' Patchem glanced at his wall clock and did the maths. 'We couldn't get them into that part of Ukraine for at least five hours, and that's flying direct from Brize Norton.'

Patchem's iPhone beat a tattoo on his desk. 'It's Snow.' Patchem glanced at Casey. 'Don't go anywhere, I'll patch you in on the call.'

Casey shrugged. 'Of course.'

'Go ahead, Aidan.' Patchem pressed a couple of buttons and took care of the e-hook-up. The call transferred to the laptop speaker. 'Vince Casey is listening in too.'

'Casey?'

'Yes, Aidan, Casey – or have you forgotten who I am?'

'It's as I thought,' Snow said. 'The device is coming to Kryvyi Rih. I located Yuriy Kozalov, one of the weapon's designers. The Al-Qaeda cell has contacted him.'

'Have you been in contact with the CIA team?'

Snow snapped. 'Yes, I bloody well have been "in contact"! They tried to shoot me!'

'Aidan…' Casey's voice was stern. 'I did not order any member of my team to take you out.'

'We believe Beck and Needham may have gone rogue and have the bomb,' Patchem said. 'They attacked the cell in Istanbul. What you're now telling us only confirms this.'

Snow tried to process the new intel. 'Beck is dead – Sergey shot him – and Needham is on his way to meet Sergey.'

'What?' Casey's voice registered shock.

'Explain exactly what happened,' Patchem ordered.

Snow quickly explained arriving at Kozalov's *dacha*, being shot at by Sergey, and what the CIA agent had said about Beck and Harris.

'So Harris is involved in this?' Casey's voice became unusually thin.

The line became quiet save for the hiss of static. Patchem was the first to speak. 'Vince… Vince, can you still hear me?'

'Jack, I can hear you all too well. First you tell me that Beck and Needham have gone rogue and now Aidan tells me Harris is in on it? I mean Jesus holy Christ! This is my friggin' CIA unit here!' Casey grabbed for a can of Coke and took a large swig before he spoke again. 'We need to act on this and act now. Aidan, I want you and Sergey to stay there. Keep Kozalov safe and apprehend Needham – we need him alive.'

'What are my orders, Jack?'

'Do as Vince says, Aidan: protect Kozalov. And if Needham shows up, subdue him.'

Casey shook his head. 'Aidan, you're on the scene, and so is Sergey. I've got Parnell with me. I'm pissed and I'm coming to you!'

The screen went blank as Casey abruptly dropped out of the call.

'What about the SBU?' Snow asked. 'I'll need them as backup.'

'You're working with Dudka's directorate only?'

'Yes.'

'Use who you have there, and for all our sakes don't mention the words "nuclear weapon". I can't get anyone else there in time. Aidan. This is down to you now.'

Chapter 13

Kryvyi Rih, Ukraine

Eliso was tired. The earlier excitement had made her nervous, not just for herself but for Kozalov. After Pavel and his band had hurriedly left the Gastronom, a steady flow of customers had arrived, all wanting their weekend drinks. And it was the women who were buying more than the men. Sometimes she wondered if she was the only person in Kryvyi Rih who wasn't an alcoholic. She allowed herself a sly smile; she liked a drink, too, she had to admit, and when all this was over, she was looking forward to winding down properly. She was just finishing up serving one of the regulars, a white-haired woman whose pink lipstick was plastered over her teeth and face, when she noticed Pavel and Kirill return. She immediately stiffened and hoped Tatyana Vladimirovna had seen them too, but the shop's matriarch had her back turned and was busily engaged in slicing sausage for another customer at the meat counter.

'What do you want?' Eliso asked Pavel.

Pavel leant against the counter. His jaw was swollen and he had changed his clothes since getting a bucket of water to the face. He opened his mouth to speak and winced as he did so. 'Who was that shit who hit me?'

'I don't know. I've never seen him before.'

Pavel glowered at her. 'You expect me to believe that a man you don't know would pick a fight with us over you?'

'She's not worth it!' Kirill spat on the floor.

'Who is he?'

'I've told you. I don't know!' Eliso's voice was firm.

Pavel raised his right fist; it tremored as the anger surged along his arm. 'You never raise your voice to me!'

'Eliso!' Someone called her name from the door.

Pavel and Kirill turned to see a large man with wild hair striding towards them.

'Who's this, another of your geriatric lovers?'

Harris reached the counter and stood next to Pavel. He got into his face. 'Are these boys troubling you, my dear?'

'The only trouble is what you are going to get!' Pavel's face took on a hard expression.

'Uncle,' Eliso exclaimed. 'I didn't know you were coming today!'

'Uncle?' Pavel said, a frown forming on his face. 'You are her uncle?'

'Uncle Vanya.' Harris managed to keep a straight face. 'I am her mother's brother. And who are you?'

'We are friends.' Kirill joined the conversation.

Harris held out his hand. Pavel shook it; the grip was firm.

Pavel relaxed slightly. 'Your niece has been having trouble with an old goat.'

'On a farm?'

'Kozalov,' Kirill said, the joke not registering.

'What type of trouble?'

'He has been trying to take advantage of her, following her, and…'

'And what?'

'Trying to sexually molest her,' Pavel jeered.

Harris feigned outrage. 'Eliso, is this true?'

She glanced down, pretending to be ashamed, but in fact hiding her amusement. 'Yes, he gave me a lift in his car, but instead he took me to his *dacha*.'

Pavel and Kirill swapped looks, incensed. They had only been guessing at Kozalov's intentions.

'Then we must go and see this Kozalov!' Harris was still outraged. 'Eliso, get your coat.'

'But my job, I can't just leave.'

Harris looked around the shop and saw Tatyana Vladimirovna, who was now standing at the meat counter observing the scene with folded arms. Harris approached her. 'Can you please watch Eliso's position for the remainder of the day?'

Her voice was gruff and indignant. 'No, I cannot. There is too much work here. What about all our customers? I only have one pair of hands!'

'Please, it would really help us all.' Harris reached into his jacket pocket and withdrew his wallet, from which he removed two $50 bills. He held them out to the shop's matriarch. 'And I am sure that this would help you too?'

'I see.' Tatyana Vladimirovna took the banknotes and studied them. This was more than she earned in a month and it was in hard currency. She pocketed the bribe. 'On second thoughts, I am sure I can manage on my own.'

'Thank you, you are very understanding.' Harris turned around. 'Eliso, I shall wait for you in the car.'

Tariq sat in the Audi SUV and watched with a professional interest the three Mafiosi who were hanging around a pair of old BMW saloons. He had known such men in Afghanistan; they were petty thugs and criminals with nothing to do and even less to lose. But unlike their Afghani counterparts they were unarmed, while he had an AK74SU across his lap. He saw Harris leave the store followed by two more thugs. Harris pointed at the Audi and then joined the rest of the men at the BMWs. A minute or so later Tariq saw a woman leave the Gastronom. She was raven-haired and extremely attractive. After a brief pause at the BMWs she took Harris's arm and they headed for the Audi. Tariq moved the Kalashnikov out of sight into the footwell as Harris opened a rear door for the woman.

'*Zdravstvyite*,' Eliso said as she clambered into the backseat.

Tariq didn't speak Russian and he didn't speak to women.

Harris got into the driver's seat and turned the ignition. 'This is Eliso.'

Tariq gestured towards the group of men. 'What's happening?'

'I'm taking us all to see Kozalov.'

'Why?'

'Camouflage. Something doesn't sound quite right about the situation at the old man's place. If there is a welcoming committee waiting for us, I want them to welcome these boys first. I've told them a good tale and said I'll make it worth their while.'

'And if everything is as East assured us it was?'

'Then we have the choice of paying the kids off or shooting them. I have no preference.' Harris sounded the Audi's horn. Pavel and his men started their cars and followed Harris in line out of the icy parking lot.

*

The Lexus 4x4 was gunmetal-grey in colour and seemed to rise organically from the discoloured snow that clung to its lower body panels. Headlights off, it whispered towards the *dacha* before coming to a halt and all but vanishing into the gloom of the forest and the falling snow. Gorodetski stepped out from behind Kozalov's Lada and approached, the crunch of his feet in the fast-freezing snow the only sound he could hear. The door lock clicked open and Gorodetski climbed in. The interior light was off but Needham was visible in the overspill from the sodium street light hanging by the next house.

'What happened?'

'I told Harris.'

'I want to hear it from you,' Needham snapped back.

'We were compromised.'

'How?'

'The guy with Kozalov, he made me as I took the shot. I hit him, he went down. When we moved in he got a round off. He hit Beck before I could stop him.'

'He killed Beck?'

'Point-blank in the chest.'

Needham drew a silenced Beretta from under his leg and pressed the end into Gorodetski's side.

'What are you doing?'

'Slowly take your sidearm out and place it on the dash.'

Gorodetski moved his right hand into his jacket and did as instructed.

'Now give me the package.'

'I don't have it.'

Needham took a breath. His eyes flashed and he pushed the Beretta harder into Gorodetski. 'Have you seen the effects of a 9mm round to the lower back? At this angle you'll live but it'll rupture all manner of plumbing. Now, unless you want to be pissing in a bag for the rest of your life, tell me the truth. Where is the package?'

'I told Harris.' Gorodetski's words were slow and controlled. 'Kozalov wouldn't tell me.'

The Beretta twitched. 'You expect me to believe you couldn't get an old drunk to tell you where his stuff was?'

'I put a round in his leg; I was running out of time. What if I'd killed the old goat?'

'OK.' Needham relaxed slightly. 'Kozalov is in the house?'

'Yes.'

'Secure?'

'Gagged and cuffed to a cupboard, but with his leg he's not going anywhere.'

'Neighbours? Eyewitnesses?'

'All quiet. That house on the left is empty and that one on the right is owned by an old woman.'

'A deaf babushka? Convenient.' Needham gave a tight smile. 'You are a royal fuck-up, James.'

'Thanks.'

'Take me to Kozalov.'

Gorodetski climbed out of the Lexus and Needham followed, his Beretta held loosely by his side. He scanned the neighbouring houses for threats but both sides were dark and silent. Needham saw the broken kitchen window and frowned. He let Gorodetski enter first, paused for a beat, and then followed. He smirked as the *dacha* reminded him of a backwoods shack. He followed the Russian left into the kitchen and, illuminated by a bare bulb, saw a figure sitting on a chair in the corner with his arms raised and held behind him. The man was gagged and had a tourniquet on his left leg. Gorodetski's Dragunov lay across the kitchen table.

'Where's Beck?'

'I put him in the next room. Take a look.'

'I shall.'

Needham collected the rifle then stepped around Kozalov and entered the living room. Beck was laid on his back. Needham moved to one side of the door and kept his back to the wall. 'Switch the light on.' Gorodetski followed him into the room and clicked the light switch. A low-watt bulb flickered into life; in the orange-tinted glow, Needham recognised his colleague immediately and shook his head. 'Where's the other one?'

'Around the side of the house, where I dropped him.' Gorodetski stood in the doorway.

Needham leant the Dragunov against the wall and then, with his left hand free, retrieved his phone from his pocket. He pressed a button. Harris's voice filled his ear. 'Go ahead.'

'I'm there. It's clear. He has Kozalov.'

'Secure Kozalov, wait for us.' The line went dead.

Needham turned his head. 'You did OK, for a Russian, James.'

Gorodetski saw the American's shoulder twitch. He had milli-seconds to react as Needham's gun arm rose. Gorodetski sprang, his right leg extended, and kicked Needham's arm. A silenced 9mm round tore into the floorboards and Needham toppled forward, but before he had time to think a tight fist connected with his jaw and he fell sideways. A second later Snow appeared in the doorway with his own sidearm trained on Needham.

'What the he…' Needham started to say as he tried to get up.

'On your stomach and put your hands on the back of your head,' Snow ordered as Gorodetski collected Needham's Beretta and the Dragunov.

'You're making a mistake.'

'Where's the bomb, Needham?' Snow demanded.

Needham was surprised; the Brit knew who he was.

Snow now pressed his sidearm into Needham's neck. 'I won't ask you again.'

'Yes, you will, unless you want to use that thing, and you won't do that. I'm Agency, for Christ's sake. And what are you, SIS?'

Gorodetski said, 'What if I put a round into your leg and hit the femoral artery? How long would it take for you to bleed out?'

'Go ahead, I'll time it,' Needham replied.

'You were right, I'm going to ask you again.' Snow pressed his Glock down harder. 'Where is the bomb?'

'I can't tell you.'

'But you have it, correct?'

'Course we do. Hey, this is an Agency operation. Now, both of you put away the pea-shooters and we'll sort all this out.'

'Did Harris order the hit on me?'

'Yes.'

'Why?'

'He said you'd gone over to the dark side.'

'And you believed him?'

'He's the boss and, hey, I don't know you from Adam, Aidan.'

Snow pushed the gun deeper; it broke the skin. 'But you know my name?'

'He briefed us.'

'OK. You and who else?'

'Me and Beck.'

Had Harris gone rogue, and then involved Beck and Needham? Did they think they were following Agency orders or were they in on whatever Harris had planned? No, Snow decided, Needham and Beck were part of it. They'd taken a nuke from a bunch of terrorists and kept hold of it. Snow moved a step backwards. 'Casey knows everything. You've got a choice to make. Help us retrieve the nuke or spend the rest of your life in a cell.'

'I keep telling ya, this is an Agency operation. Why the hell would that happen?'

'Because Harris wasn't following orders, and neither were you. Beck was ordered to kill me, an SIS officer, and you were told to dispose of Sergey – a fellow CIA operative.'

'"Theirs not to reason why, theirs but to do and die."'

'Tennyson, very apt,' Snow said. '*The Charge of the Light Brigade*, but you know damn well to question authority.'

'And what would you do, Snow? I'm toast either way. What can stopping Harris do for me? Get me a cell with a better bunk or perhaps a better view?'

'I promise, if you give up the location of the bomb, SIS will do all it can.'

Needham sighed. 'I would never have let him use it on a civilian target – you know that.'

'Do I?' Snow's mind span – what was the target?

'Harris said it was strategic. It was to be a bloody nose to the bear to teach it some manners. "Russia needs to respect its neighbours," he said, and hell, we both agreed. But then things started to change when Kishiev got involved.'

'Kishiev?' Snow said and instantly realised his mistake.

'Shit. You didn't know, did you? Snow, you almost had me

there. I want a guarantee of immunity from prosecution and I'll happily tell you all about Kishiev, his men, the target, and the nuke.'

'We don't have time,' Gorodetski said. 'Harris is on his way.'

'Cuff him,' Snow ordered. 'I'm going to call Casey personally.'

'You know him?' Needham seemed surprised.

'Why wouldn't I? He's also on his way.'

*

A steady stream of frigid air blew in through the shattered kitchen window, making the single bulb sway. Ice started to form on the worktop as night arrived and the temperature fell. Kozalov sat on a kitchen chair, wrapped in his heavy wool coat. His head was spinning; he still needed more alcohol. There was a second bottle of cognac in the cupboard but he couldn't reach it. His hands had gone numb from being cuffed to the metal handle of the kitchen cupboard, and the fake dressing on his right leg was tight. Unable to move and unable to speak because of his gag, Kozalov was angry and resentful. This wasn't how things were meant to be! How dare they treat him like this! Kozalov had no idea what was happening. The Russian and the Englishman had left together, taking the new arrival, and he didn't even want to think about the dead body in the next room! The *dacha* was still, save for the rhythmic ticking of his trusted clock and the occasional whistle as the snow blew in through the window. His head started to drop… but then another sound reached his ears: engines… vehicle engines. Their headlights beamed in through the broken window before abruptly switching off. Car doors opened and closed loudly, feet crunched in the frozen snow and were accompanied by raised voices.

'Kozalov!' A yell and the front door banged against the wall as it was thrown open.

He looked up as a group of men burst into his kitchen. He

recognised them as the local Mafiosi from the Gastronom. Kozalov's eyes went wide – Eliso was with them!

Pavel started to laugh. 'Look at him! Tied up in his kitchen! What have you been up to, you filthy old man?'

Kozalov shook his head and tried to speak but the gag stopped him.

'Search the house like Vanya told us to!' Pavel commanded.

Two of the Mafiosi raced upstairs, while Kirill and another went into the living room.

Eliso stepped forward and removed the gag. 'Yuriy, are you OK? What happened?'

'What happened?' spluttered Kozalov. 'Everything happened!'

Pavel strutted around the kitchen. 'Where is your drink?'

'Shit! Oh, my God!' Kirill reappeared, ashen-faced, from the living room. 'There's a dead body in there!'

'Dead body?' Pavel repeated. 'What, a real one?' Pavel pushed past Kirill to see for himself.

Heavy footsteps sounded on the stairs as the remainder of the group came back.

'No one upstairs,' the first stated.

'Just full of old clocks,' the second added.

'You three stand by the front door,' Pavel instructed over Kozalov's shoulder, 'and you two by the upstairs windows like Vanya told us to.'

'Why are you with them, Eliso? Why are they in my house? Who is Vanya?' Kozalov was confused, half-drunk, and angry.

Eliso stroked his head to soothe him. She then undid the top two buttons of his coat to reveal his neck and stroked the exposed skin. 'Our buyer is here. He sent Pavel and the boys to see if you were all right.'

'What are you doing?' Pavel moved back in front of the pair; it was now his turn to look confused. 'You told me he tried to molest you!'

'He did, and I encouraged him.'

'You what?'

'It was business.' Eliso reached into her pocket and retrieved a pen-like device. Without warning she plunged it into Kozalov's neck. His reaction was delayed, he tried to push her away, but she was too strong.

Alcohol and shock making his love evaporate, Kozalov yelled, 'You crazy bitch!'

'That's right, I'm a bitch…' She made eye contact with Pavel. 'And a whore.'

Pavel held up his hands, shocked. 'Whoa…'

'And Vanya is my boss, not my uncle.' She put the autoinjector back into her pocket, exchanging it for a subcompact Beretta pistol. 'And this is my friend. You and your friends are going to be paid by my boss, as agreed, to help us. So, you listen to me. Understand?'

Pavel was slack-jawed. 'Y… yes.'

'Good. Now join the others outside the house, keep watch.'

Pavel moved, his swagger gone.

Eliso dragged a second chair to Kozalov and sat down facing him. His head was rocking and his eyes were wide. She'd seen him drunk, and she'd seen men drugged before, but it interested her to see the drugs working on him. 'Where is the package?'

'What have you done to me?' Kozalov asked, his voice trembling.

'I've given you a tonic for your tongue.'

'Tonic?' He stared at Eliso; she had a strange expression on her face. What was going on? He had no idea what to say, what to think. 'Why are you doing this? We were going to leave together.'

Eliso stared into his bloodshot eyes. She couldn't be bothered to explain to him, there really was no point. The drugs would make him talk; they always did. 'I'm going to call Vanya and he is going to speak to you.'

Kozalov now had a smile on his face. 'That is good. Is he going to bring me my money?'

245

Eliso pressed speed dial on her phone and then the speaker button. Harris's voice filled the room. 'Is it done?'

'I've given it to him.'

'Make sure he can hear me.'

'Go ahead.' Eliso held up the phone.

'Good evening, Yuriy,' Harris said in accented Russian.

'You know my name?' Kozalov asked the phone.

'Of course, you are my most important supplier.'

'You are the SBU come to trick me!' Kozalov became indignant.

'Where is Needham?'

'Who?'

'The guy I sent to get the package.'

'The Russian?'

'The Russian? No, the American!'

'The Russian who tried to kill me took him away with the Englishman.'

'They took Needham away?' Harris asked.

'Yes.'

'Yuriy, tell me about the Englishman.'

'He was a tall man, he threw me on the floor – he said his name was Aidan. He knew the other man, the Russian CIA agent.'

'He knew him?' Harris's voice registered surprise. Kozalov seemed to know everything.

'Yes, it was something about saving each other's lives, and brothers. I wasn't paying much attention.'

At the other end of the call, Harris's brain frantically recalculated. How could Gorodetski know Aidan Snow? There was no possible way unless Gorodetski was a patsy, a plant, and Casey was onto him. But there had been nothing at all to suggest that his boss and friend of convenience knew anything. 'Think now, think carefully,' he asked Kozalov, 'and tell me exactly what they said to each other.'

Kozalov shrugged. 'It is as I said, I wasn't really listening.'

Harris lost his temper. 'Just tell me what they said!'

Kozalov stared at the phone that had just shouted at him. 'Sergey said he did not shoot Aidan as he recognised him.'

'From where?'

Kozalov explained as best he could. 'Will you tell her to untie me now?' Kozalov pleaded. 'I have answered your questions.'

*

Hidden in the treeline, Snow and Gorodetski had observed the group arrive, the noise and number taking them by surprise. The Mafiosi were easily recognisable, as were their cars, which were left nonchalantly parked half across the road. What threw Snow, however, was Eliso's presence. This changed things; Harris now had hired muscle and two potential hostages, both of whom were civilians. 'Harris knows something's up. He must have an eyeball on the *dacha*, but where is he?'

'Here…' Gorodetski handed Snow an IR scope. 'I came prepared.'

'Thanks.' Snow scanned the treeline either side of them and drew a blank. He then turned the scope on the *dacha*. He instantly made out 'warm' shapes by an upstairs window as well as the very visible yobs by the front door. He doubted anyone inside had IR equipment, but if so he and Gorodetski would be exposed. 'I've got one, two in the upstairs window. Three outside.'

Gorodetski shifted ever so slightly. 'So we wait it out?'

'That's the plan.' Snow had briefed Nedilko and Blazhevich on the true nature of the threat. Nedilko was in a house overlooking the back of the *dacha*, and Blazhevich was parked in the Passat along the road. They were each wearing a set of SBU comms links. 'Harris needs that component and I don't want to spook him. We have to wait and see what his move is, and the longer he takes, the nearer Casey gets to us.'

Gorodetski looked up at the sky. 'The conditions are better now; he shouldn't have any problems.'

'I agree.' He had no idea where Casey had managed to get a helo from, but he had been in the air and en route when Snow updated him on Kishiev's involvement. It was an eighty-minute flight south for someone who wasn't in a hurry, but Casey was. Snow moved his arm slowly to reveal his watch. By his estimation Casey was still an hour out. Snow handed Gorodetski the scope back and depressed his pressel switch. 'Nedilko, anything at the back?'

'Nothing. All quiet here.'

'Got that. Vitaly, where's the Audi?'

'Still static,' Blazhevich added. 'The woman got out, no one else.'

'Keep an eyeball on it.'

'Understood,' Blazhevich replied.

'Movement,' Gorodetski noted quietly. 'The front door. It's Kozalov. Human shield?'

'Perhaps.'

As the two men watched, Kozalov slowly walked down his steps past Pavel's group and shuffled into his front garden. After crossing halfway towards the neighbour's fence he stopped, turned around to face the *dacha*, and then pointed at the ground.

'What's he doing?' Snow thought aloud.

'It's not Tai Chi,' Gorodetski said.

Kozalov then walked to the side of the house and disappeared.

There was a squelch of static in their earpieces. 'I have Kozalov,' Nedilko reported. 'He's opening the outhouse. Waiting... OK, he's got a spade.'

Snow and Gorodetski observed Kozalov return. He walked back to the front garden, cleared the snow from a patch of ground, and started to dig. After several swings of his spade he straightened up and held his back, clearly out of breath. Pavel joined him and pushed him in the chest. Kozalov resumed his labour feebly until Pavel grabbed the spade and took over.

'I think we can safely say he's buried the package,' Snow stated.

'Unless he's looking for potatoes?' Gorodetski replied.

Snow shook his head; he was beginning to like the Russian. There was another reason Kozalov had been sent out, and Snow knew it. Harris was exploring, wanting to see who was outside and where they were. Snow checked his watch again; Casey was still a long way out.

After another few minutes of slow digging, Pavel heaved a bundle out of the ground and swung it over to Kozalov. He stumbled back towards the front door with Pavel at his side.

Snow had a decision to make. He couldn't let Harris acquire the missing component. 'Cover me. Don't shoot unless you absolutely have to.'

Gorodetski shifted his position. 'Copy that.'

Snow retrieved his silenced Glock, pushed himself backwards, and then leopard-crawled to his right. He put the BMWs between himself and the bulk of the *dacha*, got to his haunches, took a deep breath, and ran towards the Lada. Three, four, five quick strides through the frozen snow. The air was still and his feet seemed to clatter like hooves on cobblestones, but neither Kozalov nor the locals had noticed him yet. Snow hit the car; his arms rested on its roof and he opened fire. A 9mm round instantaneously hit Kozalov in the right leg, spinning him like a top before he fell flat on his face. The package whirled away into the snow. Immediately there was a pinging sound like heavy hail as the car and ground around Snow were peppered with suppressed rounds from an unseen shooter. The thin sheet metal offered Snow no protection; he threw himself into the frigid ground and crawled under the Russian-designed 4x4. He was pinned down; he risked a look at the *dacha*. The kitchen light had been extinguished. The Mafiosi had scattered, leaving Kozalov where he had fallen. He was groaning and dragging himself to the side of the garden, his leg leaving a bloody trail behind. Snow felt no remorse for shooting the former KGB officer; he knew what he'd been trying to sell and was well aware of what his weapon could do. As far as Snow was concerned, Yuriy Kozalov was a terrorist. Snow focused on the package; it was out in the open in front of the Lada. He couldn't reach it without being seen, but he could shoot it. Snow raised his Glock and squinted. There was no guarantee his rounds would penetrate whatever casing surrounded the firing unit decoder, but he had to try. He took second pressure on the trigger, but then he heard the ground crunch behind him. As Snow span around, a gunman came at him out of the woods, wielding a Kalashnikov. More suppressed rounds slammed into the Lada. Snow brought his Glock up as the gunman jerked sideways, taking a round from Gorodetski in the torso. Falling to his knees, he kept the assault rifle facing Snow. The man's features were now visible in the weak street lights – it was Mohammed Tariq. Gorodetski fired again and the Afghan sank.

Snow took a moment to steady his breathing.

'Aidan!' Gorodetski shouted.

In a mirror of the scene earlier in the day, Snow saw the Russian walking towards him with his hands held aloft, but this time someone was nudging him from behind with an assault rifle.

'Drop your gun, Snow, or your new friend gets it in the back of the head,' Harris said calmly.

Snow swore under his breath. By firing on Tariq, Gorodetski had given his position away.

'Ah, OK, you want me to kill him? Sure.'

Harris moved the AK towards Gorodetski's head.

'Wait!' Snow crawled out from under the Lada and threw his Glock aside.

'Smart thinking, son…'

With explosive speed, Gorodetski ducked, pivoted, and grabbed the barrel of the AK. He heaved it forward and down, pulling Harris from his feet. The American landed heavily. Gorodetski reversed the AK and swung it, but the covert CIA operative raised his arms and kicked out with his legs. Gorodetski took the impact in his shin and fell to his knees. The Kalashnikov dropped away.

'Come on, boy, or are you still a puss?' Harris goaded, getting up.

Gorodetski sprang forward and shoulder-barged Harris onto his back. Harris clung on and slammed his fists into the side of the younger man's head.

Snow saw the two men grapple. Gorodetski had now thrown Harris aside and was delivering a fist to his face. Snow reached for his Glock and got to his feet, but then something hard hit him on the back of the head. His legs wobbled, he turned, and as the ground rushed up to meet his face he saw Pavel standing over him with a shovel.

'Are you ready to die?' Gorodetski asked the American.

'Take your hands off him!' Eliso ordered, aiming her Beretta at Gorodetski. 'Now!'

Harris took a step away and brushed off his jacket; he tasted blood in his mouth. 'Never underestimate a pretty face, James.'

'My name is Sergey,' Gorodetski stated as he looked between Harris and the woman.

'Yep, and that's what I'm going to tell the militia.'

Gorodetski frowned. 'So what now? You kill us all and escape with the girl?'

'And we ride off into the sunset…' Harris retrieved his Kalashnikov. 'Now, if you'd be so kind as to get inside the house, the story for the militia works better if you're found inside.'

Harris and Eliso led Gorodetski across the frozen garden towards the *dacha*. They met Pavel halfway; he had a spade in his hand.

'Where is he?'

Pavel leered. 'He's over there. I hit him hard with this. He's never getting up.'

Harris shot a glance at the Lada and Snow's body lying motionless next to it. 'Where's my stuff?'

'Inside.'

'Then let's go.'

'Help me… I've been shot!' Kozalov wailed as they neared him.

'Leave him,' Harris ordered.

Kirill met them in the kitchen. He had found Kozalov's cognac supply and was swigging freely.

'Where are the rest of you?' Harris asked

'They got scared, they ran off,' Kirill replied. 'We were in the Ukrainian army. Nothing scares us.'

Harris knew it was an empty boast. All the Mafiosi would have been conscripted into the army for national service. 'Where's my stuff?'

'Here.' Kirill removed the package from under his coat; it was the same size as a large jiffy bag.

'You opened it?'

'No, I just took it out of the sack it was buried in. Do you have our money?'

Harris pointed at the bottle. 'Does that stuff give everyone who drinks it big cahoonas?'

Pavel became confused and pointed at the envelope. 'It's what you wanted. Now, if you pay us, we'll leave and forget all about tonight.'

'Eliso, take care of this, please,' Harris ordered.

Eliso raised her Beretta and shot Pavel in the face. Kirill's eyes went wide in disbelief; he tried to move, but then the side of his face was blown away too.

'Oh, dear, Sergey, why did you do that? That's two more innocent men you've killed,' Harris said sarcastically. He pushed Gorodetski in the back with his Kalashnikov. 'Get in the other room.'

Gorodetski allowed himself to be hustled into the living room. Beck's body was still on the ground where he had placed it earlier.

'Where's Needham?'

'The SBU has him.'

'You killed Beck, didn't you, Sergey?'

'Yes.'

'I liked Beck. I recruited him, and I recruited Needham. I don't like you, but you're actually not bad for a Russian. Perhaps if we had to do this all over again things would be different?'

Under his fleece hat Gorodetski heard a burst of static in his ear.

'Or perhaps not.'

Eliso raised her Beretta and cocked her head to one side. 'Can I?'

Another squelch in his ear and this time Nedilko's voice. 'Get down!'

'Go ahead,' Harris ordered.

Gorodetski dived sideways as 9mm rounds entered from the rear window and peppered the room. Harris threw himself back into the kitchen. Eliso screamed and fell as she pulled the trigger; her round dug itself safely into the wall.

'Get out!' Nedilko said.

Gorodetski jumped out of the window and dropped into the back garden.

*

A gunshot sounded somewhere in the far distance... and another... He felt the cold and then the pain in the back of his head. Snow slowly opened his eyes and saw nothing but shadows. He squeezed his eyes tightly shut, opened them again, and then realised his nose was touching a tyre. A familiar noise registered in his ears and then it materialised directly overhead, a black shape against a dark sky. It swooped down and almost kissed the *dacha*'s roof. It was a military helicopter and, before Snow had time to understand the implications, its doors opened and ropes dropped out of either side, immediately followed by black-clad assaulters. The downdraft forced Snow's eyes to close. This was not Casey; this was not good.

Chapter 14

Kryvyi Rih, Ukraine

Boroda was the first on the ground, quickly followed by the rest of Strelkov's men. He hurled a flashbang through the shattered kitchen window and another assaulter sent one into the hall. Weapon up, Boroda stormed the house, caring nothing for stealth or personal safety – speed and surprise were what he was relying on. Kishiev wasn't going to get away from him this time. The team split in half; Boroda steamed left into the kitchen with his half and the others charged upstairs. He scanned the room and saw three bodies on the floor, two dead, and the third lying facedown with its hands laced behind its head.

The helicopter was definitely Russian and appeared to be a Kamov Ka-60. Even in the whirlwind caused by the rotors there was no way Snow could get away without being seen. He flattened himself into the ground and slid under the Lada. The Kamov turned sharply and landed in the empty plot behind the *dacha*. Through the swirling snow he saw two commandos grab Kozalov and haul him to his feet. The old man waved his arm wildly. More commandos now exited the dacha and jogged around the side of the building. A figure was frogmarched out of the *dacha* by a single commando. The man lifted his head up and, for a fraction of a second, Snow locked eyes with Harris before a violent shove moved the American along. Snow steadied his Glock. He couldn't let him be taken like this; as a senior CIA officer he'd be a huge prize for the Russians, but the implications would run much deeper than that. Snow opened fire. His first shot went just wide, slamming harmlessly into the wooden exterior of the *dacha*; his second hit the commando high in the chest. Boroda stumbled to the ground and his AK74SU swung on its sling. Snow pushed up to his feet, adrenaline now masking the hammering in his skull, and covered the distance to Harris as quickly as the soggy ground and his groggy head would let him.

Harris scuttled away but Boroda was already on his haunches, his AK rising... and then he was propelled onto his back, hit in the chest by another round. Snow turned his head to see Gorodetski before both men gave their attention to Harris. Wrists plasticuffed together, he started to raise his arms, but then something made him freeze. More commandos reappeared from around the right side of the *dacha* and sent a barrage of rounds in their direction. Snow hurled himself at the porch, landing behind the steps, and Gorodetski bolted down the side of the building. What seemed like minutes, but was in fact seconds, later, the Kamov's engine note changed; it lifted into the air and powered away. As the noise of the helicopter faded, the sounds of the street grew to take its place. Dogs barked and a car alarm incongruously bleeped and announced a warning in English.

'Snow!' Gorodetski shouted.

'I'm here. Are you hit?'

'No, they couldn't shoot for shit.'

Snow squinted as a pair of headlights illuminated the front garden.

'Aidan?' Blazhevich called.

Standing, Snow massaged the back of his head. It hurt. 'I'm here, Vitaly… just.'

'I've called it in,' Blazhevich shouted over to the pair. 'I saw it go. It must have been the Russians.'

'It'll be too late to intercept them. They'll run straight for Crimea.'

'Did they…'

'Yes.' Snow confirmed Blazhevich's fears. 'They took Harris, Kozalov, and the parts.'

Blazhevich slammed his fist onto the roof of Kozalov's Lada in disgust. 'And the bomb?'

'I don't think Harris had it on him. He must have left it with Kishiev.'

'Well, that's hardly a sensible thing to do, is it?' Blazhevich kicked the 4x4. Snow and Gorodetski exchanged looks. 'I'm sorry.' Blazhevich shook his head. 'But we've got Needham. He'll know the plans; he'll know where Kishiev is!'

Snow's iPhone rang… Casey. 'We're twenty minutes out.'

'We've lost Harris, Kozalov, and what he was selling.'

'You've what?' Casey's voice raised an octave.

'What looked like a Russian Spetsnaz team just grabbed them. But we've got Needham.'

'OK. Stay put.'

Snow closed the phone. 'How did the Russians know to come here?'

'My guess would be a local informer in either the SBU or the militia.' Blazhevich was despondent.

'I see,' Snow said. 'I wonder if Kozalov has anything to drink indoors?'

*

It wasn't the first time he'd been captured by the Russians; it had happened in 1988 when he'd been fresh-faced and foolish. But this was far more serious. There would be no rescue this time by Mujahideen fighters. Harris lay on the floor of the helo with a black sack over his head, his ankles and wrists tightly secured. He kept his mouth shut and listened to the Russians talking among themselves. They had been looking not for him but for Kishiev and the nuke, that much was clear; but what wasn't clear was how they had tracked him to Kozalov's *dacha*. Harris ran the scenarios through his head. How would he play this? Would he claim to be an American businessman, swept up by an illegal Russian operation? That scenario did have potential. The Agency would want him back. Social media and American-funded news channels would make a meal of his abduction, his legend backed up by women playing his wife, mother, and two daughters. Campaigns would start, the embarrassment and pressure on Moscow would be huge; but, alas, he couldn't do that. Casey knew about him, the Agency knew about him, the British knew about him. What was his next option? Confess to being a senior CIA officer? Bargain with intel for his life and become the new Edward Snowden? Harris decided that was it. That's what he would do. He may even become famous and get to meet the Russian President and his celebrity friends. But then he heard groans, and Kozalov started to speak.

*

Kryvyi Rih, Ukraine

'They are like buses,' Blazhevich joked. 'You wait days for one and then two arrive within minutes of each other.'

'Let's hope this helo is a friendly,' Snow said.

Nedilko jogged over from the road where he had been talking to two militia officers. 'I've managed to calm things down and persuaded them that the Russians aren't invading Kryvyi Rih.'

'And let's pray they never try to,' Snow replied.

Gorodetski looked up at the sky. 'It's a different helo. Completely different sound.'

The four men watched their second helicopter of the night land in the empty plot behind the *dacha*. Two men quickly alighted as the rotors slowed. Snow recognised Vince Casey and Gorodetski recognised Michael Parnell.

'Where's Needham?' Casey asked without preamble.

'Inside, tied up,' Snow replied.

Casey flashed Gorodetski and the others a quick, tight smile before walking past them and into the house. Parnell followed in silence.

'Vince?' Needham was surprised to see his chief enter the room.

Casey shook his head. 'Why did you do it, Steve?'

'I was following Harris's orders.'

'C'mon, we all know that's bullshit. You've messed up big time. I'm not sure I can help you, unless you tell me everything.'

'I'm sorry.'

'For what you've done?'

'No. I'm sorry that I can't tell you – it's too late. But I can tell you I'm not sorry for taking a friggin' nuke away from a bunch of jihadis, and I'm not sorry for sending those jihadis to hell.'

Casey pursed his lips in disgust. 'Mike, he's all yours.'

Parnell had an autoinjector in his right hand and a professional look on his face. 'Steve, if you keep still you won't feel a thing.'

'Perhaps just a little prick,' Casey added, 'but I know you've felt a lot of those.'

Needham glared. He knew there was no way he was getting out of this now. 'OK, I'll talk, damn it!'

Parnell paused, his hand next to Needham's neck. 'Shall I?'

'Go ahead, he had his chance.'

Parnell pushed the pen against Needham's skin and injected the serum.

*

Russian-Occupied Ukrainian Territory of Crimea

A pair of strong hands pushed Harris down into a chair. His hood was roughly removed, causing him to squint. Bright fluorescent lights made the room look like the interior of a refrigerator. Harris shivered; the temperature made it feel like an icebox too. A man with a neat moustache, short back and sides, and several scratches on his face sat in a chair opposite him.

'Your friend, Mr Kozalov,' Strelkov said in Russian, 'has been very talkative. He has answered every question that we have posed. In my opinion it is very unusual that a man should talk so freely and look so relaxed while he is being questioned. Don't you agree?'

Harris said nothing.

'I thought initially that Mr Kozalov's candour was due to the fact that he was intoxicated, drunk on cheap Ukrainian cognac; but no, he told me himself that you had drugged him. So I think I should thank you for, in part, making my job much easier. Kozalov has told me everything he knows; however, the issue is that he does not know the answers to a pair of very important questions. I think you can answer these for me. Will you do that and save yourself an awful lot of pain?'

Harris remained silent, his face a blank mask.

'Very well, I shall ask you. Where is the bomb?'

Harris gave no visible reaction.

'Where is the bomb?'

Harris was thinking, and thinking logically. He had missed

the ERV with Kishiev, so the Chechen would now be in the process of bugging out and starting to action the backup plan. He would be on his way south to Odessa, where he would meet up with the crew of a Turkish ship breaking international sanctions by delivering supplies to Crimea. Once in Crimea, Kishiev would strike their secondary target, the Russian-controlled Crimean parliament building. But all this would take time. Harris had received anti-interrogation training, but still knew he wouldn't be able to hold out much more than a couple of days. And he imagined that the techniques the Russians had now developed would cut the time shorter still. He knew what he had to do. Resist and then drip-feed. But first he'd try to stall; there was a chance the man interrogating him did not speak English.

'I'm sorry, I don't understand you. I don't speak Ukrainian. Can you please explain to me what is happening? I am a US citizen. Who are you and why have you kidnapped me?'

'I was speaking Russian, the only true language of the Russian people.' Strelkov's eyes narrowed as he spoke in English. 'I know very well that you can understand and speak my language; it is what you used to address Kozalov. I believe that you are American and that you are an agent of the CIA.'

'I am an American citizen, and demand that you inform my embassy immediately of my whereabouts!'

'You are in no position to make demands.'

Harris didn't reply.

'Very well, it is as I thought. We have drugs that will loosen your tongue.'

Unless the Russians had improved their serum since the CIA had bought a sample to test, Harris believed he'd be able to resist. Unseen by Harris, a needle was thrust into his neck. A cold sensation streaked along the vein and his eyelids became heavy. He smirked at the Russian. 'Very relaxing; I could do with a sleep.'

'That is good. Oh, and by the way, you will be pleased to know that the man who was shot while apprehending you is fine. His body armour prevented everything but bruises.'

'Please get him some flowers on my behalf. Pansies would be appropriate.' Harris cracked up.

Strelkov scowled. 'You will now answer my questions.'

Harris felt his head loll and a smile spread across his face.

'Where is the bomb?'

'I don't know.'

Strelkov frowned; the American was resisting. 'Where is the bomb?'

'I told you I don't know.'

'Where is it?' Perhaps the drugs had been slow to work?

'I don't know exactly.'

'But you know roughly?'

Harris shrugged. 'Somewhere in Ukraine.'

Strelkov took a deep breath to control his rising anger. 'Which part of Ukraine?'

'The southern part of Ukraine.'

'Who has the bomb?'

'A friend.'

'Who?'

Harris raised his head. 'Aslan Kishiev.'

'Kishiev has the bomb?' Strelkov felt his whole body tense.

'Yes, he does, and that's bad news for you... what's your name?'

'Strelkov.' He read the American's eyes; they were still defiant, even though the pupils had dilated. Perhaps he should up the dose? But he knew what that could lead to. 'And your name is?'

'Strelkov?' Harris started to laugh hysterically, the drugs exaggerating his every emotion. 'So you're the buffoon who called your boss from Black Dolphin on an unsecured line?'

'What?' Strelkov snapped back.

'The NSA were listening in, got every word. Well, thank you, buddy, for letting us all know there was a nuke on the loose!'

Strelkov took a deep, calming breath. He knew what he had done. It was an error that might still cost him everything. 'So you are CIA?'

Harris realised that the drugs were slowly acting on him; they weren't as fast as his own, but could he beat them? He'd have to take his time and fight this, but surely a little information here and there wouldn't hurt anyone? It might even help him. 'Yes.'

'What is your name?'

'Nabiev,' Harris said, and then wondered why he had given his birth name?

'Nabiev? That is a Russian name?'

'Tatar. My parents emigrated. I'm now called Harris.'

Strelkov's mind started to whir – was it a CIA trick? Was he trying to confuse matters, or was he not grasping the whole picture? 'And you were sent to find the bomb?'

'Yes.' There was no point in denying this fact.

'Where did you find it?'

'Istanbul.' No reason not to state this.

'So you took it from the Al-Qaeda cell?'

'Yes.' Just information, not intel. He could tell the Russian this.

'Did you rescue Kishiev?'

'Yes.' A simple fact.

Something strange was happening, something Strelkov couldn't understand. Why would the CIA stay in the field once they had the bomb and the terrorist? Kozalov had told him that the man, whom he now knew was a CIA agent called Harris, had wanted to purchase parts to make the bomb function. The realisation of what was going on hit Strelkov like an iron hammer. The CIA wanted the bomb so they could use it against Russia and blame the Chechen terrorists! This was an act of war. Harris's head now lolled to one side, drool starting to drip from his mouth. Strelkov's jaw tightened; he had to find the bomb and Kishiev. 'Kishiev has the bomb in the south of Ukraine. Where exactly?'

'I don't know.'

Strelkov lost his temper; he didn't have time for this. 'WHERE IS THE BOMB?'

Harris's head jerked. 'With Kishiev.'

'WHERE?'

'It is travelling south, towards Odessa.'

'Is he alone?'

'Yes.'

'He is driving?'

'Yes.'

'What is he driving?'

'A camel.'

The man was still resisting. 'I asked you what he was driving?'

'An SUV.'

'What type?'

'Nissan X-Trail.'

'What colour?'

'Pink.'

'What colour?'

'Black.'

'Registration number?'

'BITE-ME.'

'Registration number?'

'No idea.'

Strelkov turned his head left and nodded. The interview was being recorded, plans were being made. 'Where is he going in Odessa?'

'He's not going to Odessa.' Harris smiled a wide, sloppy, drunken smile.

'What is his destination?'

'The place he'll end up at.'

'What is his destination?'

'I can't tell you that.' Harris now tried desperately to keep quiet but he felt so relaxed, and happy.

'Yes, you can.'

Chapter 15

Dnipropetrovska Oblast, Ukraine

Kishiev checked his watch and gave another nervous glance at the road. The ERV had been well chosen. It was a mothballed vehicle repair depot, on a disused road west of Kryvyi Rih. Any vehicles approaching him would be instantly seen, giving him ample opportunity to make good his escape. His own tracks had now been covered by fresh snow, as had the rented Nissan which stood outside. Kishiev thought back on the events of the last few weeks: his transferral from Black Dolphin, his betrayal of those loyal to him who had attacked Moscow, and most of all about his wife and daughter. Kishiev knew he would not see them again. His path was different, preordained by almighty Allah, peace be upon Him; he was to be the instrument of justice and vengeance against the infidels. The device stood next to Kishiev, looking innocuous in its metal case. Even without the missing components it would still be the deadliest weapon deployed in the name of Islam. As a dirty bomb it would cause chaos and render the targeted area useless for decades. The Russians would truly fear the name of the Prophet, and brothers would rise up to destroy the infidels.

This would be the start of the real war between the Caliphate and Russia.

His phone buzzed, an incoming call. Harris. Kishiev answered. 'Where are you?'

There was a pause and some static before Strelkov spoke. 'Kishiev, we have Harris, and now we are coming for you!'

Kishiev opened the handset and removed the SIM card before dropping it on the floor and crushing it under his boot. He cursed himself for not getting rid of the phone earlier. Through the window the outside world was black; no headlights or lights of any sort. Kishiev picked up the case and made for the door. He unlocked the Nissan with the remote and swore as the indicator lights flashed once to confirm his action. He carefully placed the case in the passenger footwell, raised his hand to shut the door, and then he heard it. A faint but familiar sound: rotor blades. His eyes widened and he slammed the door, turned the key in the ignition, and pulled away from the depot. He made for the small road leading into the woods around the Karachunivs'ke reservoir. Perfect. The helicopter wouldn't be able to follow him in there. He floored the accelerator pedal; the large engine pushed all four tyres hard into the fresh snow. The Nissan fishtailed before finding enough grip to propel it faster down the road. Now he couldn't hear the helicopter, nor could he see any lights in the sky. He slowed enough to make the turn and then slewed the 4x4 right and into the woods. The path was narrower than the metalled road and thick with ice. Kishiev slowed the Nissan to a crawl before finally stopping within sight of the water.

'Nice place for a picnic.'

Kishiev jerked and then the cold barrel of a handgun pressed into the back of his neck. 'Who are you?'

'My name is Aidan Snow.'

'You will never be able to stop the Caliphate!'

'Perhaps, but I can stop you. Turn off the ignition and place your hands on the wheel.'

Kishiev moved his hands slowly.

The passenger door opened. 'Good evening,' Blazhevich said. 'Cuff him, Vitaly.'

Blazhevich snapped on a pair of cuffs and then picked up the attaché case. 'Get in the passenger seat.'

Kishiev awkwardly struggled over the centre console and gear-stick; all the while Snow kept the Glock pressed against him. Through the open door Kishiev could once again hear the sound of rotor blades, and they were getting nearer. Blazhevich climbed into the driver's seat, started the ignition, and put the Nissan into reverse. He scraped against a tree branch as the 4x4 retraced its route back towards the road.

'I hope you paid extra for the accidental damage insurance,' Snow quipped.

The Nissan bumped onto the road. Blazhevich tugged the wheel left, and then they turned back towards the depot. And then a helicopter landed in the car park. Kishiev started to mumble to himself; Snow didn't recognise the language.

Casey pulled his hat down tight. He hated the cold weather and his feet were already soggy from the snow that rose above his brown brogues, but he would endure any temperature on earth if it meant reacquiring the missing nuke. He waited for the Nissan as it came to a stop a few yards away. Snow quickly got out and opened the passenger door. He hauled Kishiev by his coat collar and marched him over.

Kishiev's eyes were now wide. 'You are not Russians!'

'And thank God... sorry, Allah... for that,' Casey said with a smile.

'Any news on the Russian helo?' Snow asked.

'Safe and sound in Crimea from all accounts.'

Parnell and Gorodetski appeared from the other side of the helicopter and secured Kishiev. Blazhevich locked the Nissan and handed the device to Casey.

'Have you checked this?'

Snow shook his head. 'I doubt it'll go bang.'

'Thanks.' Casey blew his cheeks out with a huge sigh of relief as his hand gripped the handle. He gestured at the helo. 'Get in, boys; I'll give you a lift back to Kyiv.'

*

Embassy of the United States to Ukraine, Kyiv, Ukraine

The sparsely furnished conference room was dominated by a huge table in the middle and a large flatscreen monitor on one wall. For their guests' enjoyment, the monitor had been tuned to an American sports channel. Snow, Gorodetski, and Blazhevich sat on padded conference chairs drinking strong American coffee and eating imported muffins. Needham and Kishiev were being held in different rooms; both had a US Marine stationed outside. Casey had told the three operatives to make themselves at home while he spoke to Langley. Now the mission was over, the bomb retrieved, and the terrorists in custody, each man felt their body succumbing to post-action exhaustion.

Snow drained his second cup of coffee and stretched in his chair. The pain in the back of his head had been reduced to a dull throb, thanks to two codeine tablets, a mild concussion having been diagnosed by the US Embassy medical staff. Blazhevich sat hunched over the conference table, propped up on his arms and eating a muffin, while Gorodetski, who had been quiet ever since they'd landed in the embassy car park, watched the television.

Snow managed a smile. 'We won.'

'The game's not over.'

'I didn't mean the football, or whatever American sport that is.'

Blazhevich looked up. 'We won this time, but only just.'

Snow walked over to the coffee station. He helped himself to another cup, added cream, and took a muffin. 'Any more for any more?'

Blazhevich waved the request away and Gorodetski shook his head.

Snow observed the others for a moment. 'I need to thank the pair of you again.'

'For what?' Gorodetski asked.

'Both of you saved my life on the same day, on the same Kyiv rooftop.'

Blazhevich studied Gorodetski. 'It was you who shot Pashinski?'

'Yes.'

'And it was you, Vitaly,' Snow continued, 'who found me on the roof and stopped me from bleeding out.'

'Now it all makes sense,' Blazhevich noted.

'I still don't understand how you ended up in the Agency.'

Gorodetski shrugged. 'I was in the wrong place at the wrong time.'

'Doing what?' Blazhevich leaned forward.

'Shopping.'

Snow and Blazhevich traded looks.

'Do you remember the terrorist attack on that New Jersey department store?' Both Snow and Blazhevich nodded. 'I was the customer who stopped them. It wasn't that difficult; they were very badly trained. Vince approached me afterwards. My cover was blown; he knew who I really was and he made me an offer.'

'And who are you, really?' Snow sipped his coffee as he returned to his chair.

'I told you.'

'You gave me your first name.'

'My full name is Sergey Pavelevich Gorodetski.'

Snow's caffeine-assisted brain took a moment to process the name. 'Gorodetski?'

'Yes. Why?'

'And you shot Bull Pashinski because he killed your brother?'

'I told you that. He and his men murdered my brother, Misha, in Afghanistan.'

'Misha was Spetsnaz?'

'Under the command of Pashinski.'

Snow took his encrypted iPhone out of his pocket and opened his email. 'This is a little hard to believe.'

'What is?' Blazhevich queried, his mouth full of muffin.

Snow clicked on an attachment, opened a pdf file, enlarged the image, and then handed it to Gorodetski. 'Do you know this man?'

Gorodetski's eyes widened and his mouth opened. He was silent for several seconds as he stared at the image before he asked, 'When was this taken?'

'Last week.'

'Where?'

'London.'

'But it can't be true.' Gorodetski felt a lump in his throat. He swallowed as his eyes became moist. 'This is Misha.'

'Your brother Mikhail is our informer; he told us about the RA-115A. He'd been safeguarding it in Afghanistan until Al-Qaeda stole it.'

Now oblivious to the presence of Snow and Blazhevich, tears rolled down Gorodetski's face as he stared at the photograph of his brother, Mikhail 'Misha' Gorodetski. It was the first new image of his brother he had seen for over twenty-five years, but it was unmistakably him. The hair had changed colour, the face was thinner and lined, but the eyes were exactly as he remembered. He wiped away his tears angrily. 'My mother died because of Misha. She couldn't accept he was dead, it drove her insane. She was put in an institution.'

'I'm sorry. Is your father still alive?'

'Yes.' Gorodetski's features seemed softer, younger. 'He teaches businessmen in Moscow how to speak English.'

'Did he teach you?'

'Yes.'

'That's American, Sergey, not English,' Snow chuckled.

'Gentlemen, gentlemen,' Casey greeted them as he opened the conference room doors. 'Do we have a shitstorm or what?'

'What?' Snow said.

Casey poured a coffee and sat at the head of the table. 'I've been on a call with Langley's seventh floor. The Director has made it clear to me, unequivocally clear, that we must get Harris back from the Russians. Harris knows where the bodies are buried – hell, he was one of the people who made the bodies! If the Russians realise just who he is, and what he knows, it will be the start of some very dark times for the Agency. If he does a Snowden it'll blow our operations and jeopardise the lives of countless assets and operators. Neither the Agency nor our allies can afford that.'

'So what does he suggest?' Snow blamed himself for not being able to prevent Harris's abduction.

'He suggests, and I agree, that we trade Harris for Kishiev.'

'We can't do that, Mr Casey. Kishiev was captured in Ukraine, and he is a prisoner of the SBU!'

'Ya think?' Casey gazed down the table at Blazhevich. 'We'd have let you "interview" him for a couple of days first, but after that he was on a one-way ticket to Gitmo.'

'So what's the plan?' Gorodetski asked.

Casey checked his watch; it was almost 3 a.m. 'The President of Ukraine is going to have a press conference tomorrow and Russia isn't going to like what he has to say one iota.'

*

Presidential Administration Building, Kyiv, Ukraine

Ukrainian television news cameras stood side by side with those from Russia and the West. Flashes of light bounced off the faces of the men in suits as they entered. The President of Ukraine was the first onstage followed by the Ambassadors of both the United States and the United Kingdom. Director Dudka brought up the rear. They sat at a long table, set up with nameplates and microphones.

The President nodded and silence fell among the assembled members of the press. 'Yesterday, at approximately eleven-thirty in the evening, the Security Service of Ukraine, in close co-operation with our partners from the British Secret Intelligence Service and the United States Central Intelligence Agency, prevented a major terrorist attack from occurring within the territory of Ukraine.' He paused to add gravity to his statement. 'In the course of preventing this attack we apprehended Aslan Kishiev, the Chechen leader of the Islamic International Brigade, who, as you may remember, recently escaped from Russian custody. His group was responsible for yesterday's terrorist attack in Grozny and the recent attacks on the Moscow metro system.' The President paused again and this time took a sip from a glass of water. 'The attack was to be radiological in nature and was to take place within the territory of Ukraine, in the Crimean city of Sevastopol. We believe that the target was to be the base of the Russian Black Sea Fleet.'

There was an immediate storm of flashbulbs and shouted questions as the enormity of the President's last statement sank in.

He held up his hand. 'Deputy Director Dudka of the Security Service of Ukraine will now provide you with further details regarding this operation.'

Dudka cleared his throat. 'As the President stated a moment ago, the SBU, working with our partners from the SIS and the CIA, prevented a radiological terrorist attack from taking place in the Russian-occupied Ukrainian city of Sevastopol. The delivery method was to be a Soviet-era tactical radiological device.' Dudka glanced offstage and gave a nod. A man wearing a white laboratory coat over a suit entered the room. He was carrying an aluminium attaché case. He stopped to the left of the table and then opened the case to reveal its contents.

Dudka continued. 'This is an RA-115A. It is what has been referred to as a "suitcase nuke" and was designed by Soviet scientists to be used against Western targets. This is a dummy device, but I hope you will agree with me that if a real such device had detonated in Sevastopol, the casualties and the consequences would have been unimaginable.'

Snow watched the conference from Alistair Vickers's office at the British Embassy. He had a wry smile on his face. Dudka's delivery was perfect. He praised the SBU while making the FSB look incompetent. As he watched, Dudka went on to explain that the device had been made safe, and that there was no reason whatsoever to believe that any terrorist organisation, including the Islamic International Brigade, the Mujahideen of the Caucasus Emirate, Al-Qaeda, or Islamic State, could gain access to another. He then delivered the hammer blow to the 'Hammer and Sickle' by confirming that this particular RA-115A had been discovered in Afghanistan by Al-Qaeda after being taken there on Kremlin orders by the Red Army. Dudka explained in his final statement that an American intelligence officer, who had been instrumental in the discovery of the terrorist plot, had been mistakenly arrested by the Russians but was now to be exchanged for Aslan Kishiev. The Ukrainian government had consented to Kishiev being returned to Russia.

'All's well that ends well, eh, Aidan?' Vickers said in his precise, clipped diction.

'For us,' Snow replied, 'but I bet the Russians are spitting feathers.'

'Yes. I expect their foreign ministry will announce this is all a farce concocted by the CIA to weaken Russia.'

'And they'd be right,' Snow said.

A large smile split Vickers's face. 'Only we know just how true that is.'

*

Casey sat in the black, armour-plated Cadillac Escalade. The heating was on, enough to prevent a chill, but low enough to keep him sharp. Kishiev was in the back, guarded by Parnell. Both Americans were silent while Kishiev quietly recited prayers in Arabic. Through the toughened windscreen the sky was blue and cloudless, but outside the air was frigid and the wind blew viscously across the steppe. This part of Crimea was desolate, arid grasslands; difficult to farm and even harder to live on, yet the native Tatars and Ukrainians had done so. The hastily fortified border ahead now separated Ukraine from its territory illegally annexed by Russia. The border guards had vowed to protect Ukraine from all invaders, and even in the face of the Russian army had remained resolute, proud, and defiant. Via the SBU, the border guards had been advised of the prisoner exchange. The Ukrainians knew they were to let the men from the Escalade through unimpeded into the narrow strip of no-man's land between their post and the Russians'. Casey drummed his fingers on the Cadillac's steering wheel as he waited for Strelkov. The full consequences of Harris's deceit on both his CIA unit and career were as yet unknown. All Casey could do was hope the Russians kept their side of the bargain and delivered Harris. Once back in Langley he'd start to worry about his future. On the other side of the border a vehicle came into view: a square, black Mercedes G Wagon. It rumbled up to the Russian-manned checkpoint and paused briefly before proceeding onwards and coming to a halt thirty feet short of the Ukrainian side.

'Showtime,' Casey said.

Parnell shifted in his seat, opened the door, and manhandled Kishiev out of the Escalade. With Casey two steps ahead, they started to walk slowly towards the barrier denoting the unofficial border. The Mercedes disgorged its passengers. The Russians, led by a man with a neat moustache, approached Casey's group.

'You must be Strelkov.'

'And you are the elusive Vince Casey.' Strelkov extended his hand.

Casey kept his hands firmly in his coat pockets. 'I don't shake hands with invaders.'

Strelkov sneered. 'But you engineer regime change and fund mass demonstrations?'

'The Maidan movement wasn't us, Strelkov, it was the Ukrainian people. They ousted the puppet-President, not us.'

'Of course they did.' Strelkov looked past Casey at Kishiev. 'But let us waste no further time with realpolitik. Give me the Chechen and I'll give you your man.'

'That is the essence of a prisoner exchange,' Casey noted with undisguised sarcasm.

'Bring him,' Strelkov ordered.

With Boroda holding one arm and a second FSB commando the other, Harris was dragged forward. The men let go and Harris almost fell, swaying like a drunk.

'Give 'em Kishiev,' Casey called over his shoulder.

Parnell shoved Kishiev in the back and he strode forward, head held high, to greet the Russian infidels.

Time seemed to slow as Kishiev drew level with Harris. Kishiev glared at him but the American was still too drugged up to understand where he was. Parnell took Harris and hauled him back to the Cadillac. Boroda scowled as he grabbed Kishiev and marched him towards the Mercedes.

'Men like us, Casey,' Strelkov said, 'are the guardians of the people; duty-bound to protect our homes from the pernicious growth of Islamic extremism.'

'Is there much Islamic extremism among the Ukrainians in Donetsk, Lugansk, or Mariupol?'

Strelkov shook his head slowly. 'I am sure we will meet again.'

'Unlikely.'

Strelkov turned on his heels and stalked towards the Mercedes.

Casey watched the G Wagon swing lazily across the road and go back the way it had come. He waited until the Mercedes was well clear of the Russian checkpoint before he withdrew a small, matchbox-sized black box from his jacket pocket. Casey flicked the switch on its top and, just over a second later, the G Wagon was engulfed in a ball of flames, lifted into the air, and then came crashing down on its side.

'*Allahu Akbar,*' Casey said.

Epilogue

Regent's Park was home to both the London Central Mosque and Winfield House, the residence of the US Ambassador, but that was lost on the tourists enjoying the garden. Mikhail Gorodetski let his eyes drink in the flora and fauna. A simple stroll in the park was one of the things he had missed the most while living in Afghanistan. He thought back to family walks in Gorky Park and other greener places outside Moscow. That was all a lifetime ago when the Soviet Union had worked, a time when his mother and father had been happy, and he had held his little brother's hand. Mikhail didn't understand why his life had turned out the way it had; it wasn't fair he had twice lost a family. Around him Mother Nature attempted to reawaken sleeping flowers and trees dormant for the winter months, now flowing with fresh, new life. So was this to be his fresh, new life? Or was he a Soviet anachronism, a man out of time? Standing a discreet distance away, he could see his SIS 'minder' in conversation with two men he recognised: Jack Patchem and his colleague, Aidan Snow.

'Mikhail, how are you?'

'I am well, thank you, Jack.'

'We have something for you, Mikhail; it's a present from HM Government.'

'Here.' Snow handed the Russian a thick brown envelope.

'Thank you.' Mikhail opened it and his eyebrows rose as he noted the contents: a burgundy-coloured passport. He flicked through the pages and saw his photograph and, on the facing page, his details. 'So I am now British?'

'That's correct, Mikhail.' Patchem reached into his pocket and spoke into his iPhone. 'Yes, you can join us now.'

'Are you expecting someone else?'

'Yes, a couple of friends. You may recognise one of them.'

'Misha.'

Mikhail's face registered confusion as he heard the voice.

'Misha.'

Mikhail turned to see two men approaching. One was middle-aged with sandy hair, and the other was younger, with blond hair and blue eyes.

'Misha, it's me! It's Seryozha!' Gorodetski called.

Mikhail squinted. It couldn't be. His hands started to tremble and his chest felt tight, but it was true. His little brother Seryozha was standing in front of him. 'Seryozha!'

Gorodetski extended his right hand and took Mikhail's, and then he fell into what was, at first, an awkward embrace with his brother.

Casey bypassed the brothers to join Patchem and Snow. 'I hate to see a grown man cry.'

'And have you been doing much crying, Vince?'

Casey wagged his finger at Patchem. 'That, my friend, is a cheap shot.'

'So when does the investigation into Harris and his impact on the Agency commence?' Patchem asked with clinical detachment.

'There ain't gonna be an official one; Harris was blown up in Crimea. Remember? No one can confirm otherwise. He died a hero murdered by Russian-backed terrorists. But I'm still not in the clear. The Director will conduct his own "internal" investigation, and it'll hurt more than a colonoscopy with a baseball bat. So if I was a crying man I'd be balling my eyes out already.'

'We all make mistakes, Vince,' Patchem said.

'Ha, is that what Harris was? A mistake?'

'No, he was a monumental error of judgement.'

'Jack, don't you go sugarcoating it any.' He shook his head. 'Some good news, though. The girl – Eliso – is going to pull through.'

'Has Harris told you who she really is?' Snow asked.

'Yep, she's a Black Widow; her husband was killed by the Russians in Chechnya. She moved to Georgia with her mother. That's where Harris recruited her. We think she's one of many. She'll be questioned when she wakes up.' Casey extended his hand. 'Been good working with you again, Aidan. I'm sorry for Beck, Needham, Harris, and everything.'

'And so am I, Vince,' Snow said.

'*Touché!* Langley awaits. See you around, gentlemen.' Casey walked away in the direction of York Gate.

Dear Reader,

Thank you for buying *Cold East*. I hope you have enjoyed reading it. I certainly enjoyed writing it. It is said that writing is a lonely business and without your support it certainly would be.

I have been asked how much of myself is in the character of Aidan Snow. Well, we have lived and worked in the same places and speak the same languages, but I was not in the SAS. Aidan Snow and I both have a passion for Ukraine and our adopted home, Kyiv. I write the type of books I love to read, about places and people that have struck a chord with me, so if you're reading this note, I hope they have for you too.

Please let me know your thoughts and any comments you have. You can follow me on twitter: @alexshawhetman or Facebook: alex.shaw.982292

I do reply to all my messages and would love to hear from you.

Warm regards,
Alex Shaw

Dear Reader,

Thank you so much for taking the time to read this book – we hope you enjoyed it! If you did, we'd be so appreciative if you left a review.

Here at HQ Digital we are dedicated to publishing fiction that will keep you turning the pages into the early hours. We publish a variety of genres, from heartwarming romance, to thrilling crime and sweeping historical fiction.

To find out more about our books, enter competitions and discover exclusive content, please join our community of readers by following us at:

🐦 *@HQDigitalUK*

f *facebook.com/HQDigitalUK*

Are you a budding writer? We're also looking for authors to join the HQ Digital family! Please submit your manuscript to:

HQDigital@harpercollins.co.uk.

Hope to hear from you soon!

If you enjoyed *Cold East* then don't miss the first two books in the Aiden Snow series...

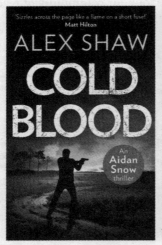

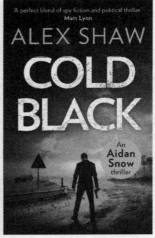